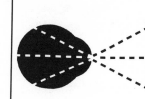

# The County Fair

# THE COUNTY FAIR

## KATHERINE VALENTINE

**THORNDIKE PRESS**

*A part of Gale, Cengage Learning*

GALE
CENGAGE Learning·

Detroit • New York • San Francisco • New Haven, Conn • Waterville, Maine • London

# GALE
## CENGAGE Learning™

**LIBRARY OF CONGRESS CATALOGING-IN-PUBLICATION DATA**

Valentine, Katherine.
　　The county fair / by Katherine Valentine.
　　　　p. cm. — (Thorndike Press large print clean reads)
　　ISBN-13: 978-1-4104-0692-7 (alk. paper)
　　ISBN-10: 1-4104-0692-X (alk. paper)
　　　　1. Catholic women — Fiction. 2. Connecticut — Fiction. 3. Agricultural exhibitions — Fiction. 4. Large type books. I. Title.
　　PS3622.A44C68 2008
　　813'.6'dc22　　　　　　　　　　　　　　　　　　　2008003677

Published in 2008 by arrangement with Doubleday, a division of Random House, Inc.

Printed in the United States of America
1 2 3 4 5 6 7 12 11 10 09 08

*To all my readers who found a home in Dorsetville*

# ACKNOWLEDGMENTS

Since this will be the last in the Dorsetville series, it seems fitting to thank all the wonderful people who have worked so hard behind the scenes on its behalf these seven years. To all the talented editors — Carolyn Carlson, Michelle Rapkin, Beth Adams, and Andrew Corbin — I am deeply indebted for your kind counsel. Thanks also to Jennifer Kim and Darya Porat, assistants extraordinaire, who have managed to keep me on track and on time with their gentle prodding. And a special thanks to Elizabeth Mackey and Kate Harris for making sure that the word got out.

Special recognition goes to Amy Berkower, whose faith in my work continues to be the "wind beneath my wings." I am truly blessed to be able to call her both my agent and a dear, dear friend.

Most importantly, I wish to thank my husband, Paul, and my children, Matthew and Heather, for their love and support. No matter what I might achieve in other roles throughout my lifetime nothing will ever be as cherished as the roles of wife and mother I have had the privilege to play in your lives.

# 1

The end of August always turned the small valley town of Dorsetville into a hive of activity.

Children, who in June had thought the summer would never end, were now flush with a sense of urgency to put in as many hours as they could down at the swimming hole by the river, or to explore new paths along the mountain range that ringed the town. Suddenly there seemed so much that had been left undone that they swarmed like bees collecting the last pollen to get it all in before summer had passed.

Men, who had spent the month enjoying the countryside filled with lush shafts of wheat and corn from the vantage of their front porch rockers, now felt the pull to get busy. As harvesttime neared, few dared to linger over second cups of coffee at the Country Kettle. They were much too busy for idle chitchat. There was machinery to grease and oil, barns and silos to be cleared, firewood to be split and stacked, and acres of corn and wheat to be gathered in before the frost.

Men worked tirelessly from sunup to sundown against the steady drone of combines that spit and sputtered up and down the fields, leaving the entire countryside to resemble a patchwork quilt. And when they were through, hundreds of circular bales of hay would dot the fields like modern sculptures left to dress the landscapes in a prelude to fall.

Women were no less frenzied as the summer came to a close. Vines bent to the ground under the weight of fist-size tomatoes. Peaches were coming so fast and furious that even the birds had had their fill. Suddenly it seemed as though every manner of fruit and vegetable was ready to be canned at once.

Women scurried about like squirrels, gathering in bushels of produce. Kitchens were off bounds to the rest of the family as women manned pots of boiling water and melted paraffin. And when the last canning jar had been lifted out from its steam bath, there wasn't a housewife among them who didn't feel as rich as Solomon as she gazed across the pantry shelves that fairly groaned under the weight of ruby red tomatoes, topaz peaches, emerald peppers, and amber corn relish, bowls of which would grace every table throughout the long winter ahead. As the snow grew higher around the doors and the temperatures plummeted to five below, the golden kernels would act as a reminder of the halcyon days of summer past and the promise of those yet to come.

But no matter how busy the season, folks in this small town always managed to fit in the annual County Fair. Although blue ribbons may have cost only fifty cents each to make, to the men and women in Dorsetville they were worth more than a king's ransom. In between their chores, men groomed their livestock entries until their coats shone like spun glass, tuned their tractors until they purred, and practiced their hog hollering until their wives thought they'd go insane. Meanwhile the women crafted items until their fingers felt as though they might fall off their hands and cooked until their kitchens were as hot as the fires of hell.

The Friday of Labor Day weekend would be the official kickoff for the fair, held at the fairgrounds about a mile and a half outside town. Although it was still called a county fair, only a few of the forty or so towns that made up Litchfield County

11

participated. Since the early eighties, much of the surrounding farmland had been sold and developed. Where acres of verdant, rich fields had once spanned the distance as far as the eye could see, the hills now sported enormous homes the locals called "McMansions." The landscape, however, wasn't the only thing that had changed with the influx of people. Taxes had soared as thousands of children poured into the school systems. It seemed that every school was undergoing some kind of renovation program. More teachers were hired. More school buses were bought. Dirt roads quickly gave way to asphalt, which was easier to plow in the winter. Of course, the increase in motor traffic meant an increase in public services, all of which required higher taxes, which began to make it increasingly difficult for farmers to hold on to their large tracts of land.

Fortunately, the state of Connecticut intervened. Realizing that the beauty of the state was in its scenic vistas, which were quickly becoming endangered, it fashioned a buyback program. Farmers would sell their land to the state, then rent it back for a dollar a year, thus eliminating all taxes. When the family no longer wanted to farm the land or died off, the farm would be turned into open space, ensuring that Connecticut would maintain its beautiful landscapes for future generations.

Several large farms had been saved with this plan, including farms in Goshen, Bethlehem, Morris, Litchfield, Roxbury, Washington, and Dorsetville, and the farmers still looked forward each year to the chance to participate in livestock competitions at the County Fair.

The fair was a tradition that had started during the depression in the hope it might keep folks' minds off their troubles. Back then it had been mostly an agricultural fair, where blue ribbons were handed out to the best in breed in poultry, rabbits, swine, horses, and cattle. Over the years it had grown and now included hollering contests, woodchopping and sawing contests, tractor pulls, a miniature rodeo run by the 4-H club, and a plethora of women's events that covered everything from fine needlepoint, quilts, hooked rugs, flower arranging, and preserves and jams to the most coveted blue ribbon of all — the Apple Pie Contest.

It was this last entry that made Father James Flaherty feel like a black cloud was hanging over him like a guillotine. Heaven help him, he had finally agreed to be a judge for this year's contest. He would have done anything short of selling his soul to the devil to have sidestepped the honor but had finally run out of excuses.

He passed the Congregational parsonage on his way downtown and remembered the year that Reverend Curtis was named a judge. The poor man hadn't had a minute's rest from the moment his name appeared in the *Dorsetville Gazette*. For the next few weeks, Father James had watched women stream into the parsonage bearing pie samples for his "opinion." When the reverend had finally insisted they stop because the activity might be construed by women of other denominations as trying to influence a judge, they took offense. Father James had heard that Reverend Curtis's church attendance dropped by 20 percent after that.

Then there was the aftermath.

"Rochelle Phillips continues to refer to me as 'the cleric' at all church meetings," the reverend had lamented when he came to offer his condolences upon hearing the news about his Catholic colleague.

Father James carefully stepped around a chalk hopscotch pattern on the sidewalk, thinking that he was already dead meat — an expression he had picked up from Matthew Metcalf, a former altar boy. Apparently, the women in his parish were well along with planning to take advantage of his position.

His head usher, Timothy McGree, had taken him aside this morning after mass. He said there were rumors flying around the parish that this year the women of St. Cecilia's had "an in," since their priest was a judge. Father James had moaned so loudly that George Benson, who besides owning a heating and air-conditioning company was Dorsetville's fire marshal and had been conducting his annual inspection, offered him a Tums and a ride to Doc Hammon's. The priest had declined both and made a beeline for the sacristy.

George's booming voice followed him down the aisle. "You'd better tell those old ladies in the Altar Society to wear their glasses when they're setting up these candles. State code says they need to be at least fourteen inches clear of all surfaces. I don't need another church fire."

George would never get over the fire that had destroyed the Congregational Church a few years ago. Since then, every time he came into St. Cecilia's he was on the look-out for one violation or another.

"The church and statues are made of stone," Ethel Johnson reminded him as her golden retriever, Honey, pulled on her leash, anxious to make their after-mass visit to the Country Kettle, where a bowl of scraps awaited her in the back kitchen. "There's no danger of anything catching on fire."

As he always did when confronted with something he couldn't refute, George mumbled, "Regulation is regulation."

Father James removed his vestments in record time, then made a mad dash out a side door, hoping that by the time George noticed his absence, he would be safely on his way to his morning cup of coffee. Like Honey, Father James looked forward to his after-mass visits to the Country Kettle.

He passed the town green, which separated St. Cecilia's and the Congregational Church. His thoughts turned back to the contest. As predicted, a string of freshly baked pies now arrived every morning, lined up on the rectory's back porch with little notes attached that read, "Hope you enjoy! Your parishioner, Mrs. Cummings" or "Just thinking of you. Your parishioner, Mrs. Florence Tate." Just as innocent as little lambs. Ha! As though he didn't know what they were up to.

He leaned back into the steep decline as the hill wound its way down to Main Street. He was in desperate need of a cup of Harry

16

Clifford's rich coffee and a plate of home fries. There was nothing like a visit to the Country Kettle to lift a man's spirits. Just the thought of his favorite eating place made him feel better. The black cloud shifted.

He spied a dime wedged between the cracks of the sidewalk in front of Second Hand Rose. He bent down and picked it up. Heads. That was a good sign, right? Who knew, maybe things weren't as bad as they seemed, he thought, smiling. He still had a week before the contest. Maybe something would come up. Maybe someone would step forward and demand to be made a judge. Not very likely, but it could happen. Or maybe the bishop would call with an urgent matter. Maybe . . .

He was so focused on the many avenues left to fate that he nearly plowed right into Barry Hornibrook as he stepped outside Dinova's Grocery's front door.

"Whoa, there, Father," Barry said, laughing, steadying a heavy brown paper bag overflowing with fresh produce.

Father James's face filled with delight. Barry was one of his many good friends here in town. "Sorry, I was lost in thought."

"Let me guess. The Apple Pie Contest, right?"

"You've heard?"

"News is all over town that the women of St. Cecilia's have the Apple Pie Contest tied up."

Father James groaned. "That's what Timothy said. I was hoping the rumor was unfounded. What am I going to do?"

Barry patted him on the back. "To use one of your phrases, this too will pass. Eventually. Just don't expect as many dinner invitations for a while."

"That's right, I forgot they hog-tied you into judging one of these darn contests. When was that? A couple of years ago?"

"Five, and Mildred Dunlop still isn't talking to me."

"Great." Father James swore. The black cloud was back.

"Look at the bright side."

"There's a bright side?"

"If none of the women are talking to you, think of all the work you'll get done."

Hmm . . . He hadn't thought about that. When was the last time he'd spent a full day on his Sunday homily without being interrupted?

"Thanks, Barry. I hadn't thought of that," he said. The cloud was starting to shift again.

"Anytime," Barry called, heading toward his car.

Father James looked straight up into a cloudless day. Why was he allowing this to get to him? For Pete's sake, it was only a contest. It wasn't like he had been asked to judge the angels, was it?

Now that things were back in perspective, this called for a cup of coffee, a plate of home fries, *and* a celebratory cinnamon bun. He headed straight for the Country Kettle, suddenly feeling famished.

Father James stepped through the restaurant door. Something wasn't right. It was just a little after nine on a Friday morning, and the place was empty. Where was everyone? Normally, he could count on the St. Cecilia morning mass crowd to be still mulling over their coffee mugs. What was going on? He asked Wendy, who was stationed by the grill with today's copy of the *Dorsetville Gazette* spread out on the counter. Wendy was fairly new to Dorsetville, having arrived just two years ago from New York. In the beginning, she had scared most of the regulars half to death with her thick New York accent and no-nonsense ways, but folks had finally come around. Even Father James had taken a strong liking to her.

"The County Fair," she said without looking up, as though that explained everything.

She licked her finger and turned a page with one hand while reaching for the Pyrex coffeepot with the other.

"A plate of home fries and a cinnamon bun," he announced, sliding onto a vinyl-covered stool.

"There aren't any."

"Any of what?"

"Any home fries or cinnamon buns."

Drats! He had been all set for a cinnamon bun, not to mention those home fries. "All right, then I'll take a blueberry muffin."

"None of those either," she said, pulling a fluorescent green alligator mug that Joe and Florence Platt had purchased during their 1995 trip to the Everglades out from a rack of clean cups. Like all of the dishes at the Country Kettle, Harry had bought it at a tag sale.

"Then make it a toasted corn muffin."

"None of those either."

"Well, what the devil *is* there this morning?"

"Toast?"

"Just toast?"

"I told you. It's the County Fair."

"Well, what the blazes does that have to do with anything?" he wanted to know, his temper rising.

"Don't get your collar all in a knot," she

said, leveling him with one of her New York don't-mess-with-me looks.

"Sorry," he said meekly, sipping his coffee. Ugh! He had forgotten the sugar. He reached for the canister.

"Apparently folks around here take this fair kind of seriously."

"Tell me about it," he mumbled.

"Do you know that yesterday I stopped in at Second Hand Rose to drop off some winter clothes, and there was a sign on the front door, 'Closed for the fair.' What kind of businesswomen would lose a week's worth of revenue for a fair?"

"Bobbie helps judge the baked goods, and Beth helps her husband set up the hog-calling contest," he said, stirring his coffee.

She looked at him strangely. "You're kidding, right?" Wendy was still having trouble adjusting to the priorities of country life.

"Nope," he said, taking a sip of coffee.

She grabbed a cloth and began to wipe the counter clean while shaking her head. "And I wonder why none of my friends back in Queens believe me when I tell them these things. Anyway, to answer your question, Lori closed the bakery for the week. As you know, little Paul is getting baptized on Sunday."

Father James smiled. He always looked

forward to baptisms, especially this one. Lori and Bob Peterson had nearly given up having another child. The adoption of little Paul was cause for great celebration.

"When that's over, she needs to finish a needlepoint pillow that she's entering and something about getting ready for a cake-decorating contest."

"And Harry?"

"He's home helping his Scout troop put the finishing touches on the float they're entering in the Main Street parade contest." She rolled her eyes. "What is it about this town and contests?"

"This year's prize is a trip to that huge amusement park, the Big E, New England's 'State Fair,' up in Springfield, Mass. I guess the pressure's on."

"So what's it going to be?"

"Be?"

"White or rye?"

Father James finished his mug of coffee but declined the toast and headed back to the rectory. He'd get Mrs. Norris to fix him a little something. Or if she was too busy, perhaps he could convince her to let him sample the ambrosia sitting in the fridge.

To his dismay, he found Mrs. Norris wilting over a boiling pot of blueberry preserves.

The kitchen smelled thickly of fruit, and the worn pine table was packed with canning jars and a host of jelly-making paraphernalia.

"Wipe your feet," she hissed without saying even as much as a hello. As if reading his thoughts, she quickly added, "And don't even think about touching that ambrosia. It's for Father Keene. Sister Claire is coming over later to pick it up."

He wiped his feet without uttering a word, although there was a stream of things just waiting to be unleashed on the back of his tongue. But experience with the housekeeper had taught him that quick-witted repartees only meant trouble. The last time he had foolishly mouthed off, she had spray-starched all of his underwear. The rash had taken weeks to disappear.

He quietly headed toward his study like a dog reprimanded for tracking in mud. He wondered if there might be a Snickers bar hidden somewhere in his desk. He closed the door so he could rummage undisturbed. To his grave disappointment, he unearthed only a near-empty container of Tic Tacs. He shook the remaining few into his mouth, then remembered he had hidden a bag of Pepperidge Farm Milanos from Father Dennis in the supply closet. He shot out of his chair like a bullet and, to his delight, found them right where he had left them — behind the box of last year's Christmas programs.

He plopped down into his desk chair and happily munched away, careful not to let any crumbs fall to the floor. No reason to add to Mrs. Norris's bad mood. Fortunately, her blue funk would eventually disappear, and she would return to her less than delightful self once the judging for the preserve and jelly contest was over. He studied the Milano, a delightful chocolate layer in between two golden ovals of shortcake and wondered if he shouldn't warn Father Dennis. Since his arrival at the parish several years ago, the younger man had traditionally gone on holiday this time of year. This would be his first experience navigating around Mrs. Norris's prefair mania. Last year she had exploded when Father James had simply asked when lunch would be ready. He still had trouble hearing out of his left ear.

He dialed his assistant's cell phone and was dumped into Father Dennis's voice mail. He left a message and hung up.

"Gosh darn it!" Mrs. Norris's voice thundered through the house. "Who put that chair there! I could have dropped a week's worth of preserves! If I catch anyone messing around in my kitchen . . ."

*My kitchen,* he thought, locking the study door. Why wasn't she cooking her preserves at her house, instead of here at the rectory? As tempted as he might have been to ask, he dared not risk it.

He rummaged through his desk again, only this time he was in search of a pair of earplugs. He had bought a set to wear at the new Cinerom over in Torrington. (Were movies theaters jacking up the sound, or was he just the only one left in New England who was not hearing impaired?) He rolled the soft bits of wax into balls and stuffed one in each ear, then reached for his study Bible. With some luck, he might find a sermon buried in all of this.

For five years straight, Mrs. Norris's preserves had taken first place at the County Fair. No other entry could touch hers. So superior was her special recipe that only a few brave hearts or newcomers even dared to enter against her. In fact, the judges had just about decided to retire the category.

Then the unexpected had happened.

Loretta Baker had discovered her grandmother's peach preserves recipe. It was the one that had won first prize at the state fair in 1935, as well as the praise of President Franklin D. Roosevelt, who'd happened to be traveling down from his summer home in Maine that year and had stopped in.

Unfortunately, Loretta's grandmother had died suddenly that following March, taking along the secret for her famous recipe, or so everyone had thought.

Loretta had recently inherited her grandmother's two-story colonial home, Riverview. It was built in 1875 and sat on five acres of land with a wonderful view of the Connecticut River. It was this river that had risen one fateful day in 1938, causing hundreds of thousands of dollars' worth of damage. Many of the stores along Main Street still bore the watermark.

A year or two later, the state had built two large dams upstream to help stop the melting snow from Vermont's mountains from combining with the spring rains and causing yet another catastrophe. When the dam was completed, the state's civil engineers assured the populace living along the river that it would prevent any further floods.

When Loretta had inherited the house, she'd had every intention of putting it up for sale. Realtor John Moran had said the location was so idyllic that it would certainly bring in a tidy sum. But as she'd boxed up her grandmother's things, she'd found the one thing she couldn't take along were the memories locked inside the old house. For as long as she could remember, the homestead had acted as her family's epicenter. The banister still bore her son's teeth marks. The room above the kitchen where she'd stayed when visiting as a child was filled with the memories of warm, happy moments. How could she possibly sell this home to strangers? It was a part of her.

So she had begun a campaign to convince her husband, Donald, to sell their condo down in Pensacola and their small Victorian here in town and, with the combined monies, fix up the old homestead and make this their year-round home.

At first, Donald had insisted that her grandmother's house was much too large for the two of them.

"It has five bedrooms, two front parlors, and a full-size dining room," he had explained. "Our last child is in college. What do we want with all that space?"

"Exactly, and soon our children will be married with children of their own. Won't it be lovely to have everyone gathered in one place to celebrate holidays and special events?" she'd asked.

Loretta had seldom persisted about anything through their twenty-eight-year marriage, and Donald could see that it meant a great deal to her, so he'd finally acquiesced.

While the contractor, Chester Platt, worked with Loretta to transform the interior, Donald spent his days trying to figure out what he was going to do about the grounds. Except for a small portion of grass that encircled the house, the rest of the five acres had been left to run wild, now thick with briars and swamp grass. Fortunately, the Bakers happened to be parishioners at the Congregational Church, whose pastor, Reverend Curtis, was the Dorsetville Garden Club president. The reverend loved a gardening challenge, and before anyone could say "chickweed," the entire club had shown up armed to the gills with wheelbarrows filled with flowers, fertilizers, and enough gardening tools to fill a barn.

Over the course of the next few weeks, the Bakers' overgrown acreage was turned into a lush, verdant landscape. Perennial beds edged the property with plumes of purple catnip; iris, with its spears of green leaves; feathery astilbes; and clusters of tall, white daisies. Down by the river, where the ground was shaded by century-old maple trees, Harriet Bedford's group had clustered several varieties of hostas, including Hadspen Blue, whose leaves were the color of midnight. Behind the house, Marge Peale (something of a master gardener herself) had fashioned a cutting garden, where gladiolus, daisies, cosmos, and mums of every imaginable color bloomed from early summer into fall. Opposite was a large vegetable garden, which Marge swore would produce enough crops to have Loretta canning for weeks.

Inside the house, things were moving along just as nicely. The kitchen renovation was well under way. Floors had been replaced, walls torn down, and partitions moved.

Occasionally, when looking at the pile of rubble forming like a great pyramid outside the back door, Donald would begin to fret that his retirement savings might be eaten up before the renovations were completed. Then one day, one of the carpenters tore down the wall behind the old gas stove and discovered an aged and barely legible recipe card. Fortunately, he had the presence of mind to handle it with care, wrapping it in a piece of plastic wrap that just moments before had swathed his ham and Swiss cheese sandwich.

Later that day, the Bakers arrived to conduct their weekly inspection. The carpenter handed the card to Loretta. She recognized the handwriting at once as her grandmother's and drew in a sharp breath as tears welled up in her eyes.

"You can't imagine what a treasure you've unearthed," she told the startled workman and kissed him so soundly on the cheek that his ears turned red. "This is my grandmother's blue-ribbon peach preserves recipe. We thought it was lost forever."

Loretta drove right down to Lori's bakery, bought a chocolate layer cake, and gathered the entire crew around a kitchen table that had seen many celebrations before. As the work crew and the Bakers sipped freshly brewed coffee and had second helpings of Lori's prize chocolate cake, they tried to figure out how the recipe card had gotten there. More intriguingly, how had it survived the flood?

One theory, offered by George Benson, who was replacing some leaky plumbing that day, was that it had somehow slipped behind the wall during the flood, floated to the top, and just stuck there when the waters had receded. The others felt it was as good a guess as any as they polished off the rest of the cake.

News spread quickly through town (as all news did in Dorsetville) that Loretta's grandmother's recipe had been discovered. Everyone was thrilled to hear it. Everyone, that is, except Mrs. Norris. She had been making a cheese soufflé for Father Dennis's return when she heard the news. It was the first time in all the years she had been cooking that a soufflé had fallen.

Father Dennis was headed back to Dorsetville after having completed his rounds at Mercy Hospital. There were only two parishioners there this week, Mrs. Daisy Fibbins and her sister, Marilyn Savage, so things went quickly. Both women were widowed and now lived together in a small cottage down by the river. Daisy had fallen off a ladder replacing a kitchen lightbulb and broken her ankle. Marilyn had strained her back when she tried to hoist her sister off the floor. They were both being discharged tomorrow at nine o'clock. He had promised to chauffeur them home and alert Sam Rosenberg that the women needed to be added to his Meals on Wheels delivery list.

The young priest drove the back roads home. He turned off the air-conditioning and rolled down the windows. A blast of hot air shot in. He didn't care. The fresh air felt good against his face, even if it was hot enough to melt the chocolate bars that he had stashed in the glove compartment. For the last three months, he had been cooped up in the executive offices of the archdiocese. He had hated every minute of it.

For some unfathomable reason, he had been chosen to act as the temporary administrative assistant to Father Dexter McCarthy, chief financial officer for the archdiocese.

Father Dennis had no experience as an assistant and absolutely no head for figures. He could barely balance his checkbook. It completely baffled him why the archdiocese had singled him out to replace Father McCarthy's regular assistant, who was recuperating from a broken collarbone. "It's one of the many mysteries of the Church, lad," Father Keene had said when Father Dennis called one night in a blind panic after hearing of the appointment.

Obediently, Father Dennis had packed his bags, even though it was with a heavy heart, and steered his RAV4 along the back roads of town, delaying as long as possible the moment when he would pull onto Route 202 and make the commitment official. Route 202 led to Route 4, which in turn led to the archdiocese, fifty miles from the safety and warmth of a town he had come to think of as home.

That day as he had driven, he had tried to memorize the color of the shutters on Ethel Johnson's front door, a door that when opened always emitted the strange combination of smells of lemon pound cake and sausage dog biscuits. Passing by the Campbells' home had reminded him of Fred, now suffering from Alzheimer's, and his wife, Arlene, who bore the burden with the grace of a saint.

The hills behind the Platts' farm had reminded him of the time Father Keene had gotten lost in a blizzard but had miraculously survived. That thought had segued into a litany of other miracles he'd witnessed since coming to help Father James manage the parish. Bob Peterson's and Chester Platt's healings of cancer. Sarah Peterson's miraculous escape from a raging fire. Dexter Gallagher's return from a coma after being trapped beneath the ice at Fenn's pond. The list went on and on.

Soon the familiar rolling hills had faded in his rearview mirror. He'd consoled himself that it was just a three-month assignment and that he would be back in time for the County Fair. It would be the first time since he'd arrived in Dorsetville to take on his post as assistant pastor that he would attend. Normally, he spent the first two weeks in September with his family. They always held a huge family reunion this time of year. He'd hated to disappoint them, but he wrote to explain that, after being away from the parish for several months, he felt it imperative to get right back to work. This was partly true. The other part was that he hated being away any more than was necessary from the folks and town that he had grown to love.

From the beginning, his appointment at the archdiocese had been ill fated. He'd felt like a sharecropper in a room of gentlemen farmers. He was forty pounds overweight, while the others worked out each morning in the gym. His breakfast of choice was pancakes slathered with butter and syrup. They all had a bran muffin and a cup of herbal tea.

The real disparity had become even more pronounced during working hours. The others had seemed completely at ease with the banks of high-tech gadgets and machinery, whereas Father Dennis didn't know one end of a computer from the other. This was why you could have knocked him over with a feather when he'd been assigned to enter the data from this year's Archbishop's Annual Appeal into the diocese's large data bank.

They had led him like a sheep to the slaughter into a windowless room, to a desk piled several feet high with donor information — name, address, phone, parish, and the amount of the gift. He'd been given ten minutes' worth of instruction and left to figure the rest out on his own, which was probably why in less than a week he would make a mistake so cataclysmic that it would be the major topic of conversation throughout the diocese for years to come.

That particular afternoon, he had been dreaming about the upcoming weekend. It was 3:00 p.m. on Friday. In another two hours he would be in his car, heading toward a small Italian restaurant in Avon, where he was to meet Father James and the St. Cecilia's morning regulars. It was Timothy McGree's birthday, and they were gathering together to celebrate. Timothy's present was all wrapped and waiting in the front of his car.

Father Dennis had been busy looking busy when the Archbishop's assistant, Father Thomas Oxford, came charging into his office. Oxford was a squat, boxy man with a bone-crushing handshake who seemed always to be in a rush.

"I need a printout of this year's donations to date," he said bluntly.

Father Dennis blinked hard, trying to clear his head of thoughts of penne with vodka sauce, fried calamari, and tiramisù, and nodded dumbly, giving the false impression that he was actually capable of executing this request.

"Have it on my desk before you leave today," Oxford said, before disappearing like a whiff of smoke.

Now what? Father Dennis wondered. When it came to the computer, the most he had been able to achieve since arriving was to learn how to turn it off and on. He still hadn't a clue how to actually enter any of the information that he had separated into small piles throughout the room. It was less intimidating that way. Several times he had been primed to ask for help, but it always seemed the others were so busy with their own workloads, he felt it unfair to burden them with his. So he had come up with a brilliant plan, or so he thought. He would just continue to shuffle the papers around and around like a carousel until his three-month stint was over and let Father McCarthy's *real* assistant figure it out when he got back.

Now, Father Dennis was realizing his plan

had a major flaw. He had not counted on someone asking him to print something out. Oxford might as well have asked him to walk on water.

He was staring at the screen, watching the cursor blink on and off like a warning light, when he came up with another brilliant idea. He might not know how to print out a file, but he knew someone who did, and when Oxford realized the document he had received did not include any of the recent data, Father Dennis would simply say he wasn't yet through collating the information. Collating . . . He liked the sound of that. It was a word which hinted that he actually knew what he was doing.

Now, to figure out how to print last year's report.

He reached for his cell phone and made an urgent call to Sister Joanna Hemmingway. Ninety-year-old Sister Joanna was a resident of the Sister Regina Francis Retirement Home and a computer whiz.

"Piece of cake," she shouted loudly enough to puncture his eardrum. Sister Joanna refused to wear her hearing aid and therefore thought everyone else was about as deaf as she was.

"I'll walk you through it. Are you at the computer? Okay, then. Take the mouse, move the cursor toward the toolbar, and drop down the box under File."

"Take the mouse . . . ?" He scanned the desktop for anything that might resemble a rodent.

Sister Joanna sighed. "Have you been living in a cave all of these years? Never mind. We'll have to start from the beginning . . ."

Over the next hour, the nun led him through some computer basics, and he began to feel a little less like a raft adrift at sea. Soon he was double-clicking and shifting through files. In fact, he was enjoying himself.

This wasn't so hard. What had he been afraid of? he remembered thinking right before he came to the place where he was supposed to open the donors' file and print it. He double-clicked several times, but nothing happened.

"What am I doing wrong?" he asked, glancing nervously at the wall clock. He was meeting Father James at five, and it was already quarter to.

"Sometimes things like this happen," she said. "Maybe the original file has been corrupted. Let's go into Windows Explorer, the file manager, and move the old file into a new folder."

In hindsight, Sister Joanna realized that

she should never have led him here. This was memory central. Every bit of data was stored within this program. But he had said that time was short, and this was the quickest way.

She instructed him on how to create a new folder.

"Now go into the file that's labeled 'Directory of Donors.' We'll make a copy, then move the copy into the new folder. Then when we're done, we'll delete the old one."

Father Dennis had never been good under pressure. His mind had a tendency to seize. While Sister Joanna was explaining all of this, all he heard was the word *delete,* and so he did. Not one file but everything that had been stored in the archdiocese computer network. Gone.

He would never have guessed that a priest of Father Oxford's caliber knew so many swearwords.

It was days before anyone would speak to him. He sat alone in his windowless office feeling like a leper of biblical proportions. Then one day he was led to the reception desk by the front entrance and given what Father Oxford claimed was a simple task. He was to take charge of directing all incoming calls. As Sister Joanna would have said, this was a piece of cake.

He was handed a carefully detailed chart listing all the extension numbers and a "simple" format to follow. He was to press the red (or was it the yellow?) button before transferring a call (or was it after?). The instructions weren't all that clear, and he was afraid to ask, so he muddled through as best he could. For the remainder of his tenure, all those calling the archdiocese would find themselves transferred to departments that had absolutely nothing to do with why they were calling. Even the Pope's secretary found himself one day speaking to the janitor.

So Father Dennis was not the only one with a grateful heart when his assignment with the archdiocese was over and he was reassigned to St. Cecilia's. Even the sight of St. Cecilia's pseudo-Gothic, misshapen exterior couldn't dampen his spirits. To him, seeing it was like gazing at the Sistine Chapel. Tears slid down his cheeks as he pulled up in front, and if he could have been assured that no one was watching, he would have gotten out and kissed the ground.

But the experience at the archdiocese had not been without merit. During those lonely nights and seemingly endless days, Father Dennis had made a decision. If God would just give him another chance, he'd be the best, most dedicated, single-minded priest in the entire archdiocese.

And good to his promise, Father Dennis jumped right into parish work with two feet. Within a few weeks of arriving back at the rectory, he had taken on daily mass at the retirement home and at the hospital, begun a coat drive, started a Bible study class, and insisted on heading the weekly bingo games, leaving Father James plenty of time to act as a judge for the Apple Pie Contest.

# 2

On Sunday a heat wave blew into town, making folks feel as though they had just been plowed over by a steamroller. It is a noted fact that New Englanders can't handle the heat. Give them a winter storm with windchill factors below zero, and they'll just pile on another sweater or some thermal underwear and soldier on. But subject Yankees to anything over seventy degrees, and they begin to puddle.

That morning most of the women in town made it very clear that their husbands were not to expect the standard Sunday fare of roast chicken, country fried potatoes, hot buttermilk biscuits, and French onion and string bean casserole. Until the heat wave broke, not a hot meal could be found in all of Dorsetville.

Sensing the discomfort of their congregations, both Reverend Curtis and Father James hurried along their sermons. Even though George Benson had made it his business to ensure that both air-conditioning units were pumping to full capacity, people were melting in the pews.

Fortunately nothing, however, could dampen the spirits of those about to attend the baptismal celebration of Paul Edward Peterson.

"I baptize you, Paul Edward Peterson, in the name of the Father, the Son, and the Holy Spirit."

Father James stood in front of the baptismal font with a smile as wide as the Texas plains. Next to the Petersons stood the beaming godparents, Stephen and Valerie Richter, previously Valerie Kilbourne. She and Stephen had been married this past summer, and folks couldn't have been more pleased for the young couple.

Valerie and Stephen had once been college sweethearts, but before they could go on with their plans for marriage, Stephen had been wrongly accused of a crime. Not wanting Valerie to know, he'd disappeared, spending several years in prison completely unaware that he had fathered twin girls. Then, two years ago, a series of events miraculously reunited the couple, who decided to make Dorsetville their home.

43

As Stephen and Valerie gazed into the face of baby Paul, their eyes met, and a silent message was passed. The Richters were hoping that soon they, too, might announce an upcoming addition to their family. For certain, their daughters, Linda and Leah, who couldn't seem to get enough of the infant, would be greatly pleased.

The sanctuary was filled with friends and neighbors gathered to share in this happy event. In the silence of their hearts, each one prayed that baby Paul would bring much happiness to the Petersons' small family. Bob and Lori had been through so much these last few years, with Bob's cancer, then nearly losing their daughter, Sarah, in a fire, and finally Lori's miscarriage last year.

"I still can't believe it," Lori whispered to Valerie as she looked with rapture down at her new son. He lay peacefully in his godmother's arms, swathed in a white embroidered gown that had once been worn by his big sister.

"When the adoption agency called to say they had a two-week-old baby boy with Down syndrome and asked if Bob and I would consider adopting him, I couldn't speak through the rush of tears," she had told Valerie the day she introduced their new son for the first time.

Tears gathered thickly in her eyes again this morning and spilled down her cheeks, but unlike the tears in the past — tears of fear that Bob was dying of cancer, tears of anger when she had miscarried — these tears were of pure joy.

Father James glanced at the Petersons as his heart swelled with thanksgiving for this young couple, who had been through so much yet had maintained their faith. And God had honored their steadfast faith with this special child. It was especially poignant since the child they had lost had also been diagnosed as mentally challenged.

"Can I hold Paulie?" his sister, Sarah, asked with outstretched hands. Big Sister couldn't seem to get enough of her new baby brother.

"Be careful," Lori said, gently handing him over.

"Oh, *Mommm,*" Sarah complained. "I know."

"Of course you do, pumpkin," Bob said, running a hand along her cheek. "You're just going to have to give your mom a little slack. She's still a little nervous. After all, it's been nearly ten years since either of us cared for an infant."

"Yes, but now you have me to help," Sarah

reminded them.

"And don't forget us," the ten-year-old twins, Linda and Leah Richter, cried in unison as they leaned over Sarah's shoulder to get a closer look. Baby Paul cooed with delight.

The guests murmured their approval.

"So, who's up for a party?" asked Harriet Bedford, seated beside Sam Rosenberg and Ethel Johnson in the first row. "There's enough food to feed a small third world country."

"Count me in," Father James said, hoping that Harriet had made her special barbecued chicken and Ethel her crabmeat casserole.

As the group made their way toward the reception being held in the basement of the church, Father James thought what a fortunate man he was. As pastor of this wonderful church community, he had access to endless good food, good conversations, and cause for celebration.

Over the next twenty-four hours, a blast of humid tropical air sealed in the town. People kept their radios tuned to the weather, hoping for a forecast of rain. Anything to help cool things off. Those who were able stayed indoors with the shades drawn and a good book. Those who had to venture outdoors found themselves dripping in perspiration within minutes of stepping out the front door, and dogs made peace with cats as both sought shade under the front porch.

It seemed the hardest hit were the elderly, like the residents of the Sister Regina Francis Retirement Home. Even pumped to the max, the air conditioner could not keep up with the heavy load. Around ten o'clock, the nuns closed off portions of the home and moved residents into the common areas, where large, rotating fans roared like jet engines, making conversation and television watching near impossible. Few, however, complained. Anything was better than wilting alone in their bedrooms.

Father Keene, whose health had been on a steady decline for months, couldn't be moved, so Sister Bernadette brought in a small portable fan and hooked it up at the foot of his bed. The elderly priest smiled his thanks. He often said that there was only one thing a son of the Emerald Isle could not tolerate — the summer's heat.

Mother Superior had made certain that each of the residents was comfortable, but by noon her concerns had shifted over to the nuns. Their blue woolen habits were just too heavy to be worn in this heat. The last thing she needed was someone suffering from heat prostration.

She called Sister Claire and told her to have the others change into the lightweight cotton housedresses that were kept in the attic for just such occasions. The nuns sighed in relief, happy to peel off their thick black stockings and itchy wool jumpers.

"Why, I feel ten pounds lighter," Sister Theresa said, smiling as she passed the others on her way to the kitchen. She was dressed in a yellow-flowered print.

There was only one who refused to comply with Mother Superior's order — Sister Joanna.

"I've haven't worn anything other than my habit since I took my vows over seventy years ago, and I'm not changing my ways now," she said, flinging the paisley cotton dress back at a startled Sister Theresa. After having had her say, she went into the kitchen to soak her feet in a bucket of ice water.

Meanwhile, outside, children's lemonade stands proliferated. Leah and Linda Richter claimed the choicest spot, beneath the shade of a maple tree outside the town's park, and did a landslide business after morning mass. This irked the Gallagher twins something fierce, especially Dexter, who figured they could make at least ten dollars a day set up in this prime location. The boys had their eyes on the camping gear displayed in Stone's Hardware Store window and needed the money.

The Gallagher twins were happy finally to have put the events of the past winter months behind them. The brothers had fallen through the ice at Fenn's Pond. Rodney had been retrieved, but it had taken the rescue workers over an hour to pull Dexter from the icy waters. He had lain in a coma for several weeks as the town prayed without ceasing for his recovery. Miraculously, Dexter had pulled through.

A lot of folks felt that the twins, who were always in trouble, had more lives than a cat. If there was trouble, you could bet that those two would be in the thick of it. Why, just about everyone in town had suffered from their pranks at one time or another. Fortunately for the boys, every time their antics caused yet another calamity, Father James would lace his sermon with a parable about forgiveness. Even so, Barry Hornibrook, who owned the Old Mill's Hotel and Conference Complex, was still having a hard time forgiving the twins for the time they blew up his boat.

On Tuesday, Dexter arrived early and had

his brother help him set up on the girls' spot. They were just about to pour a glass of lemonade for Father Dennis when Rodney spied Leah crossing the street with murder in her eyes.

"I think we're in big trouble," he told his brother, hiding behind Dexter. Rodney figured since this was Dexter's idea, *he* should take the heat.

"What do you think you're doing?" Leah challenged. "This is our spot."

"I don't see your name on it anywhere," Dexter said defiantly.

Rodney tried to caution his brother. After all, this was the girl who had given Andy Martin a shiner over a dispute concerning a favored fishing hole. Dexter finally caught his drift when she rolled up her sleeves and threatened to "beat them to a pulp" if they didn't move their stand.

Mumbling that they didn't need the girls' stupid spot and that they'd find an even better one, the boys gathered their things and what was left of their machismo and headed down to Main Street. They found a shady spot just outside the Japanese restaurant, set up their stand, and waited.

A few feet away from their impromptu lemonade business, the town crew labored to replace an old water line outside Second

Hand Rose. The Hamilton sisters had requested the work be done while the store was closed for the County Fair.

As the men's thirst increased in proportion to the rising temperatures, the boys began to do a landslide business. Within a few hours, they had sold out.

"The crew chief said that they'd be here all week. Geez, we could make a fortune," Dexter told his brother, counting a wad of one-dollar bills. "I just hope the heat wave keeps up."

"I just hope Leah doesn't find out," Rodney countered.

But as the heat wave continued, entrepreneurial spirits waned under the relentless sun. Lemonade stand signs were tucked away among the broken aluminum chairs and old tires at the backs of family garages. Children sought relief down at the river, floating amicably along on the currents, having left territorial battles for cooler days.

Sam ambled into the Country Kettle, shaking his head.

"What's up?" Timothy McGree asked, watching his friend slide into a booth.

"Guys doing my roof just took off, leaving the entire north side exposed."

"What do you mean they 'just took off'?"

asked Ben Metcalf, pushing his half-eaten order of whole wheat toast aside. The crumbs kept getting caught in his dentures.

"They said that the tar melts in this kind of heat, which means they leave footprints all over the shingles. So, unless I wanted my roof looking like it was put up by Bigfoot, they'd better wait and come back when it wasn't so hot." Sam reached for a paper napkin and wiped his brow. "I sure hope the temperature drops and the rain holds off."

"The heat won't end until we get some rain," Timothy reminded him, reaching for a piece of Ben's unfinished toast and slathering it with orange marmalade.

"They put some tarps up, but if we get one of those nasty summer storms with the driving winds and rain, those tarps won't keep the inside of my house dry."

"It's a real catch-twenty-two situation," Ben said sagely, watching marmalade drip down Timothy's chin.

"So . . . if it rains and your house gets flooded, sue them," offered Wendy, who had a habit of entering conversations uninvited. "Anyone want more coffee?"

Sam held up his cup. "We don't sue folks around here, Wendy."

"And why not?" she asked with her thick

New York accent.

"Because they are our neighbors and friends," Sam reminded her.

"Then let me get this straight. You're saying that folks in Dorsetville can sue only strangers?" She waited for an answer.

"Who are you going to sue?" Father James asked, sliding into a booth alongside Ben.

"Sam's roofers took off without finishing the job," Timothy said.

"How's Mildred?" Sam asked. Mildred Dunlop was a retired elementary school teacher. Most everyone in town under the age of fifty had once been her student. Sam knew that Father had been to visit her this morning after mass.

"Uncomfortable, like the rest of us. I'll have a mug of coffee and something to eat," he told Wendy.

Mildred had recently been diagnosed with a heart ailment. Doc Hammon had ordered her inside until the weather broke. Until then, she had been added to Sam's Meals on Wheels clients' list.

"Still just toast," Timothy offered, pushing Ben's plate aside. "I can't wait for things to go back to normal around here."

Feeling that he should set a good example, Father James tried to sound upbeat, even though he would have given anything for a

53

plate of bacon, eggs, and home fries. "I'd love toast. Make it rye. Second thought, give me a double order."

The three men looked at him with raised eyebrows. He couldn't fool them, not for a minute.

"So what are you all up to in this heat?" Father James asked, watching Wendy plop four pieces of bread into the toaster.

"Carl wants us to scope things out at the fairgrounds," Timothy said. He and Ben were volunteer cameramen for the local cable station, WKUZ. Carl Pipson was the station manager.

"He's thinking of doing a special on the carnival people who just pulled into town," Ben said. "We're supposed to snoop around and see if we can dig up any dirt."

"Dirt?" Sam repeated. "I thought Carl leaned more toward positive programming. What made him think up an angle like that?"

"George Benson," Timothy said.

That explained it, Father James thought, sipping his coffee.

As fire marshal, George had the duty to inspect all carnivals and give them clearance to open. Over the years, his inspection had uncovered a wide range of violations. George made no secret of what he thought about carnival people.

Wendy delivered the toast. The edges were burnt to a crisp. Father James stared at his plate.

"The toaster's on the fritz," she told him without any hint of apology.

"I don't know how much longer I can stand this heat," Timothy said, adjusting his straw hat. It was one he had pulled out of the town hall Dumpster last spring after a craft show. It still bore the remnants of a pink daisy on the brim.

Ben wasn't feeling any too comfortable, either. The back of his neck felt like it was on fire. He had forgotten the Coppertone in Sam's car.

"When is Sam picking us up?"

"After he delivers his meals." Timothy looked at his watch. "We've got another thirty minutes."

"I'll be fried by then."

"Then stay in the shade."

"What shade? We're in the middle of thirty acres of open fields."

"Darn George Benson for suggesting this," Timothy said. "It'll be his fault if we both get heatstroke."

"What's that?" Ben asked, cocking an ear. In the distance, voices were being raised in a heated discussion.

"It's coming from one of those trailers," Timothy said.

"Sounds like one doozy of a fight," Ben said.

"I suppose we could sneak over there and listen in," Timothy offered, not moving. "Maybe it's something we could use."

"Yeah, and maybe not," Ben said, tucking himself farther into a small wedge of shade.

"Don't lie to me, Jed. The money is gone. Four thousand dollars is missing, and you're the only one who knows the combination to the safe besides me, and I certainly didn't take it," Suzanne Granger said, holding back the storm of anger that was about to hail down on Jed Mullen. He had taken the payroll money. Now the trick would be getting him to tell her where it had gone.

She knelt on the worn linoleum floor in front of the metal safe, staring into its empty interior. Yesterday she had divvied up last week's accounts. Money for expenses — insurance, gas, and food — had already been deposited into the bank, but payroll was doled out in cash. Carny people didn't believe in banks. As far as she knew, not one of them had a checking account.

She continued to stare into the twenty-

56

four-inch-square hole as though she might have missed the small brown envelopes, representing two weeks' worth of wages, that she had placed in there yesterday. Sweat ran down her face and dampened her hair into tiny rings that clung to her forehead and down the nape of her neck. It also collected between her breasts, which she was astutely aware Jed was watching.

She was dressed in shorts and a halter top, but even so, the office trailer still felt as hot as the Sahara Desert. Jed's stench — a combination of sweat and fuel oil — only increased her discomfort. She got up and moved behind the desk to glare at him.

"What did you do with it, Jed?"

"Do with what?" he asked, pretending an innocence they both knew was a lie.

"Don't play games with me," she said hotly. "The payroll is missing, and I know that you took it."

"Goddamn, it's hot in here." He swore, peeling off his cotton T-shirt and wiping his face. "What's wrong with the air-conditioning?"

"It's broke . . . again. And we don't have any money to repair it."

Suzanne noticed his tight-fitting jeans had slipped down to reveal his tapered waist and rock-hard stomach. She hastily looked away.

This was no time to be sidetracked by Jed's phenomenal body.

There'd been a time, when they first met, that the sight of a nearly nude Jed Mullen would have sent her hormones raging. There was something raw and primal about the man. He also carried an edge of mystery and danger that had fascinated her. But now, two years later, he had all the appeal of tripe.

Jed had no sense of decency, no concept of right or wrong. His concerns centered entirely on himself, which was why she was certain that he had taken the payroll money. He didn't give a darn if the others, who worked their butts off making the carnival run smoothly, went without their pay. He'd probably used it to buy some new piece of equipment for his truck. Last time money was missing, she had noticed the pickup was sporting an expensive new sound system.

So, what were her options? She couldn't prove he had taken it. Even if she could, calling the police would only risk another round of negative publicity. Clients were just now starting to forget the scandals that had nearly destroyed the business a few years ago. Scandals that had cost the carnival tons of lost revenue and were the reason she had been forced to take him on as a partner.

She hated being in this position. The first chance she had to buy him out, she was taking it. That was, *if* she ever found enough money. It seemed each year things got worse.

She looked at him staring at her with that insolent smile. He had her cornered, and he knew it. God, if she could breathe fire, he would be toast right now.

"I know you took the money," she began again, feeling her face grow hot with rage.

"Oh, ya?" He struck a match on the heel of his boot.

Suzanne loathed cigarette smoke, and he knew it.

"If you don't return it, the employees we depend on to keep this place running will walk out, and then we won't have any business. Where will you get your spending money then? Let's face it, it's not like you have some fancy college degree and can get a job on Wall Street. Heck, I don't think you could get a job at McDonald's with your IQ."

His eyes narrowed.

Bingo! She had hit a nerve. Jed hated when people talked down to him. She felt a semblance of satisfaction.

He flexed his muscles and glared at her.

She glared back.

If he was trying to intimidate her, it wasn't going to work. He had stepped over the line this time. He had stolen money from *her* people. *Her* family, all of whom had needs. Mick Brady, who ran the concessions, supported a mother in a nursing home. Terry Landon had diabetes and used her paychecks to buy her insulin. Without it, she could literally die.

All these things ran through Suzanne's mind like flash cards. She looked at Jed, with his insolent who-gives-a-damn attitude, and wanted to pummel him.

"When I made you a partner —"

"After accepting a nice chunk of change, without which you would have lost all of this," he reminded her, making a feeble attempt at finding some high ground.

She ignored the dig. "We agreed that I would handle the finances and whatever profit we made *after* expenses we would split, fifty-fifty."

"So, I took my share in advance. What's the big deal?"

"You can't take your share in advance."

"And why not?" He laughed as though this was all a big joke.

"In the first place, how would you know how much your share *was* until we added up the expenses, which, in case you're unaware, are considerably higher than just six months ago? In fact, it seems like everything has gone up but our revenue," she concluded, grabbing the ledger.

"Look here. The insurance money is past due. The coaster ride needs repairs, and one of the fuel tanks for the fried dough stand needs replacing. All of this was supposed to have come out of the advance money for this gig. The gig you insisted we take even though the one in Providence would have yielded us twice the revenue. I still don't understand what was so important about this particular fair."

In fact, she had fought tooth and nail against coming to Dorsetville, but to no avail. She had too many memories associated with this town. It was much too risky to return, especially for her son, Billy, but she couldn't admit that to Jed.

"I need that money paid back now, Jed," she said, slamming the ledger shut.

"I don't have it."

"What do you mean, you don't have it?"

"It's gone, Suzanne, so get over it," he said, opening the screen door and stepping outside.

"Jed! You come back!" She raced to follow.

He stood on the other side of the closed screen door. "I don't know why you're getting yourself all worked up. Relax. You'll have a heart attack. Besides, the fair is opening in a few days, and this place will be swarming with people. You'll make it up. Just tell your people they have to hang on till then."

With that he turned around and walked away.

"Jed! Jed Mullen, get back here!"

He kept walking.

"Jed!" she screamed, watching him disappear around the trailer.

In a fit of rage, Suzanne kicked the bottom panel of the screen door so hard that the aluminum buckled. Oh, great! Her hissy fit had cost her a screen door.

She stomped over to her desk and sank down into an old swivel chair. If only she could sock someone, she'd feel better. The chair listed heavily. Like everything else around here, it was broken.

She glanced out the window. The top of the Ferris wheel and the striped tent rose in the distance. How many skylines had that scene framed down through the years? Thousands? Even in the midst of despair, the sight gave her a thrill.

*Admit it, kid, you're a carny through and through.*

She closed her eyes and tried to imagine what she could do to save the business. She had been holding on by her fingernails for months now. A stack of unpaid bills sat in the wire basket. State Farm was threatening to cancel their insurance. If she did close down, what would become of her employees? Most had been with the outfit for years. Where would they go? Carnies didn't fit in with regular folks. They were different. They were also her family.

They had welcomed her with open arms when she was ten years old. Both of her parents had been killed in a freak train accident. Her uncle Brad had owned the carnival back then. He'd been her only living relative, so the courts had sent her to live with him.

It had been a strange lifestyle, especially for a child accustomed to a normal life. They were always on the road and used a trailer for a schoolhouse. There were few children to play with, but she never lacked for entertainment. There was always someone willing to show her a card trick, or give her a ride on the elephant, or teach her how to swirl a perfect cone of cotton candy. As strange as it might seem to the outside world, the lifestyle had suited her, and in time, she'd come to think of the carnival as home.

It was this strong sense of belonging that had driven her to keep the business going after her uncle died, and for over a decade, she had managed to do quite well. She still wasn't sure what had started the downturn, although she had her suspicions. The carnival had been making good money up until the time Jed was hired on as a driver. Soon afterward, machinery had started breaking down. Then there was that suspected rape of a young girl. Once the accusation was made public, they faced cancellations from venues they had serviced for years. Now they did mostly out-of-the-way places that other carnivals didn't want.

The real mystery in Suzanne's mind was how Jed had gotten his hands on the fifty thousand dollars he had used to buy in. He'd saved it, he told her. But after seeing his spending habits over the last two years, she somehow doubted that. And who were those men who sometimes came to visit? They always arrived in mammoth SUVs with dark tinted windows. What were they so afraid people might see? She had asked Jed who they were a couple of times.

"Just friends," he'd told her.

Funny, Jed had never struck her as the type who had any friends.

# 3

"Al . . . pick up the phone," Betty Olsen shouted to the sheriff, her voice echoing through dispatch and bouncing down the linoleum-tiled hallway. She rubbed her throat. One of these days, she was going to burst a vocal cord, and all because the sheriff refused to use the intercom.

"Who is it?" Al Bromley bellowed back from inside his office.

"A man named Fillmore. Says he's from the FBI."

"FBI? Tell him to hold on." He grunted as he wrestled with his office window, which looked out on the back parking lot.

Some idiot had turned the air-conditioning off during the night, and his basement office was as hot as a clambake. Topping that off, the only window in the office had been painted shut. He swore under his breath. That would teach him to allow maintenance crews to paint his office when he was away on vacation. Last time, he had come back to find it the same color as the bottom of the high school pool. All it had needed was a fish mounted on the wall to be mistaken for SeaWorld. He supposed he shouldn't complain about the window having been painted shut. At least he could tolerate the neutral beige color.

"Al! That FBI guy is still waiting!"

"All right, all right. I hear ya."

He gave the window another sound slap, more from frustration than from any serious hope that it might budge. Sweat poured down his back, and large, wet stains circled his underarms. This heat was going to be the death of him yet. He hated summer. Give him four feet of snow and a good old nor'easter any day.

He turned back to his desk and was nearly bowled over by a smell so foul that for a moment he thought the sewers had backed up. It was Harley, his German shepherd. Darn his wife, Barbara. She must have slipped the dog some breakfast sausage again. How many times did Al have to tell her that pork gave Harley gas?

"Should I tell him to call back?" Betty asked, standing outside his office door. "Ugh, gross."

"No, I'll get it. Hill!" Bromley bellowed,

picking up the receiver, finger poised over the flashing red light.

Sergeant Frank Hill rushed in, then reeled back. "What's that smell?"

"Harley," the sheriff and Betty said in unison.

Betty picked up the phone. "Agent Fillmore, the sheriff will be right with you. I'm sorry for the delay." She pushed the *hold* button and shoved the receiver toward the sheriff.

"Did I just hear you say *Agent* Fillmore, like in the FBI?" Hill asked, his eyes as big as saucers.

"Never mind that. Here." Bromley reached in his desk drawer and pulled out a thick leather leash. "Take him for a long walk." He grabbed the receiver out of Betty's hand.

Both Hill and Betty remained rooted. It wasn't every day their department got a call from the FBI.

"You may both go. And Betty, pump up the air on your way out, then call the maintenance crew. Tell them I want this window fixed ASAP or I'll open it myself with a hammer."

"All right, I'm going. You'd think after all these years working for the department, he'd trust me more," Betty mumbled as she

68

trudged down the hall.

Hill remained behind.

"I've got someone waiting on the phone here," the sheriff reminded him.

"I just want you to know that if there's anything you and the FBI need, and I mean *anything, even* surveillance work, I'm free."

"I'll pass it along. Now I have a call to answer . . ."

The sergeant began backing out of the office. "Maybe I could —"

"Go!"

"Yes, Chief. Come on, Harley." The dog got slowly to his feet.

Bromley waited until he heard the door click shut before picking up the phone.

"Sheriff Bromley here."

"Sheriff, this is Agent Fillmore. Thanks for taking my call. I know you must be busy. I wonder if you have a spare minute?"

"Sure. What can I do for you."

"We've been tracking a suspect involved in some heavy interstate drug trafficking, and we just traced him to your area."

"Go on."

"The guy's name is Jed Mullen. We've been trailing him since he got out of prison about two years ago."

"What was he in for?"

"Loaned some money to a guy who got a

little testy when Mullen tried to double his interest without warning. There was a fight."

"Don't blame the guy. Credit card companies do the same thing," Bromley quipped. He had recently been shocked right down to his socks to discover that a late payment of one day had sent his interest rate soaring to 28 percent.

The agent laughed, then continued. "Mullen beat the guy up pretty bad. The guy pressed charges, and Mullen did some time. While he was there, he made friends with Fred Covas, who was in for transporting a load of coke up from Miami. We'd been trailing this guy for years, hoping that he would lead us to his source."

"How did Covas get busted?"

"A state trooper pulled him over outside of Savannah, Georgia. Noticed a taillight out on his Lexus coupe. Covas gave him some lip. The trooper cuffed him and figured he had probable cause to search the car. He found half a kilo of coke stashed behind the backseat.

"This put a serious damper on our investigation, but we figured we had to let it play out. If we intervened, Covas's friends might have gotten suspicious. So we worked out a deal with the D.A. We let Covas believe he was being charged with a reduced crime due to some technicality over the search. He got three years instead of twenty-five. He was released in fourteen months."

"Not a bad deal."

"While in the pen, he makes friends with Mullen."

"The guy you tracked here, right?"

"Right. Mullen gets out a few months later, and suddenly he's got money to invest in a carnival."

"Let me guess. The carnival is the one that's setting up right now at the fairgrounds."

"That's the one."

"So what's Mullen's part in all of this, and what's the connection with the carnival?"

"We've been keeping tabs on the two of them. A few weeks ago, Covas contacted Mullen. They met in a striptease joint on Manhattan's Lower East Side. From what we've been able to put together, there's a large shipment coming up from Colombia by way of Miami. We believe it's marked for three of the main drug dealers here in the Northeast. We've also heard that this time there's to be a sharp increase in prices."

"I guess even drug dealers have overhead expenses," Bromley said sardonically.

Fillmore snickered.

"What does Mullen have to do with all of this? I thought he was just a small-town hood."

"Since 9/11, getting anything into this country has grown more risky. The waterways are heavily guarded by the Coast Guard. Part of Homeland Security. Our sources tell us that the dealers are not happy and that a big meeting is planned to hash things over before the drugs exchange hands.

"A few years ago, Covas's people had to come up with another route, so they started transporting the stuff the old-fashioned way, by cars, trucks. The problem was the state troopers seemed to be able to spot them at fifty paces. So someone thought up the carnival angle. It was the perfect cover. How many cops that you know would think to search a caravan of carnival trucks for drugs?

"He might be small town, but he's ambitious, and he's clever," Fillmore went on. "He's been using the carnival to traffic drugs up and down the eastern seaboard since buying into the business. We're pretty sure that the owner, Suzanne Granger, is clean. Apparently she inherited the carnival from her uncle. She's a single mom. Got a teenage son. We did some checking with the

IRS. Looks like she's done pretty well for herself since taking over. According to her tax returns for the years 1999 through 2002, she made a cool $150,000 to $170,000 annual profit.

"Most of her crew have worked with her and her uncle for years. She ran a tight ship and was a stickler for making certain that all health and public safety codes were met."

"You said *was*. What changed?" Bromley asked, leaning back in his chair. The springs groaned under his weight.

"Mullen. In the beginning, he was hired on as a driver. You know, those big rigs they use to transport equipment. But as soon as he comes onboard, things start to take a downturn. Machinery breaks. Accidents happen. Then a new employee — guy hired to drive another rig who later turned out to be one of Covas's people — was charged with statutory rape. News gets out on the Internet. Old clients start canceling left and right. Pretty soon the carnival is in financial straits. Then Mullen suddenly steps in and offers to save the day by buying a part ownership. I guess Ms. Granger didn't have much of a choice."

"I don't get why Mullen chose Dorsetville," Bromley said.

"The river. Our sources say he already has

the goods hidden somewhere in the carnival and he's in charge of putting this meeting together. Apparently, he feels that a meeting by boat is the safest. If something goes wrong, there are a dozen small outlets along the river where someone could disappear. It also makes it much harder to put together a sting operation. That's where you come in."

"Tell me what you need, and I'll make sure it gets done."

"We've invested over three years and countless man-hours in this sting. If we play our cards right, we might be able to do some serious damage to the entire northeastern drug trade. We have everything we need except one thing."

"What's that?" Bromley asked.

"We need to know the exact time and location of the meeting. And, Sheriff . . ."

"Ya?"

"Keep your eyes and ears open for any unusual activity along the river. I'm betting that Mullen is staking out an inlet deep enough to accommodate some good-size boats but hidden enough not to attract any attention."

Sergeant Hill wandered along Main Street with Harley's leash in one hand, barely aware of his surroundings. Normally Hill prided himself on his keen observation skills, but right now, nothing registered. Not the car parked too close to the fire hydrant or the town construction crews breaking down for lunch. His thoughts were a million miles away.

He was running an imaginary conversation between him and the sheriff through his mind and was just about to make several brilliant points on why he should be included in the FBI investigation when the German shepherd planted his feet as firmly as tree stumps and refused to budge.

"Come on, Harley," Hill said, tugging on the leash, which was about as effective as trying to move a boulder with a garden spade.

Harley stared at a stack of boxes piled behind Dinova's grocery store.

"Woof. Woof." The dog tugged on the leash.

"What is it, boy? You see something?"

"All right, go ahead." Hill snapped off the leash and prayed it wasn't a skunk who had bedded down for the day. Last time the shepherd had tangled with one, it had taken repeated shampoos and several gallons of tomato juice just to curb the smell, and it was six months before the odor stopped resurfacing every time he got caught in the rain.

Harley darted through the alley, making a beeline for a large cardboard box with a Foxy Lettuce label. Hill followed in hot pursuit. It wasn't until he was nearly on top of the carton that he heard the first soft, plaintive *meow.*

"Well, I'll be darned," he said, staring into the heart-shaped face of a small tabby kitten.

Harley nuzzled the box and stuck his head inside to investigate.

"Don't scare her," Hill said, feeling suddenly protective of the tiny feline. She couldn't have weighed more than one or two pounds. He gently scooped the cat into his arms. She tucked her head underneath his chin and began to purr.

"Hey, listen to that, Harley. I think she likes me."

Hill wondered who the kitten might belong to. He checked for a collar or a tag, but there wasn't any. Next he examined the box, hoping it might provide a clue. It was filled with fresh shredded newspaper and a clean towel as a makeshift covering. Someone clearly was concerned for the animal's comfort, but who would have just left her here? It certainly wasn't someone from

Dorsetville. He'd bet a week's salary on that. Everyone around here would rather cut off a leg than abandon an animal, which was why the town didn't have an animal shelter. There was no need.

Harley nudged Hill's arm, trying to get in closer. He hadn't known many cats and found this one terribly interesting.

"Back up, Harley. You'll scare the poor thing."

Harley looked disappointed but did as he was told.

"Now what am I going to do with you?" Hill asked the cat. "I can't just leave you out here all alone."

What *was* he going to do? He couldn't take the kitten back to his apartment. His landlord, John Moran, had a strict no-pet policy. The cat shifted her weight, curling herself up into a tight little ball in the crook of his arm. He studied the sweet little face, with its long white whiskers and the tuffs of orange hair that sprouted from the tips of her ears like antennas. He looked down into the trusting gold eyes. His heart gave a lurch.

He gently returned the animal to her makeshift bed. He'd just leave her here while he asked around town, and if someone didn't claim her, well . . . he'd think of something.

Father James waited for the heavy oak door to Merrybrook, the Holmes family mansion, to open, feeling like the common laborer about to be given an audience by the queen. His stomach was making those strange gurgling sounds that it did whenever he was anxious. Visits with Mrs. Marion Holmes always had that effect on him. This visit was especially nerve-racking. He had been summoned to talk about giving the Blessing of the Hounds, scheduled for this Friday, and he planned to try to wangle his way out of it.

Mrs. Holmes's butler, Hudson, opened the door. He was a thin, stately man with salt and pepper hair who seemed as timeless as the estate he managed. Father James figured he must be well over seventy and probably should have retired years ago. Running back and forth along the marble-floored corridors of this immense mansion would tire a man half his age. Hudson, however, would not consider retiring. Unbeknownst to Father James, he was much too fond of his employer ever to leave.

"Good afternoon, Father James," he said in his stiff English accent.

"Good afternoon, Hudson," the priest

replied, stepping into the entrance hall paneled in rich mahogany.

"Please follow me into the library, sir."

After having been in the bright glaring sun, Father James felt as though he were threading his way through a dark cave. He squinted. Now where did Hudson go? Drats! He had lost the butler. There had to be at least six doors leading off the main gallery. He remained rooted like a rutabaga.

"This way, sir," Hudson called from the third door on the left.

"This place is so big, you should give out maps," Father James joked, walking past a tall, gilded mirror. He could have sworn he had seen its twin displayed at New York's Metropolitan Museum of Art.

"I'll pass your suggestion along to madam," the butler said, drolly.

Father James had never been in this room before. Most of his brief encounters with Mrs. Holmes had taken place at the rectory or in the front parlor. The artwork was incredible. Was that a Remington on top of an inlaid table? He noticed a fresco painted on the ceiling and was arching his neck to trace the outline of two cherubs when he collided with a delicately shaped chair. The chair leg scraped across the floor. Hudson gave him a sharp look of disapproval.

"Sorry."

"I'll tell Madam that you have arrived," Hudson said before disappearing like a whisper behind the closed door.

Father James glanced slowly around the room, trying to take it all in. He didn't know a lot about art, but he had taken enough classes in college to know that the Renoir above the fireplace was real and that the vases flanking the floor-to-ceiling windows were Ming. Even the furniture looked as though it had stepped out of Louis XVI's fabled French court.

He had just come from a visit at Ethel Johnson's, so Father James carefully brushed the backside of his pants before lowering himself onto a brocade settee. It would never do to leave a trail of Honey's dog hair on one of Mrs. Holmes's priceless antiques.

He waited for a sign that his hostess was coming. She had the most annoying habit of making him wait, and the longer he waited, the more nervous he became. He ran a finger around his collar. The white plastic tab felt as though it were cutting into his throat. Just nerves, he figured. He was afraid of what Mrs. Holmes might say when she heard that he was about to renege on his offer to pinch-hit for Father Keene. He would simply tell her that after much thought (should he add "and prayer," or should he keep the Good Lord out of this?) he had decided he just couldn't condone the blessing of horsemen who were about to run a poor, defenseless fox into the ground.

How he wished that Father Keene was well enough to take over. In fact, the elderly cleric had seemed to enjoy this annual event — the riders, the huge Hunt Breakfast afterward, especially the Irish whiskeys served when the weather turned unseasonably cold, as it was wont to do this time of year. There was one thing to say about New England weather. If you didn't like it, just wait a minute. It would change. And change it did, quite often this time of year. One moment it was so hot that you were shedding clothes the way a dog sheds hair, and the next the temperature would plummet to forty and you needed a heavy cardigan just to run outside for the mail.

"Nice of you to come, Father James," Marion Holmes said, stepping through the doorway.

At the sound of her voice, he jumped as though a rifle had been fired. He quickly recovered and stood to greet his hostess.

"Good afternoon, Mrs. Holmes. It's always so nice to see you," he said, thinking he was going to burn in hell if he kept telling lies. "I won't take up much of your time; I know how busy you are. I just wanted to speak to you about the blessing on Friday."

Might as well get on with it.

Father James watched her slip delicately into a wing chair. For a woman past seventy, she still carried herself with a great amount of grace.

"Please sit down, Father. Hudson, we'll have our tea in here. Do you like Darjeeling, Father?"

"Darjeeling?"

"It's a blend of tea."

"I don't know."

"I have this one specially blended by the Harvey Brothers in Millertown, New York. Do you know anything about teas, Father?"

"I know enough not to put a tea bag in the microwave," he joked. He'd never forget the time he had had one of his tiffs, tired of being bossed around by his housekeeper, and in a rare show of defiance had put a cup of water and a tea bag in the microwave against her dire warnings. When the buzzer went off, he'd discovered tea leaves plastered over every square inch of the interior.

Mrs. Holmes frowned slightly, apparently not quite certain how to respond. "Yes. . . . Perhaps we should begin."

Before he could get one word out about the blessing, she had donned a pair of tortoiseshell glasses and referred to a folder Hudson had left on the coffee table.

"I thought we would go over the judging process for the Apple Pie Contest. Have you ever judged a contest like this one before, Father?"

He had forgotten that Marion Holmes also chaired the County Fair each year. In fact, a Holmes had chaired the fair every year since its inception. Perhaps it had something to do with the fact that they owned the large tract of land the fair sat on, which was also the reason the annual fair was held here and not in another part of the county. Large tracts of land were scarce. The Holmeses, however, refused to entertain any development proposal for the fairgrounds property. They considered it their civic duty to provide the annual event, and since they didn't need the money, local developers had stopped asking.

"No . . ." For one fleeting moment Father James thought about trying to wangle out of this event as well but then thought better of it. Doing so might weaken his position on the Foxhunt, and of the two, he definitely wanted out of the Foxhunt more than he did judging the contest.

"It's really quite simple," she began, handing him a piece of paper so he might follow along. "Each judge is given a tally sheet like the one you're holding. Notice that several categories are listed, all related to pie baking. You are to assign a numerical score from one to five, five being the highest, to each category. When you are finished tasting each of the entries, the sheets are collected, then tallied, and the entrant with the highest score wins the blue ribbon. The second highest, the second-place ribbon, and so on. Simple, isn't it? Oh, good. Here's our tea. Set it down here, Hudson. I will pour. Cream or sugar, Father?"

"Both please. About the judging —"

"One lump or two?" she asked, holding the silver sugar tongs above the sugar bowl.

"Six."

A flicker of shock flashed across her face, but she quickly recovered, counting out six sugar cubes, then handing him the delicate porcelain cup.

"I was wondering, who is in charge of the event?"

"In charge? Why, you are, Father. I thought that was clear. Your position as a cleric naturally lends itself to taking on a leadership role, don't you agree?"

No, he didn't, but that was neither here

nor there. He hated being in charge of anything. Being in charge always meant trouble. As far as he was concerned, he had agreed only to put a mark on a scorecard and let someone else be responsible for adding it all up and handing out the ribbons. Let the losers vent their anger on someone else.

Suddenly, he had a need for something sweet. In all the years he had visited this house, he had yet to be served as much as a cookie. As he took a sip of his Darjeeling, he glanced over the rim of his teacup and spied a small Picasso in the corner.

"Now, Father James, I wish to talk to you about the Foxhunt," she said, delicately folding her hands in her lap. "The invitations went out a few weeks ago, and I must say that the response had been overwhelming. It looks as though we will top the numbers of riders that have participated in all other years."

"Yes, I was hoping that we might discuss this." Here goes, he thought.

"Pity that Father Keene is so ill. He has always done a superlative job. The riders will be so disappointed that he can't be with us this year. But then, I'm sure you'll conduct the ceremony with just as much aplomb."

"About the ceremony. I wish to request that I be exc——"

"You'll need to confer the blessing at seven forty-five sharp," she said, taking hold of her teacup again. "I'll have Hudson set a small area by the arbor that you can use. Father Keene always requested that spot. He liked to be out of the sun."

"Mrs. Holmes, I really can't —"

"This year the proceeds will go to the soup kitchen at the Daughters of Mary of the Immaculate Conception of the Blessed Virgin Mary in Granby," Mrs. Holmes said.

The sinking feeling in the pit of his stomach had returned. Which was worse? Offending the animal lovers in his parish or offending Mother Superior? Either way he was a dead duck.

"Did you want to comment?" she asked.

"No," he lied. "You seem to have everything covered."

She placed her teacup back on the table and rang a silver handbell.

Hudson appeared as though by magic. "Yes, madam."

"Please get Father James his hat."

"He didn't wear one, madam."

"No hat? Oh, well, yes, I do suppose it's too hot outside for a hat." She rose and handed the priest the manila folder containing the tally sheets. "I've had my secretary attach the names and phone numbers of the other judges on the inside. I suggest you give them each a call so you can coordinate everything."

"Yes, I'll do that as soon as I get back to the rectory."

"Well, then, I guess that concludes our business for the day. I will see you at seven-thirty sharp on Friday. Good day, Father."

"Good day, Mrs. Holmes."

He watched her leave, then followed Hudson to the front door, said his good-byes, and hopped inside his Jeep, which was about as hot as a pizza oven. He turned on the engine and flipped the air-conditioning to high. A blast of hot air like the winds of the Sahara shot through the vents, hitting him square in the face. He sat there dripping, waiting for the cold air to kick in, and studied the folder.

Nigel Hayes, the town historian, was listed as a judge. That was good. He and Nigel had worked on other committees. He enjoyed working with Nigel.

He scanned down to the next name.

"Oh no . . ."

Listed just below Nigel's name was that of George Benson.

■ ■ ■ ■

Mrs. Holmes stood watching the driveway until the priest drove away. A sudden tiredness — no, it was a deep weariness — washed over her. What was wrong with her? She hadn't done a lick of work other than make a few phone calls. There was a time when by noon she would have ridden her favorite thoroughbred along the three-mile trail that swept across the estate, conferred with her business manager, dictated a dozen letters, mostly responses to social invitations that she steadfastly refused to attend, and made plans for dinner. Now she could barely make it up the stairs to her room without feeling as though she had just climbed the Matterhorn.

Maybe she should take Hudson's advice and make an appointment with Doc Hammon. How long had it been since she'd last had a checkup? Two, three years? She never used to let these things slip by before. Lately, she felt it wasn't worth the bother. She had made the mistake of saying so to Hudson and had received a stern lecture about the need to "carry on," as he put it.

She smiled. Dear, dear, sweet Hudson. Their relationship had certainly changed over the years. Now he was more cherished friend than servant. In fact, he was the only friend that she had left in the world.

She looked down on the town below and thought how its inhabitants perceived her. To them, she was the Lady of the Manor, someone who lived an idyllic life, filled with social events frequented by society's most celebrated families. At one time, perhaps. Now she mostly spent her days alone, wandering Merrybrook's empty hallways, trying to catch a ghost of a memory of happier times, when her son, William, was alive.

She should have sold the estate after he died. Gone someplace warm and exotic, distanced herself from the pain that had eaten at her soul like a cancer. But how could she leave? This was their home, the only home William had ever known. Those were the stairs that he used to climb every night after kissing her good-night. The drawing room had been host to his childhood games of checkers, and later chess. The stables down below were where he kept his old pony, refusing to sell it even when he had grown too big to ride it.

So many memories were encapsulated inside this house. She had grown up here. No, she could never part with it.

Merrybrook sat atop the hills that encircled Dorsetville. From the library window, Marion could chart the town by the rooftops that peaked between clusters of trees — oaks, sugar maples, pines. The Congregational Church spire marked the town green. To their left, she traced the stores along Main Street, counting off the wood-shingled roofs, until she came to the Country Kettle. Her gaze lingered there. She smiled with a rush of warm memories, hardly dimmed by the passage of years.

It was the summer right after high school graduation. She was dreading the last week in August, which signaled the end of the enchanted life she had been allowed to enjoy. In September, she was to begin classes at Vassar, where it was joked that marriage was the most popular course. There she would meet a classmate, Jacqueline Bouvier Kennedy, whose life would follow an equally tragic curve.

Marion had not been accepted to Vassar on the basis of her grades. She had always been a poor student. But academic prowess mattered little. Her mother was an alumna, as were her mother and her mother before that. It also helped that Marion's grandmother had just given Blanchette Hooker Rockefeller a hefty donation. At the time,

Blanchette had been spearheading the renovations of Vassar's main building.

Academics had always bored Marion. She saw no reason to clutter up her mind with the chemical properties of hydrochloric acid or how to calculate the area of a right triangle. What did either of those facts have to do with her real passion, art? She planned to spend a semester at the Sorbonne, feeling that all great art was rooted in Parisian soil.

But she wasn't going to study just art. She wished to study Parisians as well, to learn of their passion, their romance. Above all, she wished to throw off the shackles of her provincial New England upbringing and learn about life.

She had it all planned out. She would find a café far from the tourist trade, linger over cups of steaming black coffee, daintily fingering a *pain au chocolat* in the morning or a glass of ruby red wine after dusk. Perhaps she would seek out where Robespierre played chess, or where Napoleon was forced to leave his hat in lieu of payment when he forgot his purse.

She ran images round and round her mind that summer, hoping each revolution might soften the pain of leaving her boyfriend behind. The cause of her angst was a raven-haired boy whose father owned the local bar. His name was David Kelly, and they had fallen madly in love while walking through the town park one summer night before their senior year in high school.

Funny, she had known him all his life, but it wasn't until that night, with the peepers sounding in the distance and the smell of new-mown grass in the air, that she realized what a rare and sweet boy he had become. She was smitten.

Upon discovering the romance, her father had cautioned her that she must not grow too fond of the boy. After all, she came from one of the finest families in all of New England. Her affection was not to be wasted on the son of a local bar owner.

All that last summer after graduation, she'd campaigned, hoping that her father would change his mind, see it her way. She'd pleaded with him to allow her to stay here in Dorsetville. She loved David. He wanted to marry her.

But during that era, daughters, especially those of the privileged, were not permitted to pursue their hearts. Fathers knew best. Dorsetville may have been a wonderful town to grow up in, her father told her, and its citizens the best in the world, but her course had been set before she was born, and it did not include a boy from a working-class family.

The time came to leave for Vassar. Marion cried and pleaded and threatened, but all to no avail. Her belongings were sent on ahead, and she was instructed not to make a scene as she slid into the family's limousine. As the long, black Cadillac drove through Merrybrook's tall iron gates and wended its way toward the main road that would take them on to Poughkeepsie, New York, she watched her childhood disappear along with the familiar landscape. She was a young lady of substance. She would follow the course charted by the other women in her family. Go to Vassar. Find a socially acceptable husband. Take her proper place among society.

With time, she forgot the raven-haired boy who had made her heart sing. She studied hard at school, made passable grades, and in her junior year was rewarded with a year of study abroad. Paris waited, and with it the hope that something magical would happen before she was consigned to a life of prescribed boredom.

In Paris, she met Benson Reginald Holmes II. He, too, had been sent to enhance his studies, although he was seldom seen on any campus. Most of his courses were conducted along the Moulin Rouge.

He was handsome, debonair, and possessed a sense of danger foreign to the sheltered young woman. And for some reason she could not fathom, he seemed to be mad about her.

Of course, it helped that her girlfriends were all green with envy. In hindsight, perhaps the allure of being in possession of something that others coveted had been too heady to resist. This had never happened to her before. Perhaps it explained why she elected to ignore her nagging doubts — the concerns over his excessive drinking, and his euphoric highs and dark, manic lows. She should have walked away. Not let things get too serious. But she was young and desperate not to live the boring life her parents led.

Against the romantic Parisian backdrop, it was easy to ignore Benson's imperfections. She encouraged his attentions. He proposed that Christmas. She wired home to her parents, who booked seats on the very next plane. It just so happened that both fathers had attended Harvard. Both families couldn't have been happier. A match made in heaven, they said.

The marriage was a fiasco from the first. Benson's fondness for wine and women grew more obsessive. His mother later confessed to Marion that her son had been a compulsive drinker for many years, and after a rather embarrassing episode with questionable women in one of Boston's noted hotels, they had sent him abroad with the warning not to return until he had straightened himself out. They had thought this marriage was evidence that he had finally decided to walk the straight and narrow.

Divorce was out of the question in that era. High society would put up with any kind of deviant behavior as long as it was discreet, but never condone divorce. By now both of her parents were dead. Marion convinced Benson to move into Merrybrook. She took control of the family fortune and, much to her surprise, discovered that she was quite good at making money. Within five years, she had doubled their wealth. It was all a game to Marion. The wealth itself was secondary. It was a way of keeping her mind off her husband's many infidelities, as were the endless array of social events she hosted and the charities and the tennis matches and the golf tournaments and the polo matches.

The busier she became, the less she felt the sting of Benson's rejection. He came home less and less frequently, until except for a cable requesting the transfer of more funds into his account, months could pass without a word from him. Then one day his car would charge up the driveway. He would dash breathless through the front door, acting as though he had just gone out to pick up a newspaper, as though they enjoyed the most normal of marital relationships.

Marion grew to dread these visits. Benson would drink. She would escape to her room. Then, sometime during the night, he would slip into her bed. She would feel his hands seeking her out. There was never any passion, only a sense of connubial duty. It never occurred to her to refuse him. Good wives didn't do that. Instead, she let her mind drift to other things. She would study the wallpaper and the drapes, wondering if she should redecorate this fall, or if she should sell her Olin stock or hold on to it until the end of the quarter.

Three months after the last of these visits, at precisely nine o'clock in the morning, Doc Hammon called to tell her the pregnancy test she had taken three days before had come back positive.

At four o'clock that same day, a state trooper knocked on the front door. He had come to inform her that her husband had driven his car off a bridge and was dead. An autopsy would later show that his blood alcohol level was three times the legal limit.

She buried him on that Wednesday and on Saturday went forward with the formal dinner party she had planned for the ambassador of Spain. Marion's friends all said she was holding up beautifully, a shining example of good breeding and social grace that always showed during moments of great duress.

What others did not know, however, was that Marion showed no grief because she felt none. Whatever love she once had for Benson had died long ago. If she felt any sorrow at all, it was for what could have been, a sadness that sometimes deepened when she spied David Kelly and his new wife strolling along Main Street.

That could have been me, she would think. I could have been the one gazing lovingly into David's deep green eyes, feeling the tender touch of his hand on my arm, hearing the music of his laughter.

A deep sadness would clutch her chest, and she would rush upstairs and throw herself across her freshly made bed to cry tears for unrequited love, tears that would not abate until the day she first laid eyes on her son, William, and knew that finally all the love she had sealed away in her heart had found an outlet.

Marion came out of her reverie at the sound of Hudson's voice.

"Madam, there is a phone call from the mayor's office."

"What does he want?"

"He wishes you to meet him at the fairgrounds. There seems to be a problem about fencing."

"Fencing?"

"Yes, madam. A portion of the fence at the fairgrounds had given way sometime during the night, resulting in the escape of the carnival's petting zoo creatures."

"What does Mayor Martin wish me to do about it?"

"I wouldn't know, madam."

# 4

Ethel Johnson had just fed Honey her noontime meal and was washing up a roasting pan that had been soaking in the kitchen sink when she noticed a small goat eating her prized hydrangeas.

"Good heavens!" What in the world was a goat doing in her flower bed? She grabbed a towel and headed for the back door.

"Shoo! Go away!" she shouted, stepping onto the back porch, waving the dish towel like a matador would his red cape.

The goat looked up briefly, calculated that she represented no real threat, and went back to ripping a cluster of flowers from their stems.

"Go away, you scoundrel," she yelled, bounding down the stairs. "Those flowers are promised to Reverend Curtis!"

What was she going to tell him? she wondered, pounding down the porch steps, ready to do battle, if need be, to save the

2534113

reverend's flowers. He was counting on those perfectly shaped hydrangeas to complement his floral entry, which he was bound and determined would take first prize at this year's fair. As a member of the garden club, Ethel knew how much it meant to him, and her heart just sank as she watched the goat ripping off bloom after bloom.

*Woof! Woof!*

Darn blast it. She had left the kitchen door open.

"No, Honey, stay!"

The golden retriever completely ignored the command, leapt off the porch, and joined Ethel in defense of their territory.

The goat spied the dog and lowered his horns. Ethel gasped. "Leave it alone, Honey! Come back here!" She tried to snag her collar, but the dog outmaneuvered her, snapping and nipping at the goat's rear legs.

The goat bucked, missing Honey's snout by mere inches.

"Leave it alone and come back here!" But she might as well have been talking to a clump of dirt. Honey continued her campaign.

The goat sensed the dog was ready to do battle and took off in a flash with a large, pink blossom still gripped in his mouth and

Honey in hot pursuit.

And at that moment, the woman who championed animal rights and would do anything to save an animal in need took a distinct dislike to goats.

Ethel wasn't the only one visited by an unwanted guest that day.

Lori Peterson had just finished hanging a row of diapers when an Angora rabbit sporting a tag that read "Rex" hopped into her clothes basket en route to the vegetable garden, leaving two large, dirty rabbit prints stamped on Paul Edward's brand-new suit, the one she had bought on sale at Kmart last week. She had planned for him to wear it this coming Sunday at mass.

Odis Tunis, who had just left Kelly's Bar, was weaving his way toward his trailer parked about a quarter mile outside town when he spied a miniature donkey kicking its heels up in a patch of clover by the old Hawkins place. Never having seen a miniature donkey before, he figured he was having one of those alcohol-induced hallucinations he had read about. He had also read that once you started seeing those kinds of things, it was time to get on the wagon.

He rubbed his eyes, hoping it would disappear. It remained. A very bad sign.

When he got home, he told his wife, Viola, that he wanted her to drive him to the nearest AA meeting. He was taking the pledge.

"Viola, you have my *saakke* . . . my *saakkid* word that I'm done with drinkin' . . ."

Viola eyed him suspiciously. This wasn't the first time that he'd sworn to quit, but he had never taken to joining AA before. She asked him what happened, and he told her about meeting a donkey, no taller than his knee, on the way home. The alcohol had finally frazzled his brain. It was time to lay off the sauce for good.

She drove him into Torrington and waited in the car while Odis attended his first AA meeting. While she was waited, she happened to tune in to Tom Chute's radio program just as he was announcing the escape of an entire menagerie of animals (including a miniature donkey) that had broken free from the carnival that was setting up in the fairgrounds.

Viola had been praying up a storm for Odis to stop drinking. She even went as far as attending morning mass over at St. Cecilia's on Tuesdays. That was the day they venerated St. Anthony, who was in charge of miracles, and even though she wasn't Catholic, she sure did need a miracle.

She loved Odis more than dirt, but it was

hard living with him when he was drinking. Last week he had stolen her cleaning money to pay his bar tab. They had been living off boxed macaroni and cheese for breakfast, lunch, and dinner ever since.

As she waited for Odis to come out from his first AA meeting, she decided to keep the news of the runaway menagerie secret. No sense in letting him discover that what he had seen was real. Might drive him right back to the bottle. No, let him continue to think that he had been having a hallucination. Maybe that and her new dedication to St. Anthony might keep him off the booze long enough for her to get a little rest.

For the next twenty-four hours, members of the escaped menagerie were spotted throughout the town. Tom Chute continued to interrupt the day's programming to issue updated reports of sightings or captures.

Meanwhile, the Boy Scouts, led by Scoutmaster Harry Clifford, abandoned their work on the float they were building for the prefair parade to comb the woods. No animals were captured, but the Gallagher twins managed to catch a bad case of poison ivy. Mary Pritchett's Brownie troop fared a little better. They caught the miniature donkey by offering him Leah's peanut butter and molasses sandwich.

Pete Carlson caught the ducks. He was getting ready to leave on an excavation job when he spied a line of webbed-footed trespassers waddling across his back lawn. He was duly upset to see them pecking away at the new grass seed he had laid down the day before. Thinking quickly, he threw some scratch feed his wife used to attract the chickadees at the bird feeder into his kids' wading pool. The ducks quacked their delight and hurried over. While they were busy exploring this new plastic pond, he encircled the convoy with some chicken wire he had stored in the garage, then called the radio station to announce their capture.

By early afternoon, there were still a dozen animals at large, so some local farmers (who were no strangers to capturing runaway livestock) got together and rounded up the rest. They threw a couple of bales of hay and some fresh feed into an open field behind the fairgrounds, sat back, and enjoyed a couple of sodas. Within an hour, not only the animals from the petting zoo but several deer, a family of wild turkeys, and Joe Platt's Angora rabbit, Rex, who had been missing since the Easter Egg Hunt, showed up. (Rochelle Phillips over at the Congregational Church had gotten it into

104

her head to showcase a bunch of caged rabbits along the egg hunt route. Somehow Rex had managed to escape.)

By nightfall, the animals were once again safely caged within the newly repaired chain-link fence, which had been donated by Marion Holmes.

All, that is, except one.

Pepper Pot, the potbellied pig, was still at large. His owner, Sticks Hopson, who ran the petting zoo, was nearly frantic with worry.

"That pig's my star attraction," he told Ben Metcalf and Timothy McGree, who had been sent back to the fairgrounds to do a piece on the missing animals. Ben later confided to his station manager that he never thought he'd see a man so broken-hearted over a pet pig.

Pepper Pot, however, was not just any pig. He was a star, known up and down the East Coast for his ability to "sing" a medley of Beatles songs. It wasn't exactly singing, more like a monotone type of snorting, but he kept a steady beat, changing tempo with each melody.

"Twice he's appeared on David Letterman's 'Stupid Pet Tricks,' " Sticks said, leaning into the camera, as Ben made certain he was centered on the viewfinder.

"And six months ago I was contacted by a Hollywood producer. He wanted to cast Pepper Pot in a Charlie Chan feature film. Imagine that!"

Timothy asked when the movie was scheduled to start filming, and Sticks admitted he hadn't heard a word since, but added that he was still hopeful and that he planned to buy a new trailer with two slide-outs to expand the living area with the money. Every time he thought about it, his eyes shone like streetlamps.

When Pepper Pot was still missing at dusk, Sticks was nearly panic-stricken, berating himself for having spilled the beans about that Hollywood deal all over the airwaves.

"Someone's probably kidnapped him," Sticks lamented to Suzanne. "It's just a matter of time before we get a ransom call. I wonder if I should call the FBI."

"That might be a little premature," she said kindly. "I'm sure Pepper Pot's found himself a soft bit of ground and a patch of wild turnips. He's probably tucked away somewhere safe for the night. Why don't you go back to your place and try to get some sleep? If he hasn't returned by morning, I'll have Billy resume the search."

She saw him hesitate. "Is there something else?"

Sticks stared down at the toe of his boots. "Just wanted to thank you for keeping me on."

"There's no need —"

He waved off her objections. "It's been something that I've been wantin' to say for a long time now. This seems to be about as good a time as any. Anyone else would have sent an arthritic old man packing a long time ago. I know I ain't good for much anymore."

He swallowed hard and cleared his throat. "Now, you tell Billy that before he leaves in the morning, to come see me. I've got some treats I want him to take along. That pig's partial to Cheez Doodles. He can smell them a mile away."

Sticks started toward his trailer as thunder boomed in the distance. Halfway there, he paused and looked up at the darkening sky. It near broke his heart to think of Pepper Pot out there all alone in a storm.

"Why can't you go to the concert with me?" Matthew Metcalf asked Stephanie Costello, trying not to let the panic he was feeling filter into his voice. Night Hawk, a local country-western singer, was performing.

Although his concerts were kind of lame, all Matthew's high school friends were planning to attend. How was it going to look if he showed up without a date? Besides, Stephanie and he had set these plans weeks ago.

The two were standing in the middle of the produce aisle at Dinova's. Matthew was working the nine-to-four-o'clock shift and was conscious of the fact that the store's owner, Gus Dinova, did not pay him to spend time talking to his girlfriend.

Stephanie turned to study a crate of apples, enjoying her steady boyfriend's reaction. Good. She wanted him upset. That was why she had spent so much time in front of the mirror, trying to decide what to wear. She'd finally settled on a midriff blouse that matched her eyes and the pair of white shorts that showed the navel ring she had just gotten at the Brass City Mall. She wanted to remind him just what he would be missing if they broke up.

Breaking up with Matthew was something she tried not to think about. She loved him. But something had changed between them. Lately, it seemed as though she were invisible. He hardly noticed anything about her anymore. Not her outfits or her new hairstyle. (Her bangs had finally grown out enough to brush them to one side. What had she been thinking when she'd had them cut?) Heck, he hadn't even noticed the navel ring! Every guy she had met on the street since she got it had noticed. What was going on? Why was he losing interest? Did he have another girlfriend on the side?

Matthew was eighteen and ready to start college in the fall, although it seemed kind of funny that he hadn't decided on one yet. Maybe with his grades he didn't have to decide until the last moment. Stephanie was a little fuzzy about how these things worked. She had just turned sixteen. College seemed light-years away. Besides, the few times she had asked Matthew why he hadn't picked a college, he'd grown quiet, like he didn't want to talk about it, so she had let it go.

College choice, however, had nothing to do with her dilemma. Every time they went out, Matthew's mind seemed a million miles away. Maybe he didn't think it was cool for a college freshman to date a high school junior. If that was the case, she planned to show him that she was just as hip as those college girls, even more so . . . hence the navel ring. It had really hurt, but she figured it was worth it. She'd do anything not to lose Matthew.

In a rising panic, Stephanie had begun to

spend inordinate amounts of time on the phone, soliciting her girlfriends' advice. They'd suggested romantic picnics, walks in the park, a moonlight boat ride down the river, anything that might reignite the romantic flame. Stephanie had tried them all, but to no avail. Matthew had remained as distant as ever.

Finally, her friends had concluded that the situation called for extreme measures. Stephanie should do what women had done throughout the centuries. If she wanted to evoke a commitment from an evasive male, she had to pretend there might be someone else, and that was what had brought her here today.

"I didn't say I *couldn't* go with you," she said coyly, picking up an apple and studying it closely. "I said I had other offers."

"From who?"

"Whom," she corrected. Stephanie was a budding journalist. "But that's not the point."

"Not the *point?*" Matthew began to unload a crate of peaches, bruising several as he forcefully stacked them into a pyramid. "I thought we were a couple."

For the first time in weeks, she felt a surge of relief. They were still a couple. But wait a minute. Why was he ignoring her? She decided to press on. "I don't remember either of us ever agreeing not to see other people."

He grew very quiet, focusing his attention on the peaches. She held her breath. Had she gone too far?

"Hey, Matthew," his boss called. Gus had come up behind them.

Matthew swung around too fast, sending peaches scattering all over the floor.

"Sorry, Gus. I'll pick them up." He chased after several that had rolled into the aisle.

"After you're finished up here, I want you to go outside and break down those cardboard boxes. Garbage pickup is tomorrow, and the weatherman says we're in for some severe thunderstorms. Bundle them up tight. I don't want them flying into the next county."

Gus noticed Stephanie standing to one side. "Oh, hello, Stephanie. I didn't recognize you without your bangs."

"Hello, Mr. Dinova."

"Tell your mom we got a shipment of that soap powder she likes."

"I will."

She waited until he disappeared toward the back of the store, then bent down to help Matthew with the peaches.

"Matthew, I really —"

111

"Listen, Steph, I can't talk now. I'll call you tonight after work. We'll talk about the concert then. Okay?"

So that was the way it was going to be, huh? She handed him the peaches she had gathered and stood up. "You can try to get me if you want, but I don't know if I'll be home. I might have other plans."

Matthew stood several inches taller than she was. She noticed that all the lifting he did here at the store had defined his broad shoulders. He was such a hunk. She felt her throat catch. God, she'd just die if they broke up. But she couldn't think of any way of keeping him other than to make him see what it would be like if he lost her.

Matthew glanced into her eyes for a brief second as a range of emotions rippled across his face. She grew uncertain. Had her plan backfired? Was he going to tell her that it was over between them?

He grabbed the empty grate and headed toward the stockroom at a brisk pace. "Then I guess I'll see you when I see you," he called over his shoulder.

Stephanie stood among the peaches watching the heavy metal doors close in his wake. Maybe this wasn't such a good plan after all.

The sky had turned the color of pewter. The air was so still that not a leaf moved on any of the trees that lined Main Street. Sergeant Hill looked up. Rain was in the air. A big storm was coming.

The alleyway behind Dinova's was piled high with cardboard boxes. Hill waded through them waist-deep before finding what he was looking for.

"How are you doing?" he asked the cat, reaching inside her box. He rubbed her ears and smiled as the tiny creature closed her eyes in ecstasy. "I see you've finished off all the milk I brought you, and most of the food."

Throughout the day, he had stopped to question people. Was anyone missing a tabby kitten? No one had heard about a missing cat, but they said if they did, they'd be certain to let him know.

Lightning flashed over the mountain range, followed by a roll of thunder. A splattering of raindrops bounced off the asphalt. The cat edged closer to the side of the box and looked up at Hill with fearful eyes.

"Poor thing." He reached in and lifted the tabby gently. She was shivering. He opened his shirt and laid her against his chest, feeling the tiny heart beat wildly. The little thing was frightened half to death. He buttoned his shirt, leaving just her head sticking out. The kitten began to purr.

"What am I going to do with you?" He glanced around the alley. "I can't leave you out here."

The wind had increased. The thickening clouds overhead were ready to pour down torrents of rain. There was only one thing to do. He'd have to risk it and take the kitten back to his apartment. His landlord's offices were downstairs. He'd just have to hope that John had gone home early.

A bolt of lightning lit up the sky; then a clash of thunder made the ground vibrate.

That did it. He was not leaving the cat out in this storm. He would just have to take care of her until he could find her a good home. After all, how hard could it be to find a home for a sweet little kitten like this?

He looked around to make certain that no one was watching. Just to be on the safe side, he decided to keep to the back alleyways. No use risking someone spying him with the cat. There were no secrets in this town.

The cat meowed softly against his chest

but didn't try to break free.

"It's going to be all right," he told her.

He'd smuggle her up to his apartment, warm up a nice bowl of milk, then try to figure out what he was going to do next.

There was one thing Billy had noticed about this town right off. Folks sure did like to garden. It seemed as if every house he passed along the route from the fairgrounds into town had some flowers growing in the yard. There were flowers draped over moss-covered hanging baskets on nearly every front porch, and flower boxes filled to overflowing beneath front windows, and riots of mixed plantings displayed in the rows of clay pots that lined the front stairs, not to mention the flower gardens that stretched from the fronts of the properties all the way to the rears.

Main Street also bloomed. Containers were placed at every street corner, and hanging baskets hung from the wrought-iron lampposts. Some stores, like the one called Second Hand Rose, had entire front gardens lining their portions of the sidewalk. It certainly made the place cheerful, he thought, even on a gloomy day like today.

Thunder boomed in the distance like a muted set of cymbals. The air had gotten thick with moisture, the sky so foreboding that the light sensors were triggered, causing the streetlamps to flick on.

"And one . . . and two . . . and three . . . ," he counted between flashes and clashes, estimating how far away the storm lay to the south. Seemed about seven, eight miles. There was still time to continue his search.

Billy had spent the better part of the day recombing the area around the fairgrounds for the lost Pepper Pot. This time of year there were plenty of roots and leaves to eat. He figured the pig couldn't have gone far. Maybe the other search teams had missed him.

Six exhausting hours of climbing up and down mountains later (he had even followed an old logging road that went all the way to the river), there was still no sign of the pig. He decided to head into town, even though he felt it was highly unlikely the pig had traveled this far. Most probably he was still hiding out in the woods by the fairgrounds. But not wanting to leave anything to chance, Billy decided to give the town a quick once-over.

Billy turned into the alleyway by the grocer's and spied a police officer slip behind a row of stores. Looked like he had a kitten tucked inside his shirt.

Billy pulled out the last few Cheez Doodles. The rest he had eaten on the way into town. He owed Sticks a new bag.

"Here, Pepper Pot," he called softly. "Here, pig . . . here, pig . . ."

He paused outside the grocer's back door and looked around. If the pig was here, he was doing a pretty good job of hiding.

Without warning, the back door flew open, and a boy about Billy's age came barreling through, his arms filled with boxes, knocking Billy to the ground.

"Gee whiz, I'm sorry. I didn't see you. You all right?" Matthew asked, dumping the boxes and helping Billy to his feet.

"Yeah, I guess so," Billy said, dusting himself off.

A strong gust of wind swept across the asphalt. The boys scrambled, grabbing boxes with both hands.

"Thanks," Matthew said as Billy handed them over. "I'm Matthew Metcalf. I work here. I'm a stock boy."

"Billy Granger. I work at the carnival. I'm out searching for a potbellied pig. You didn't happen to see one hanging around here, did you?"

"A potbellied pig?"

"Yeah, they're short and round and make

an oinking sound. They're kinda hard to miss."

Matthew laughed. "I'm sure I would have noticed one if it passed by. Hey, wasn't he part of the petting zoo that got loose?"

"Yeah, we rounded up all the rest. He's still on the lam."

A gust of wind lifted the stack of boxes that Matthew had leaned up against the building and tossed them into the neighboring alleyway.

"Oh, great!" Matthew raced after them.

Billy caught one as it whizzed by.

"My boss wants all of this bundled up before the storm hits," Matthew said, restacking the boxes beside the Dumpster. "Doesn't look like I'm going to make it."

"Need some help? I bet if the two of us tackled it together, we could get it done in no time."

"You wouldn't mind lending a hand?" Matthew asked.

"Beats looking for a pig."

Thunder crashed behind the mountain range. "We'd better hurry if we're going to make it in time," Billy said.

The sky turned gunmetal gray, and the air suddenly grew still, as though nature was holding its breath, waiting for just the right moment to unleash a torrent. The boys made a good team, working feverishly to beat out the rain. They had just wedged the last bundle safely behind the Dumpster when the heavens opened.

"Come inside and let me buy you a Coke," Matthew shouted above the storm. "It's the least I can do for all of your help."

"Thanks, but I still have a pig to catch."

"In this weather?"

"Sticks — that's his owner — is going to have a coronary knowing that his pig is out in this."

A lightning bolt speared the sky. Rain droplets increased their tempo, beating a new rhythm against the asphalt.

"Listen, you can't search in this kind of weather," Matthew said. "I'm almost done for the day. You hungry? We could go grab something at the Country Kettle and wait this out. When it's over, I'll take you around in my car."

Except for the Cheez Doodles, Billy hadn't eaten all day. A cheeseburger sounded awfully good. "Okay."

"That's my car parked over there." Matthew dug into his pants pocket and tossed Billy his keys. "Start it up. I'll be right out. I just have to tell my boss that I'm leaving."

Billy watched Matthew slip inside the back of the store. He was barely cognizant of the rain that was now coming down in sheets, plastering his shirt to his chest like a second skin. His thoughts remained elsewhere, rooted in the question What kind of person would just hand over a set of car keys to a perfect stranger? Dorsetville was filled with mysteries, and the strangest one was that he felt a strong sense of déjà vu, like he belonged here.

Water raced along the gutters, charged down the drainpipe, and spilled over onto the asphalt, forming a river that converged with another stream, the runoff from the building next door. Billy jumped out of the way and raced for the Firebird beside the No Parking sign. He liked Matthew's style.

He fumbled with the key in the lock, the driving rain making it nearly impossible to see. Finally, the key slipped inside. He gave it a slight turn. The lock clicked open. He dove inside and shook himself like a mongrel dog.

Within seconds he had turned over the engine, thrown on the defroster, and found the windshield wiper switch, but even with the wipers beating across the glass at maximum speed, the world outside remained shrouded in mist. Billy carefully maneuvered the car beside the grocer's back door to wait for Matthew, feeling the oddest sense that this stranger and he were somehow fated to become really good friends.

The rain pounded against the front windows of Hill's apartment, obscuring Main Street below. Occasionally, the soft peal of telephones filtered up through the floorboards. He listened carefully for voices. Yep, John Moran and his receptionist were still busy at work.

His bedside clock read four-twenty. John closed the office at precisely five o'clock every day except Saturday, when he went home at three. John and his wife played bridge with another couple on Saturday night. They met for cocktails first. Sundays, of course, the office remained closed. None of the shops in town were opened on Sundays.

Now if he could just keep the cat quiet for another forty minutes, he'd have the rest of the night to try to figure things out. That shouldn't be too hard, right?

"Right, kitty?"

Oh, no. The cat was missing.

"Kitty? Here, kitty, kitty, kitty."

No response.

Hill had placed the cat on his bed when he came in. He looked under the bed. No cat. He searched the floor of his closet. No cat. Where had she gone?

He checked the living room, then the kitchen.

"Here, kitty, kitty," he whispered. If that didn't beat all. Where could she have gone?

The bathroom door was slightly ajar.

"Kitty?"

The smell hit him like a brick wall.

"Oh, no . . ."

The cat was using the tub as a litter box. Hill clamped a hand over his nose and shimmied over the tub edge. It didn't take a genius to realize that this cat was very, very ill.

He rushed to his bedside phone and called Dr. Neal, the local vet.

"Good afternoon, Sunnyside Veterinary Hospital," an equally sunny voice proclaimed.

"Help!" was all he could think to say.

"Excuse me?"

"My cat. I mean, not my cat but a cat I just found. It's really, really sick. I think it might be dying."

"Now calm down, sir, and tell me what's wrong."

Hill thought a moment, then relayed as delicately as possible the current state of his bathtub.

"Hmm . . . That could be anything. You

say the cat was a stray you found?"

"I brought it home out of the rain."

"That's commendable, Mr. . . . ?"

Oh, Lord. He couldn't give her his real name. What if it got back to John?

"Smith."

"How's its nose?"

"It has one."

"No, I mean is it warm and dry, or cool and moist?"

"I don't know. Wait a minute. I'll be right back. Don't hang up."

He charged back into the bathroom. The poor sick cat was valiantly clawing the porcelain tub, trying to cover up her embarrassment. Hill gently lifted her up and touched her nose.

"Warm and dry," he reported, balancing the cat on his hip.

"That's not good."

"It's not?" He felt flush with fear.

"We normally close at four-thirty on Tuesdays. It's the doctor's poker night. But considering the circumstances, you'd better bring that poor thing right in. We don't want it to dehydrate."

Dehydrate!

Images of dried pieces of fruit and beef jerky filled Hill's mind with terror. He looked at the cat and instantly saw this small bundle of fur shriveled to the size of a dried kumquat. There was no time to waste.

Fearing that the cat was in imminent danger of dying, he hurriedly bundled her in the quilt he'd won at last year's church raffle and dashed out his apartment door, praying as he rushed down the backstairs that he would not bump into John.

Fortunately, the landlord was nowhere in sight as Hill hopped into his truck. He quickly placed a seat belt around the cat swaddled in the quilt and revved the engine, wishing he had access to the police cruiser. That baby could go from zero to eighty in 7.2 seconds.

He threw the truck into reverse and floored it. Wait a minute, he thought, coming to a screeching stop. He was a volunteer fireman. The blue emergency light was tucked underneath his seat.

He stuck it on his dashboard, flipped the On switch, and tore out of the parking lot. Cars parted in front of him like the Red Sea.

The sheriff was reading the updated report that Agent Fillmore had just faxed over when Betty knocked lightly on his office door.

"What is it, Betty?" he asked, not bothering to look up.

"You know anything about a fire in town?"

"No. Should I?"

"It's strange, that's all."

"What's strange?" Al Bromley hated it when she made him fish for information.

"I just got two calls. One from Nancy Hawkins and another from Sirius Gaithwait. They said they saw Sergeant Hill barreling down Main Street in his truck with the emergency lights flashing."

The phone rang. Betty reached across the sheriff's desk and answered it on the second ring.

"Dorsetville Police Headquarters. Please state your emergency. Oh, hi, Chester. Yeah, I just asked the sheriff. He doesn't know anything about it, either. I'll ask him."

Betty covered the phone with her hand. "Chester says George is out on a job, so firehouse protocol says you're the next in charge."

"So?"

"He wants to know if he should sound the sirens and call in the volunteers as a precautionary measure. Just in case there really is a fire and Hill forgot to pull the alarm."

# 5

"Go in peace to love and serve the Lord," Father James intoned, concluding the morning mass.

He felt a heaviness of heart as he looked out over the sanctuary, which was normally filled with laughter and happy chatter but now was shrouded in silence. This was the third Wednesday in a row that Father Keene had not presided over the morning mass. According to Mother Superior, he had had a relapse of the pneumonia that had nearly taken his life this past winter.

Amidst the pain and sorrow, Father James called up a happier memory. He and Father Keene (then pastor of St. Cecilia's) were standing in the kitchen, waiting for a kettle of water to boil, since Father Keene wouldn't let anyone, including Mrs. Norris, make his tea.

The bishop had announced Father James's appointment as St. Cecilia's new pastor. He was still feeling slightly awkward over the announcement, even though he had insisted that the elderly priest continue to reside at the rectory. Such arrangements were not uncommon in country parishes. They allowed priests who had served long terms in their communities to finish out their days among familiar people and places.

The parishioners were pleased as punch to hear that their favorite priest would be staying on. After all, Dorsetville had been his home for as long as anyone could remember, and they shared a cache of rich memories and warm friendships. Father James had hoped that the arrangement would put the gleam back in his predecessor's eyes, but there was something deeper troubling the elderly cleric. After having discussed this shift in titles beforehand, Father James felt confident that the elderly priest held no ill will, or misgivings about him taking over the reins. But he was at a loss to understand why he sensed a deep sorrow.

He took the matter up with the Lord, and as the Father is wont to do by way of the Holy Spirit, He sent back the answer through a simple thought.

Father Keene was deeply disturbed because he feared now that he was no longer officially attached to a church, he had lost the gift of publicly celebrating mass.

How could Father James have missed that?

He quickly suggested that Father Keene take over the Wednesday morning mass, adding it would be a great service to him, since he would be so busy with so many other duties. As soon as the offer had left his lips, the light in Father Keene's eyes was rekindled, and through the ensuing years, he never missed a Wednesday morning mass.

From that week forward, on Wednesday mornings, St. Cecilia's pews were filled, with the overflow lined up against the side walls. No one wanted to miss Father Keene's homilies, sprinkled with an eclectic mix of spiritual wisdom derived from a lifetime of walking with the Lord, the simple musings of a country priest, and dashes of Irish wit.

His congregation cherished the gift of sharing this sacred sacrament with the priest who had baptized most of them, married a few, and buried more relatives than he liked to remember. As one eighty-four-year-old man said to Father James, "He's the only one left that I can turn to and say — 'Remember when.' "

Father James finished mass. He raised his hands in a final blessing, kissed the altar, then walked through the side door into the sacristy, his heart still heavy with thoughts of Father Keene's declining health. A knock on the door brought him around.

"Do you have a moment, Father?" Matthew Metcalf asked.

"I always have time for a former altar boy. Come on in and take a seat," the priest said brightly. "Come on in."

Matthew's presence at mass this morning had not gone unnoticed by St. Cecilia's pastor. It always made his heart sing to see young people seated among the weekday regulars, even if he knew that more than likely their presence signified some kind of crisis in their lives.

He watched Matthew slide into a chair and suddenly realized that the boy had been replaced by a young man. He counted back through the years by way of the sacraments: first Holy Communion, confirmation. He had presided over both. He also had had the honor of being seated among the Metcalf family this June as Matthew gave the valedictory speech at his graduation. His grandfather Ben had been so proud that Father James thought he might burst at the seams.

It was hard to believe this was the same boy who had once turned the town into a three-ring circus by creating a hologram that had been mistaken for a Martian apparition. Where had the time gone?

Father James removed the silk stole from around his neck, folded it carefully, and placed it neatly inside one of the built-in cabinet drawers.

"I need to talk to you about something that's really bothering me," Matthew began. "It's about . . . God."

"Then you've come to the right place," Father James said. "How can I help?"

"Read this," Matthew said, handing him an opened letter.

Father James slid the chasuble over his head and hung it on a hook inside the closet before taking a seat next to Matthew. He studied the piece of paper.

"I got turned down for financial aid," Matthew said. "I was counting on it. You know what they said? They said that my parents make too much money. Is that a laugh or what? They should come visit my house at the end of the month, when the mortgage is due."

"This is very serious. I can see why you're upset," Father James said.

"I don't get it. What makes the Financial Aid Office think that my parents can afford thirty thousand dollars a year in tuition without any assistance? They saw what my dad makes . . . or made."

Father James reached over and laid his hand on the boy's shoulder. "I heard about your dad's job being downsized. It must be very hard on the family."

"There goes my shot at MIT." Matthew hung his head in frustration.

Father James studied the form letter. His heart ached for the boy. Attending MIT was all Matthew had talked about during his high school years.

"I'm sorry, son. This is a terrible disappointment. I know how much you wanted to go there for college."

"I don't get it," Matthew said, anger spilling into his voice. "I studied hard. I kept up my marks. Well, except for a small glitch last year. But I came right back. I got first prize at last year's state science fair. I aced the SATs. I was chosen valedictorian."

"I know. That was a wonderful speech you gave."

"A lot of good any of it did me," Matthew said bitterly. His disappointment was almost palpable as he studied the tile floor.

Father James knew that Matthew's anger was really because God hadn't intervened as the young man thought He should. The poor Lord, Father James thought. He was always the fall guy for people's crumbled dreams. Why did people insist on interpreting unanswered requests as God's show of indifference, when they were really His way of preventing us from settling for second best? It had always been Father James's experience that when God closed a door it was because there was something infinitely better a little further down our spiritual path. Few of God's children, however, had the patience or the faith to wait it out.

Matthew leaned forward in his chair, resting his elbows on his knees, and slowly looked up at Father James with equal amounts of torment, disappointment, and rage.

"What did I do wrong?"

"Seems to me you did everything right."

"I prayed real hard."

"Yes, I imagine you did."

"And so did my grandfather and my parents and my sister. So why did God refuse to answer our prayers? He could have done something on my behalf, you know, like influenced the Financial Aid Office to give me the money I needed. It's not like I'm asking for a gift. I'd pay it back. I don't understand why He wouldn't help me out."

There it was.

"God doesn't withhold the realization of

our dreams as a form of punishment. That's not His way," Father James said earnestly.

"Then answer me this," Matthew said, bouncing out of his chair. "All that talk you're always giving about God's love and His faithfulness. Where was that faithfulness when I needed it? He knew how much this meant to me. I've wanted this since I was a kid. I always dreamed about going to MIT, and I worked my butt off to get good grades so I could get in."

"I know you did, Matthew. Your grandfather was always bragging about how you repeatedly made the honor roll," the priest offered.

"I know it sounds hokey, but I really thought I could make a difference. They're doing all kinds of things now with computers. You know how Mr. Peterson had bone cancer a few years back?"

Father James nodded.

"MIT is developing a scanner that can read a person's DNA, like the scan used to read your groceries at the market. It's fast and simple. No more painful bone marrow biopsies. Pretty soon, every child born in a hospital will be scanned and logged into a huge database. That means everyone's DNA will be registered at birth, creating a worldwide registry of possible donors. Just think how exciting that would be," Matthew concluded, his face flushed.

It was almost painful for Father James to watch. The boy held so much promise. It really wasn't fair that a lack of funds should keep him from going to the college of his choice. Still . . . the God he served often closed doors that it was not in our best interest to step through, even though our rational minds might make us think other-wise.

"Have you considered that perhaps God might have something better in store for you?" he asked the boy.

"Better than a shot at MIT? Like what?" Matthew slid back into his chair, sullen and angry. "Maybe God thinks that being the head stock boy at Dinova's is a far better career? That's a job that would really make a world impact," he sneered.

Father James felt the boy slipping further into an abyss of self-pity. It was time to get a little tough. "And what if He did? What's wrong with being a stock boy?" he asked. "St. Paul wrote in Colossians, 'Whatever we do in word or deed, do all in the name of the Lord Jesus, giving thanks to God the Father.' We are to be thankful for the op-portunity to serve humanity no matter what job God gives us. There is no lesser or more important job in God's eyes. It's how we use those jobs to help better the lives of others that matters."

"I'd have a much better chance at helping better others' lives if I had been allowed to graduate from MIT," Matthew said petulantly.

Father James's heart softened. "I know you've been given quite a blow, but don't give up on God. I guarantee, He's not done with you yet."

Matthew arched an eyebrow.

"Remember how he took David, a lowly shepherd, and turned him into a king? There's no telling what God can do with a man if his heart is right, even if that man stocks shelves for a living."

"You're supposed to say stuff like that. You're a priest," Matthew replied angrily. "If God really cared about me, He'd fix this. I worked hard for this chance. I don't do drugs or alcohol. I stay out of trouble."

Father James lifted an eyebrow.

"Well, okay. Maybe that one time with the hologram, but does that cancel out all the good things I did, like helping my grandfather at the television station or donating time at the senior center to teach the seniors how to surf the Net or e-mail their grandchildren? Would God rather I be someone like Carrie Sanderson?"

Father James knew all about the girl. She was living with the Pitchetts as part of an intervention foster program. Carrie had grown up in one of the industrial towns along the river and gotten involved with drugs at an early age. Last spring she had been arrested for breaking into a neighbor's house looking for some easy cash. She was sentenced to the juvenile detention facility in Bridgeport, where a counselor intervened and recommended her for a new foster care program. As far as Father James was concerned, the state couldn't have chosen a better set of foster parents. Mary and Jack Pitchett were parishioners of St. Cecilia's and active members of the Dorsetville community. Mary ran the Brownie program, and Jack coached Little League. Carrie was their first foster child and doing splendidly.

"What about her?"

"Come on, Father. Everyone knows she's a druggie. That's why she was sent here. And look how things are working out for her. She's got a great job with Mr. Pitchett at his country club. She goes around town bragging that she's making ten dollars an hour. He even lets her drive his new Mustang. So why does God let people like her breeze by while guys like me who try to live a decent life and follow the rules, He ignores? Heck, it wasn't like I asked Him to win the lotto. All I wanted was one lousy break."

"Faith isn't about keeping score."

"Then what good is it?" Matthew asked, slumping in the chair.

"Faith is a matter of trusting when everything tells us to do otherwise. It's about believing in a loving Father who won't let us accept anything but the best for our lives, even when it makes us lash out at Him when our plans have been derailed."

"The best for my life would have been to get the money so I could go to MIT," Matthew said stubbornly.

Matthew left Father James pondering how he might help the boy overcome his anger toward God and headed right out to the fairgrounds. He had a date to meet Billy so they could resume their search for the missing potbellied pig.

Just a few miles out of town, his thoughts shifted to his girlfriend troubles. What was going on with Stephanie, anyway? They had been dating since last fall. Things had seemed to be going along all right, but now, all of a sudden, she was hinting that there might be someone else. What was up with that? And why had she acted so strange yesterday when they met at the Country Kettle?

He and Billy had looked like two drowned rats after dashing through the torrential rain. All the parking spaces close to the restaurant had been taken.

Stephanie had been seated in a booth surrounded by six of her girlfriends. Why did girls always travel in packs? he wondered. As soon they'd spied him and Billy walk in, they'd huddled together and started whispering while throwing shy, furtive glances his way. He'd been about to say hi when Stephanie noticed him and deliberately turned away.

If that's the way she wants it, he'd thought, then that's okay with me. "Come on, Billy, let's sit up by the counter."

Matthew had taken a seat next to George Benson, who smelled strongly of fuel oil. He was telling Wendy about some pie contest he'd been asked to judge.

Matthew had ordered cheeseburgers and Cokes. Harry Clifford had been stationed behind the grill. The rain had washed out his plans to finish the Scouts' float.

Matthew had focused on his cheeseburger while trying to ignore the ripples of laughter he felt certain were aimed his way. He'd glanced quickly over his shoulder. Sure enough, the girls were looking straight at him. Stephanie had caught his eye and flushed with embarrassment.

Billy had followed his gaze. "You know her?"

"Yeah, she's supposed to be my girlfriend."

"Supposed to be? You don't know?" Billy had asked, smiling.

"Not at the moment I don't. Wendy, can we have a large order of fries?"

What was she telling her friends? he'd wondered. That he had missed a few phone calls because he'd fallen asleep. Yeah, that was a real gas. If she had any kind of a heart, she would have forgiven him. She knew he had been putting in a lot of overtime at Dinova's. He had been saving furiously for college expenses this fall. A lot of good that had done him, he'd thought wryly.

He had also worked extra hours to save money for their dates. Stephanie had been his first steady girlfriend. He'd discovered that a big date once a week (which was expected) didn't come cheap. A movie plus a couple of Cokes and a supersize bag of popcorn set him back thirty bucks. A couple of cheeseburgers, fries, and shakes afterward could bounce the tab up to fifty. It was discouraging to think that working all day Saturday at Dinova's at minimum wage was barely enough to cover the costs of one date.

Dating, however, wasn't his only expense. There was car insurance and maintenance. Matthew also bought his own clothes and school supplies so his parents could use what was saved on him to buy stuff for his younger sister. Things at home had been rough since his dad's job had been downsized. Everyone was pitching in, trying to help out. His sister babysat for Lori Peterson while she worked at the bakery. His mom had gone back to work as a clerk at the town hall. Even his grandfather had tried to pitch in. Last week, Matthew had overheard his grandfather try to get his dad to take his Social Security check. His dad wouldn't hear of it. "If things get that rough, I'll let you know," he had said with tears in his eyes.

Matthew could tell by the look on his dad's face that he was worried, although he tried to hide it. He was such a great guy. Matthew wished there was something more he could do to help out. That was why he hadn't made a big thing about losing out on MIT. He didn't want his dad to feel any worse than he already did.

Matthew had been secretly putting in

some overtime at Dinova's, making money he used to help his mother out with the grocery bills. He stacked shelves after the store closed and ran delivery orders, although with the price of gas, he figured he made only two dollars a run. Still, it was something. He also pumped gas over at Tri Town Auto when Nancy Hawkins was shorthanded, and in between he helped his grandfather with editing at the cable station. Mr. Pipson gave him a couple of dollars for each show. All together, he had little time or energy left for late-night phone calls.

Maybe he should tell Stephanie about what was happening at home. Maybe then she'd cut him a little slack. But family pride kept him silent.

Now, as he coasted down Route 63 heading toward the fairgrounds, he wondered how life had become so complicated. If things were this hard now, what was it going to be like when he got old, say in his thirties? It was depressing just thinking about it.

The sign announcing the dates and times of the County Fair was just up ahead. Matthew slowed down. A man wearing a pair of dust-covered overalls, a strained smile, and a tag reading "Volunteer" was talking to the driver of a flatbed truck. The bed was stacked with chain-link fencing.

The volunteer spoke into his walkie-talkie. "Where should I tell him to go?"

The response was garbled. The volunteer rolled his eyes. "Darned if I know where they want this stuff delivered," he told the trucker. "Just take her around to the barn by the rear of the fairgrounds. Maybe someone over there will be able to tell you where it belongs."

Matthew was next in line. "I'm here to pick up someone who works for the carnival."

"Park it over there, by that patch of grass." The volunteer pointed to a tangle of open-bed trucks and cattle trailers haphazardly parked among the weeds. He waved Matthew through.

Matthew carefully maneuvered the Firebird through the gates, and the familiar scent of hay and manure brought on a smile. For just a moment, he was ten years old again and stepping through these gates with a stack of quarters in his pants pocket and the freedom to explore the fair at his own pace. That year he was old enough to be on his own, his father had said. Matthew had felt ten feet tall.

He slowed down to a crawl, trying to avoid the potholes. Every year the fair committee spent hundreds of dollars leveling out the parking grounds, and every year the place was filled with crater-size holes as soon as the horse and cattle trailers had pulled through the gates. Most folks wondered why they even bothered.

Matthew was especially careful to avoid the giant holes. He had a trunk full of groceries, including several dozen eggs. Gus had asked him to drop off an order at Merrybrook after he picked up Billy. There was also an "extra" canned ham, which Gus said he had ordered by mistake, for Matthew's family.

"Take it home. Maybe your mom could use it. It will only go bad on my shelves," Gus had said. Like most folks in Dorsetville, Matthew's boss knew when a family in town was having a hard time making ends meet. It was difficult accepting the handout, but Matthew made certain to express his family's deep appreciation.

He made a wide arc, circling around the vehicles until he came to a small clearing and thought how lucky he was to live in a small town. There was a sense of peace knowing that, no matter how bad things got, there would always be someone around who cared. He wondered what it must be like for Billy. From what he had seen of life, he was pretty certain that hard times knocked on just about everybody's door at one time or another. At least Matthew's family could take comfort in their community and friends. But what must it be like for carnival people, always traveling around? What did they do when times got rough? Who cared for them? It sure wasn't a lifestyle that he'd ever want to try.

Trucks and trailers parked helter-skelter in the tall grass displayed familiar signs: MARCUS DAIRY, PLATT'S FARM, MUNSON'S POULTRY, PAINTER'S RIDGE PRODUCE, MARCH FARMS. Their owners, all vying for blue ribbons, had come early to wangle the best stalls — those closest to the manure truck, water supplies, and hot dog stands.

Matthew finally found a spot near the poultry barn alongside Mrs. Stilton's aging station wagon but decided to keep on going. Mrs. Stilton was ninety-two years old and could barely see or hear. When folks saw her weaving down the road, they pulled off and let her pass. Last year she had backed up into a stack of shopping carts at Grand Union, forcing them through a front window. She had been reaching for the brake when her foot hit the gas.

Sheriff Bromley said she was a menace on

the road and should have her license revoked, but when he tried, the folks over at the senior citizens' center staged a sit-in at the motor vehicle department, claiming age discrimination. Nothing came of the sheriff's complaint. It was the first time Matthew had ever seen Sheriff Bromley back off. His grandfather said he knew better than to mess with the Grey Hornets.

Matthew finally found a safer parking space alongside one of the aluminum sheds. He got out, stretched his legs, and looked around. The place was bustling with workmen. Some were making last-minute repairs on one of the barns. Others were stringing rows of lights. A few feet over, the portable potty team were lining up row after row of blue vinyl stalls.

Billy had said to meet him by the circus tent. Matthew spied it right away. It was hard to miss, sitting behind the Ferris wheel, to the right of the roller coaster, its center arching toward the sky like some sacred shrine. Matthew headed out, his boots quickly covered in dust.

The fairgrounds was separated into two segments. One side housed the County Fair portion, the other the carnival. He made his way through a string of barns and outbuildings until he came to the archway decorated in three-foot-high letters reading RIDES AND GAMES OF CHANCE. Stepping through the portal, Matthew felt a familiar thrill. What child hadn't felt his heart race with wild anticipation as he spied the sights of the carnival spread out before him like a magic carpet?

Up ahead were rows of booths, each sporting a different game of chance. There were roulette wheels, numbered boards, pyramids of milk glasses, backdrops with circular cutouts through which patrons would toss sandbags. All vied for attention with brightly colored banners and rows of stuffed monkeys, giant bow-tied bears, long-eared rabbits, and a plethora of small black-and-white cats.

Last year Matthew had won a three-foot-tall gorilla for his sister. It now sat in the corner of her room alongside her bookcase, wearing a Huskies cap, Nike sneakers, and a pair of men's boxer shorts with little red valentines that his dad had been happy to donate.

Interspersed among the games were dozens of food booths decorated with elaborate signs listing their menus. Chili dogs, deep-fried turkey legs, fried onion blossoms, cheese nachos, cheesy fries, double-dipped chocolate ice creams, shakes, funnel cakes, sausage and onions on a bun, corn dogs, and Philly cheesesteak sandwiches, plus the standard hot dogs, hamburgers, and fries. Matthew smiled, remembering last year. His grandfather had decided to ignore Doc Hammon's orders to avoid fatty and fried foods. He was in bed for a week with the gout.

From inside a trailer parked to one side, a giant generator roared to life. It belched black smoke, sputtered, and died. Seconds later, a man with a heavily pockmarked face dressed in dirty denim overalls charged out, cursing up a storm. He kicked the door to the trailer and threw a wrench onto the ground.

Matthew made a turn at the cotton candy machine and spied Billy standing to the left of the circus tent, his long blond hair draped over one eye as he studied the foot of a huge pachyderm.

"There's nothing wrong with his leg," he said, running his hand along the elephant's thick gray skin. "Let's have a look at the bottom of his foot."

The trainer lightly tapped the elephant's right leg. The elephant lifted his foot. Billy examined the underside closely. "I don't see any cuts or abrasions that would make him limp. I think it's just a case of old, tired feet.

Soak them in some Epsom salts and warm water, and try and keep him off the hard turf for a few days. Maybe you can stake him in that back pasture. The ground looks pretty soft over there."

"Thanks for looking at him, Billy. That's what I thought, too, but I wanted a second opinion. I wonder how long before he's feeling better." The trainer tapped the leg again. The elephant gently lowered his foot.

"Hard to say. He's an old guy. His problem could be coupled with a touch of arthritis," Billy told him, patting the elephant's upper thigh. "You know, he's really way past due for his retirement. Maybe it's time you started thinking about getting a new partner."

"You got about five thousand dollars you don't need?" the trainer quipped, then looked up into the elephant's face. His eyes softened. "Truth is . . . even if I had the money, I wouldn't want another partner. We've been together for too many years, right, old fellow?"

The trainer caught himself before he grew too sentimental. "Meanwhile, I'll have to find a way to fill in his act. Too bad you haven't found that pig. He's always good for a few laughs. No sight of him, unh?"

"Not yet, but we plan to keep on looking," Matthew said, coming up from behind.

"Hey, man, I'm glad to see you," Billy said, all smiles. "Lou, this here is Matthew Metcalf. He lives in town. He's offered to take me around to look for Pepper Pot."

"Nice to meet you, Matthew."

"And this is Bogie," Billy said, rubbing the elephant's trunk.

"Like the old actor?" Matthew asked, laughing as the elephant searched his pockets for peanuts.

"I watch a lot of late-night TV," Lou offered.

"I guess we'd better get going," Billy said. "Sticks won't rest until we find that pig."

"Sticks?" Matthew asked.

"He runs the petting zoo. Pepper Pot is his main attraction."

Billy reached inside his pants pocket and brought out a handful of peanuts. The elephant didn't hesitate. He arched his trunk over Billy's shoulder and scooped them up, then poured them into his mouth.

"You'll feel better in a few days," Billy said, ruffling his ear.

The elephant leveled his large black eyes at Billy, then slowly leaned forward and made a deep bow.

"Hey, look at that," Lou said, excitedly. "In all the years we've been together, I've never seen him do anything like that before."

"You're welcome, buddy," Billy told him.

Hudson placed the rare first edition of *de la démocratie en Amérique,* by Alexis de Tocqueville, inside the tall glass bookcase, beside an equally rare first edition of J. R. R. Tolkien's *The Hobbit.* It had arrived an hour ago by special courier from Bauman Rare Books in Manhattan.

The specially made case would hermetically seal once the lock was engaged. Hudson made certain all was in order before inserting the delicately shaped silver key. Both temperature and humidity were well within range. Should a disruption of either occur, an alarm would sound. It was a necessary precaution, considering the value of the books housed inside, which included rare first editions such as *A Christmas Carol, Life of Samuel Johnson, Principia Mathematica,* and *The History of the Expedition Under the Command of Captains Lewis and Clark.* The collection housed inside the case was valued at almost $5 million.

Hudson slipped the key in his vest pocket, neatly placed the invoice requesting payment of $42,000 on Mrs. Holmes's leather-topped desk, and adjusted a small Waterford bowl filled with Charbonnel et Walker cappuccino truffles from the world-famous English chocolatier. They were Marion's favorites and quite difficult to obtain. Hudson had called every day for two weeks before he was able to ensure a shipment, which would cost him a week's salary, but he didn't care. Just to see the smile on her face when she discovered the delicate sugared morsels would prove well worth the expense.

The buzzer outside the servants' entrance sounded. The delivery boy had arrived, a fact that did not require Hudson to hurry. Instead, he glanced around the room. Nothing missed his scrutiny, not a picture frame that might have been moved a millimeter out of place or a chair cushion bearing an indentation of its previous occupant. He had a keen eye for detail.

A piece of lint on the antique Farahan Sarouk Persian carpet caught his attention. He removed the offending article, which appeared to have come from a dustcloth used by the cleaning women. They came once a month to give the mansion a good going-over. Not that it needed much cleaning. The entire west wing had been closed off for years. His mistress seldom received visitors anymore. In fact, there were only five rooms in use at present — the dining room, kitchen, front parlor, library, and Mrs. Holmes's upstairs bedroom. The other twenty-four rooms lay slumbering, like Sleeping Beauty awaiting the touch of a loving hand to restore them to life.

Hudson had lived in a spacious apartment above the garage until recently. Several weeks ago, he had suggested to Marion that he take over one of the rooms in the east wing. "I feel it might be more convenient should you have need of me in the middle of the night," he'd said.

He had held his breath waiting for her response. His mistress was an independent woman and could easily be offended by the implication that she might not be able to fend for herself. But he'd had reason to be concerned. Over the previous months, he had noticed a sharp decrease in her activity level. Normally, she took a daily walk around the grounds and the adjoining woods. Now she seldom ventured out of doors. He'd also noticed that even the smallest amount of exertion left her winded. His deep concern for her health had made him override proper servant-employer etiquette. He'd expressed his concerns. Hang the consequences.

In the end, he needn't have worried. She seemed to be greatly relieved by his sugges-

Within six months of saying "I do," the couple had moved to Merrybrook and Benson had gone back to drinking and carousing. His young wife had done her best to hold up the illusion of a respectable marriage, but it was evident that others in their social circle knew the truth. Invitations to functions had begun to decrease after Benson's repeated embarrassing displays. Social calls had stopped soon after as well. Hudson had watched with growing compassion as Marion found herself isolated and alone, left to suffer unjustly for the sins of her husband.

Then one day, as Hudson was mending his master's favorite summer suit (needed for a secret rendezvous with a divorcée he had recently met at their fifty-thousand-dollar-a-year country club), word arrived that Benson Reginald Holmes II had been killed in a terrible automobile accident.

The funeral had been a horrible strain on the widow. Her husband was laid out in the front parlor. For the next three days, the same people who had shunned Marion had streamed through the grand entry hall to offer their condolences.

Hudson had watched from the sidelines, the consummate servant, ready with a crisp linen handkerchief should anyone be overcome by grief, or a glass of sherry. Not surprisingly, there had been little call for the former and a great deal for the latter.

Hudson, as unobtrusive as the potted palms, had observed everything, especially the way Benson's parents' eyes sought Marion out yet slid away whenever she glanced in their direction. Even their posture — as rigid as a wooden ruler — had spoken volumes. It was clear to everyone, even the most casual observer, that they blamed her for their son's passing. Perhaps if she had been a better wife, their son wouldn't have had to seek comfort in the arms of another woman, wouldn't have needed to drive to the next town in search of a warm smile and words of encouragement, wouldn't have drunk to excess in his despondency over his failed marriage, wouldn't have driven off that bridge. Marion had endured it all — the whispered comments, the hard stares — with grace.

After the funeral, a week had passed before she summoned Hudson to the library. He had assumed he was to be dismissed. The family no longer had need of a valet.

Marion was seated behind the Sheraton desk that fit so neatly in the space between the tall windows. It had been a gift from her parents on her last birthday. She glanced up briefly as he entered. She was dressed in a simple navy sheath with a single strand of pearls. Her hair was neatly arranged in a chignon at the nape of her neck. The timeless style fit her.

"Please close the door, Hudson, and take a seat."

He silently did as requested, but not before noting that, when she spoke, the slight tremor evident during her short marriage was gone. It had been replaced with a new parlance, one of confidence and resolve.

"I would like you to stay on at Merrybrook as my butler," she began. "Now that my husband is gone, I will be concerned with running the financial end of our estate, and I need someone dependable to look after things here. Your loyalty and . . . discretion . . . have not gone unnoticed all these years. So, if you are willing, I would like to hand over the running of this household to your most capable hands."

Hudson blushed with pride at the accolades and eagerly accepted the position. Within weeks he had Merrybrook running like a well-oiled engine through both his mastery of time management and his superb people skills.

Thus began a continuous stream of parties and weekend functions, especially after the arrival of William, born six months to the day after the death of his father. It was as if Marion were trying to exorcise her husband's shortcomings, determined that her son's life be free from the taint of his father's indiscretions.

From the time the child was born, he was surrounded by some of the world's most influential and socially upstanding citizens. Roosevelts, Astors, Goodriches, Rockefellers, Kennedys, and Piedmonts were just a few of the families who spent weekends at Merrybrook, along with world leaders and noted scientists. Hudson remembered one memorable afternoon tea when he was summoned to the drawing room with a request to find Truman Capote a clean shirt. William had spit up on his collar.

Hudson's thoughts had returned often to those days over the last eighteen years as he walked Merrybrook's silent halls in his highly polished, rubber-soled shoes. Occasionally he would enter the ballroom or the sixty-foot dining room and stand quietly, trying to hear the ghostly whispers of those who had once graced these finely appointed rooms.

Perhaps he should have left right after William's death, as soon as it had become apparent that his mistress would spend the rest of her life turning her home into a shrine for her dead son. The hairbrush William once used still bore strands of his hair, the color of summer wheat. His nightstand with its half pitcher of water and the upholstered chair where a shirt had been carelessly tossed all remained frozen in time, as though, should William ever return, he could step back into his life without having missed a frame.

William, however, was not returning. He had been killed while climbing a mountain in Tibet, where he had gone to escape both a domineering mother and a broken heart.

Why had Hudson remained? Simple. Kept in a carefully guarded place in his heart was a deep, romantic love for his mistress.

The service entrance buzzer sounded again. Now Hudson was duly incensed. What was wrong with young people today? Didn't they have any sense of decorum?

He squared his shoulders and strode across the highly polished kitchen floor. The scowl he wore spoke of his deep displeasure as he opened the door.

"Good afternoon, Mr. Hudson," Matthew Metcalf said, stepping inside before the butler could utter a word. The boy's arms were filled to overflowing. "Gus asked me to drop this stuff off."

"Stuff?"

"It's for tomorrow's Hunt Breakfast. Father Dennis wanted it delivered early, so it would be here when he arrived to set up the buffet."

"Father Dennis?" What did the priest have to do with anything? Hudson had hired Emily Curtis to run the Hunt Breakfast.

"He's working for Mrs. Curtis, helping her set things up. Where do you want this?"

"In the subfreezer," Hudson said, then pointing to the rubber mat, he added, "Please, wipe your feet."

"This way," Matthew called over his shoulder. "Hudson, this is Billy."

"Hello, sir," Billy said, careful to wipe his feet.

"Hello, young ma——" the butler stammered. The resemblance to Master William Holmes was uncanny.

Billy shifted uncomfortably under Hudson's steady gaze. "Can I go now, sir?"

Hudson caught himself. "Yes, just follow Matthew."

The butler pretended to be busy folding napkins as the boys made quick work of the produce, carefully separating tomatoes, onions, peppers, muskmelons, lemons, oranges, blueberries, and cherries into bins.

From his vantage point, Hudson was able to study the boy, tracking every detail of his face, the way he held his head, the shape of his nose, his cheekbones. It was as though he were being visited from the grave.

"I guess that does it," Matthew said, stacking the empty crates. "Want us to put these outside behind the shed?"

"Yes, that would do nicely," Hudson said, trying not to stare at the boy yet finding it difficult to turn away.

"Good-bye, sir," the boy said and gave Hudson a slightly crooked smile. He knew that smile.

Hudson watched from a side window as the teenagers neatly stacked the crates, then slid inside the fire-engine red sports car parked beneath the portico. He zeroed in on the blond-haired boy.

"Amazing."

He had once heard that everyone has a double somewhere, but he had never believed it until now. It was absolutely uncanny. This young man was a carbon copy of Master William.

# 6

"I'd like a word with you," Ethel said after mass.

"Sure, come on in." Father James had just finished disrobing and was getting ready to leave. It was his day to give communion to the shut-ins.

"I hear you have been asked to give a blessing for Mrs. Holmes's Foxhunt."

He knew where this was going and tried to head her off. "Did you know that the proceeds for the event are going to the soup kitchen over in Granby?"

"Don't you go trying to sidetrack me, Father James Flaherty."

The use of his full name. That was never a good sign.

"What I want to know is how you, a man of the cloth . . . a man of the Church . . . committed to issues of inhumane suffering, can condone such a barbaric practice."

"I . . . er . . ."

"I thought you were a man of peace . . ."

"I . . . er . . ."

"I thought you believed in the sanctity of life."

"I . . . er . . ."

She waggled a finger in his face.

"You disappoint me greatly, Father James. If you were a *sincere* man of compassion, you would refuse to take part in this . . . this . . . travesty against God's innocent creatures."

"I . . . er . . ."

"If you decide to go through with this, Honey and I might have to consider crossing the street. I hear Reverend Curtis is strictly opposed to all forms of animal abuse."

"Now, Ethel, you don't really mean that." Although there were a dozen parishioners he wished *would* cross the street, Ethel Johnson wasn't one of them.

"Good day, Father James. Come along, Honey."

The golden retriever leaned forward to lick the priest's hand. Ethel pulled her sharply away and marched out the back door of the church.

Father James and Mother Superior met every Wednesday afternoon for tea, a ritual they had started several years ago, when the nun began the retirement home. That tea had become his oasis in the storm-driven life of the parish priest. He especially looked forward to it today. His ears were still vibrating with Ethel's dressing-down.

Mother Superior's orderly office always smelled of equal parts lavender and Lysol. It was stationed in the eastern wing of the facility and included a set of double-hung picture windows that looked out onto the town green across the street. A stone fireplace was tucked smartly at an angle in the corner between the windows and a pair of French doors that led to a small, private courtyard. A grape arbor shaded a flagstone patio, which kept the space cool even on the hottest days. Ringing the inside area were huge pots of lush flowers, their leaves trailing like tendrils broken free from an old-fashioned upswept hairdo.

This was Father James's favorite place in the summer, and as his hostess poured tall, slim glasses of freshly made lemonade, he marveled once again how removed this space felt from the rest of the neighborhood. Although the town green was often filled with Rollerblading children or mothers pushing carriages as they yelled out warnings to older siblings, the noise never seemed to penetrate here. It was like watching a silent movie.

"Canapé?" Mother asked, passing him a plate laden with a rich assortment of shrimp and lobster meat encased in puffed pastry, succulent scallops wrapped in something green that smelled of lemon, and paper-thin cheese wafers bearing dollops of a rich, fragrant pâté.

"Father Dennis is gearing up for tomorrow's big event," she explained. "I told him I thought the assortment rather ambitious for a breakfast, but I'm afraid he's so glad to be back among the living, as he puts it, that he's gone a little overboard."

Father James laughed. "Poor guy is still having nightmares over his stint at the archdiocese. But it does look as though he's outdone himself this time." His fingers hovered over the plate with indecision. "I hear it's going to be quite an event. Someone told me the governor had agreed to come."

"I wouldn't be a bit surprised. Mrs. Holmes has gone all out for our cause. You did hear that she's donating all the proceeds to our soup kitchen in Granby?"

"Any idea how much it might bring in?" He was still hoping to weasel out of the event.

"I'd never come right out and ask, of course, but I've heard through the DV grapevine . . ."

"DV?"

"Dorsetville. I've heard that each rider is paying five hundred dollars."

Father let out a low whistle.

"Extraordinary, isn't it, that people would pay that much just to chase after a rodent."

"I don't think foxes qualify as rodents," he told her.

"Well, whatever they are, the efforts tomorrow will be well spent. I understand that over fifty riders have been signed up. That will feed a lot of homeless people."

"Yes, I suppose it would," he said, washing down the last piece of shrimp he'd finally chosen with a sip of lemonade.

Well, one thing was for sure. With that kind of money at stake, Mother Superior would not be happy should he refuse to participate. It looked like he'd just have to risk Ethel "crossing the street."

"I missed Father Keene at mass today. That makes three weeks in a row. May I have some more of that lemonade? It sure does hit the spot."

"He's not doing well," she said, swinging her veil to one side as she refilled his glass. "Of course, it could just be this awful heat.

168

You know how bitterly he complains whenever the temperature rises above seventy." She set the glass pitcher on the wrought-iron table. "Doc Hammon was here this morning."

Father James felt his chest tighten. He held his breath. "And?"

"It's not good. His kidneys are starting to shut down."

"What about dialysis?"

"He refuses."

"Refuses? Why?"

"His wish is for nature to take its course."

"He can't really mean that. Why, he's only eighty years old." Father James's eyes filled with an unexpected rush of tears. "People live well into their nineties today. Have you tried talking to him?"

In a rare show of emotion, the nun reached over and took his hand. "It's time, James. He's tired. He's had a good life, and now he wants to go home."

He nodded, not trusting his voice.

Father Keene was like a father to him. He thought about the first time they met.

He had been assigned as an assistant pastor at St. Cecilia's. The archbishop had made it clear he thought that the current prelate needed to retire, that he had let the church become run-down, unsafe, and that

169

James was being positioned to take over his duties and, if necessary, close the church.

It hadn't taken an engineer to know that the church building was coming apart at the seams. That had been evident the day of his arrival. But Father James had quickly perceived that people, not buildings, were Father Keene's main priority. Yes, the church was in desperate need of repairs, but the people, well . . . they were doing just fine.

Memories of those first few years filled his heart with gratitude as he later made his way toward the priest's room. How blessed he had been to be mentored by such a fine disciple of the Lord. Father James had met many older priests down through the years and spoken with a great number of other young priests, many of whom had not found such a warm welcome or a superior whose life so exemplified the life of Christ.

In all fairness, many of these pastors had begun their careers wanting to make a difference in their small part of the world, and were just as fervent in their commitment to extending Christ's teachings to the masses of troubled souls. Unfortunately, they had allowed the daily grind of running a parish, and the constant battle to stay the course directed by the Church against a fast-moving modern society, to turn their zeal to ashes.

Somehow, however, Father Keene had never lost his early priesthood passion, a deep, abiding love of God and the Church that radiated through everything he did. Much of it had to do with his background, Father James supposed. He had grown up dirt-poor in Ireland and as a young boy had found himself the family's sole supporter when his father suddenly died. With a heavy heart, he had left home to work as a farm-hand in a town several miles away. There the owners had taken him into their hearts and later helped him attend seminary. Those had been hard and anxious times for Father Keene, but as in so many lessons God sends disguised as tragedies, the deep sorrow and despair he had felt was later fashioned into a reliance upon God that forged a strong inner faith, turning a simple Irish lad into a great shepherd for Christ.

Throughout his priestly ministry, people came from all around to drink in the special peace that emanated from Father Keene, and to hear his simple homilies, not words couched in fine grammatical discourse but stories of his boyhood or those he loved who had dared to rely upon God's faithfulness and been rewarded by His grace.

Never was that faith more sorely tested than when St. Cecilia's was slated to close. With the departure of the woolen mills, many parishioners had moved away, and the church buildings were quickly turning to rubble.

Father James remembered one day both priests were just finishing mass when a low rumble, like that of an earthquake, shook the altar. Father James, who was presiding, sped up the final blessing and dashed from the altar into the side room, where a portion of the wall beneath the window that looked out across the town green lay in rubble, a fine mist like baking flour rising in the air.

"Glory be!" the elderly priest cried joyously. "It's a sign for sure."

"A sign of what?" Father James asked.

"A sign that the Lord Himself has begun the renovations," Father Keene offered, examining the pile of rubble up close. "This could mean only one thing, laddie. The Lord has decided to honor our prayers. St. Cecilia's will not be closed. The money we need is on its way."

Six months later the miracle they sought appeared. St. Cecilia's was saved, and Father James had never doubted Father Keene's prophecies again.

Was Father Keene's work truly finished here on earth? he wondered. Should he respect his mentor's wish to let nature take its course, or should he try to encourage him to continue on, knowing how much this wise saint of God had left to share? Above all, how did one know when it was time to let a loved one go?

Father Keene had been moved to the west wing of the building, which housed a fully equipped nursing facility. It was a small area that held twenty beds and was designated for those who needed full-time care. The good sisters had tried to eliminate any demarcation between this section of the home and the others, but there were small signs that those who resided here were in poor health and in need of greater assistance. The area was entered through a set of double doors wide enough for a gurney. Sturdy handrails separated the wall sections painted in different shades of green. The air hung heavy with the pungent smell of antiseptic.

Father James trod softly across the highly polished square tiles, passing the open door of eighty-eight-year-old Sister Anna, whose mind had returned to that of a young child. She was dressed in a white cotton robe with a cascade of blue violets embroidered on the lapels, her white hair tied up with a bow. She slept peacefully in front of a television; her earphones had slipped down around her neck as a game show contestant silently mouthed words of jubilation, clutching the show's host and pointing to a shiny new red automobile.

Father James continued his lonely trek. Occasionally a slight snore filtered through a partially opened door, or the sounds of a baseball game being played out over a radio. He glanced inside other rooms, where supine shapes were silhouetted beneath cotton blankets in tulip yellows and rosy pinks, chosen to infuse energy and hope into a sad place.

How hard it was to imagine these former priests and nuns as vibrant beings, busy about their Father's work. Now they lay waiting to be released from the imprisonment of bodies broken down through years of use and to be transformed into His image.

Finally, he came to Father Keene's room. The old priest lay still, deathlike. Father James took in a breath, fearing the worst, and thought about calling for help, but then he spied a slight movement beneath the blanket. He exhaled and tiptoed in.

Is it truly time for Father Keene's final

journey? he asked God within the secret chambers of his heart. If it is, please give me the grace to release this dear mentor and friend, mindful that he is about to meet You face-to-face, even if his passing leaves a hole in my heart.

Father Keene peered up through half-opened eyes and smiled weakly. "I've been praying that you'd come," he said, the soft Irish lilt of his voice never rising above a whisper.

"Always happy to play the part of an answered prayer," the younger man countered, forcing gaiety into his voice. "How are you doing, my old friend?"

"Not so good on this side, but I expect to be doing just fine when I cross over. Sit down, Jimmy. I'm in need of a priest."

How many of these bedside conversations had he had over the years with those about to die? he wondered. He never got used to them. They always made him feel so inadequate. Now, at the side of his dear friend, he felt even more humble. He had brought along his satchel and removed his stole, placing it around his neck.

He quietly pulled up a chair and sat down, then reached out to clasp Father Keene's hand. How frail it felt, as delicate as a bird's wing. He held it gently, as one would a treasured and fragile object, his eyes traveling along the white sheet to the bandages that covered the IV pumping saline into this withering body.

He made the sign of the cross and waited.

Father Keene's eyes twinkled with an old spark. For just a moment, Father James felt renewed hope.

"Forgive me, Father, for I have sinned. It's been a week since my last confession," said Father Keene. He paused as though trying to gather his thoughts.

"Since we've last talked, I've been busy packing," he began. His throat caught, and he started to cough.

A metal pitcher, wet with condensation, sat on the nightstand. A glass wrapped in cellophane sat alongside. Father James removed the plastic wrap, filled the glass halfway with water, placed a straw in it, and offered it to Father Keene, whose lips, he noticed, were cracked and dry.

Father Keene took a small drink, then waved it away. "That's better, Jim," he said, his head falling back against the pillow. "Now where was I?"

"You were packing," Father James reminded him, setting the glass back on the nightstand.

"Oh, yes, that I was. I was going over my

inventory of memories, sorting through the ones I want to take along and the others I wish to leave behind."

Father James smiled. "You must have stored quite a few over the years."

"Aye, that I have."

"So, what have you decided to take?"

The elderly priest thought carefully. "Some childhood memories. The green of the hills of Ireland. The way the mist rolls in off the sea, then covers the cobblestone streets in soft down. My family, of course."

"Of course."

"I can't wait to see them again." He gave a devilish little laugh. "I can see them all now. The Father has told them that I'll be arriving soon. Ma is busy bustling around in the kitchen, making my favorite soda bread. Pa is outside sweeping the path. My brother and sisters will be arriving soon. They live just over the hill now. An easy walk for Ma and Pa to visit. Ah . . . laddie . . . what a celebration we'll be having when I arrive."

The childlike vision of heaven made Father James openly weep. He could easily see his own loved ones someday preparing for his homecoming in much the same way. Once again he marveled at Father Keene's rare gift of making the things of God appear so simple. Who could possibly be afraid of dying when holding on to this image?

He grabbed for a tissue and blew his nose.

"What's your fondest memory?" Father James asked, trying to regain his composure.

"Oh . . . there are so many," Father Keene replied. "But I suppose the one I will cherish most is my day of ordination."

"Hmmm." Father James nodded. This was true for most priests.

"You know, Jimmy, I can't for the life of me understand why more young men aren't joining the priesthood. 'Tis the greatest joy a man can know. It's like Christmas every day."

"Christmas?" Thinking of his recent confrontation with Ethel, Father James didn't know if he would go quite this far.

"What's the greatest joy of the Christmas season?"

"The birth of the Lord, Jesus Christ."

"Yes, that's true, but there's more. Something about His birth that God shares with man."

Father James thought a moment. He knew all the theological reasons, but he had a feeling that wasn't what the old priest meant.

Father Keene saw his puzzlement and offered, "It's the unselfish gift of giving without expecting anything in return. Think how wonderful it feels to help feed a starving family, or provide a toy for a child who would otherwise be without. There is no greater joy and fulfillment than to know the inner peace of having helped your fellow man.

"As a priest, you get to live out that joy every day. In thousands of ways, you help the lost find our Savior Jesus. Oh . . . such a lovely Savior, filled with compassion and love, who gave His life so unselfishly so we could be reunited with the Father. My heart swells with joy every time I think of His grand plan." He turned to glance out the window. "And as priests, we get to be part of it. I don't know of any greater profession than ours, James."

"I agree. Well, that's quite a suitcase full of memories. Will you have room for them all?" he joked.

Father Keene smiled. "Oh, there's room. I only wish there were more of them to pack."

"You've done a fine job as a priest and a pastor and as a friend."

"You're good to say that, Jimmy. But I do have my regrets. Did you ever wish you could go back and do something differently?"

"I guess we all do, but I can't imagine that you have many."

"No, but even one soul lost saddens the Lord. Remember the parable of the ninety-nine sheep? He left all to go search for the one who was lost."

"And is there a lost soul in particular that comes to mind?"

Father Keene nodded. "Yes, there is. One. A young girl. She got a raw deal, Jim, and I allowed it to happen."

That was hard for Father James to imagine. Father Keene had always been the champion of the down-and-out.

"Her name was Suzanne Granger," he said, whispering it softly. "And lately, I see her face every time I close my eyes."

Suzanne couldn't sleep. The trailer was as hot as Hades. She sat up and fumbled for her watch. The luminescent dial read twelve forty-five.

From the front of the trailer, she heard Billy's gentle snores. God bless that kid, she thought. Since he was an infant, he had been able to sleep through almost anything. It had sure made it easy raising him with her peripatetic lifestyle.

She got up and threw on shorts, a rumpled T-shirt, and a pair of flip-flops. There was no sleep for her tonight. Besides the oppressive heat and the payroll that was due tomorrow morning, she felt a steady uneasiness. It was also this town. She hadn't wanted to come here, and the sooner she and her son were gone, the better.

She slipped outside, holding the screen door, letting it close gently behind her. She heard a soft *click,* then turned and started down the dirt path that wove its way around the nest of trailers. She continued along, working her way toward an open field.

A slight breeze rustled a small copse of trees off to the north. She turned in to the gentle wind and felt a hint of dew cling to her legs and arms. The sky was amazingly clear. The stars sparkled like white diamonds. From her distant past, she heard his voice explaining . . .

"That's the Big Dipper, which really isn't a constellation. It's actually called an asterism. Now, see where the edge of the dipper points straight up? Follow the two end stars east and you'll find Polaris . . ."

She felt a tug at her heart. It didn't seem to matter how long ago they had parted, just the hint of his name still brought it all back, emotions so large that their imprint would forever remain upon her heart.

She looked toward the trailer, highlighted against a full moon, and thought of their sleeping son. He knew so little about his father. She had deliberately remained oblique. The less he knew, the better it was for him, she told herself. But was that really true? Or was it herself she wished to protect?

The air grew still again. Off in the distance a raccoon called its bevy of cubs. She hunched down, hoping to spy them.

William had once professed a passion for wildlife. "If I had my way, I would take off for the Appalachians and become a mountain man," he'd professed.

The thought made her smile now as it had then, because it had been inconceivable for William to be anything less than what he had been groomed to become — the heir apparent to the vast Holmes Empire.

They had met at the hardware store here in Dorsetville. Over the years, she had often tried to remember its name, but it remained elusive, like the blue heron that she had seen standing like a sentinel in the dawn's early light down by Bantam Lake the morning her uncle's carnival had arrived in town.

Later, she had told William about the bird. He insisted, in the tone that he reserved for stating absolute certainties, that they were too far north for herons. That was one of the things she loved about him. William had few doubts about anything in life.

He had been wrong. She did see it again. On the day of his funeral.

She had forgone the graveside service, not wanting to chance a meeting with his mother, whose only real crime had been to voice what Suzanne had already known in her heart. She could never fit into William's lifestyle. As in the heavens he had loved to explore, they were galaxies apart. Even though for one brief moment their diverse lives had aligned, the radiance of young love illuminating the wondrous facets of unexplored celestial bodies, it would have been just a matter of time before they both were pulled back by the forces that governed their separate worlds.

She had known that since their first meeting.

That day her uncle had sent her in search of some one-penny nails. Too shy to ask for help, she must have appeared lost among barrels filled with nuts, bolts, and nails. William had sensed that she was adrift and waded his way through a tide of male customers, all of whom seemed to her to be speaking in other tongues.

"Need some help?" he'd said simply.

His eyes were the first thing she'd noticed. They were as blue as the waters reflecting a clear winter's sky. They were intelligent, probing eyes, but also warm and inviting. They held no ridicule, they registered no judgments. She would have spied it right away if they had. As a carnival kid, she had grown up with the judgmental stares of others. Why did people assume that because you lived in a house on wheels you were somehow inferior?

He helped her find the right nails, then insisted on walking her back to the fairgrounds. It was early September, and her uncle's carnival was booked for the next six weeks in area towns.

Although they hadn't spent a great deal of time together, it was just enough for both of them to fall in love.

From the beginning, she had warned him that it couldn't last. Their backgrounds were too divergent. He'd scoffed at her objections. Take education, she had said. She had been home-schooled. Her high school diploma had come in the mail. He had attended the best of private schools and was now a senior at Dartmouth, with plans to get his law degree from Harvard and someday open a law clinic in downtown Boston.

He'd teased her. Wouldn't she like playing the role of a lawyer's wife?

The truth was, she couldn't imagine it. What would she say to all his highbrow

Billy to that kind of humiliation.

The night air was growing damp. She headed back toward the trailer.

She had guarded Billy from the truth for nearly eighteen years. The fact that Jed's personal agenda might have put that protection at risk infuriated her. She just hoped that their stay in Dorsetville was brief enough that Billy wouldn't happen upon any reason to suspect this town carried the secret to his past.

Sheriff Bromley sat at a corner table in Kelly's Bar and Grill, nursing a Budweiser and halfheartedly watching a ball game between the Red Sox and the Chicago Cubs. His faithful German shepherd, Harley, lay by his side, enjoying the cool tile floor and the air-conditioning. Summer heat was murder on the breed.

The bar was nearly empty. The regulars, mostly blue-collar workers, had already come and gone, dropping in after work for a cool beer and a few one-liners before taking off for home, just enough male bonding to ensure their place among the hierarchy in town was secure, but not so much that it would give their wives cause for complaint.

David Kelly's grandfather had opened the bar in the early nineteen hundreds as a way of drawing together the immigrants who had come to town to work in the mills. It had been a daring and risky enterprise. Fights were common among tradesmen back then, especially since nepotism was the rule and anyone trying to break into a trade without the proper ethnic credentials was likely to be blackballed.

But Emmett Kelly had also come from Ireland, a land accustomed to disputes. He knew the power of a pint of beer, good conversation, and some healthy laughter to help bind a diverse group of workingmen. He also knew the prudence of keeping a baseball bat, which he casually referred to as "the enforcer," behind the counter to ward off the occasional rabble-rouser. In all the years that Emmett had reigned behind the twenty-four-foot mahogany bar, there had been only one occasion that he had had need to use it, and the thirty stitches it had taken Doc's father to close the wound had been enough of a deterrent to keep disagreements to the streets from that moment on.

Kelly's sat catty-cornered between Main and a side street. It had two picture windows, one facing each thoroughfare. The doorway was angled between the streets; when the bar was built that orientation had caused some confusion down at the post office as to what street it actually fronted. Was mail to be sent to 48 Main Street or 23 Tyler Avenue? folks wanted to know.

For several months, the highway and building departments had joined with the zoning committee and the postmaster to debate this quandary. Meanwhile, Connecticut Light & Power was threatening to turn off Kelly's lights if he didn't submit an address where he could be properly billed. This in turn caused the health department to get involved, raising concerns over water temperatures used to wash glassware and dishes. "If the electricity is turned off, the hot-water tank goes with it," health officials warned.

Kelly's Bar and Grill, which had been open less than two months, was in peril of closing when Father Keene had stepped in. He was fresh off the boat from Ireland and not about to let a bunch of bureaucrats gum up his enjoyment of a pint of beer with friends at the end of a long day. So he rallied the men and marched down to town hall, where he proposed the type of commonsense answer as elusive as a winged bluebird to most politicians.

"Number the building 1 Kelly's Way."

"But there's no such road," the mayor said stubbornly.

"Then declare one," Father Keene retorted.

It had been that simple.

The bell above the front door jingled. David Kelly, Marion Holmes's high school flame and a third-generation barkeeper, looked up and shook his head. Odis Tunis had just walked in.

"Coke," he told David, acknowledging the sheriff with a nod before sliding onto a vinyl-covered stool.

Harley lifted his head a few inches off the floor and glanced at the newcomer but, sensing no reason to stay alert, went right back to sleep.

Bromley watched with wry amusement as David filled a tall glass with ice, then took the metal hose attached to the soda dispenser and filled it with soda. Apparently, Odis was still on the wagon. The sheriff couldn't help wondering what had brought on this sudden case of sobriety.

The vintage yellow and green clock advertising Ballantine Beer read seven-twenty. George was late. He was supposed to have been here at seven.

Might as well order something to eat while I wait, he figured. Tonight was Barbara's quilting group, the Clothesline Quilters, which meant Bromley was expected to fend for himself.

The game was over. The Cubs had won 4 to 3, in a thirteen-inning victory over the Red Sox, which meant he'd owe Chester Platt five bucks. David flicked off the television and threw a fistful of quarters into the jukebox.

"We need something to liven up this place," he said to no one in particular. The peal of steel drums and Alan Jackson intoning that "It's five o'clock somewhere" flooded the empty space.

"My profession's theme song," David said, joining in on the lyrics as he danced his way back toward the bar.

The gentle rhythm of Jackson's song was suddenly interrupted as George Benson came thundering through the door. "I see that your air conditioner is on the fritz again," he shouted over the music. "When are you going to break down and buy a new one?"

"There's nothing wrong with the temperature in here. It's all that hot air you carry around with you," David countered. "You want a beer?"

"Sure. And turn down that blasted music. I hate it when you have to shout to be heard."

Bromley and David exchanged an incredulous look that said, And this from the man who always speaks as though he's addressing the hearing-impaired.

"Sorry I'm late," George told the sheriff, pulling out a chair and hitting Harley on the head with a chair leg. The dog yelped and scrambled out of the way. "The Hendersons' kitchen sink was clogged again."

George belched as he positioned himself across from the sheriff.

"Damn cabbage. Those sisters' cooking is going to be the death of me yet. I've got to stop scheduling their work around suppertime. Hey, Dave, bring me some bicarbonate, a jar of those pickled pigs' feet, and a beer."

"Are you through getting settled in yet?" Bromley asked. It was a wonder the guy had any stomach lining left.

"What's got your knickers all in a twist?" George asked, sipping his beer. "And what's so darn important that I had to miss the fire department bowling league tryouts?"

"I need a favor."

"You and half the town," George quipped. "Listen, if your AC's broken, you'll have to stand in line. I gotta finish up at the retirement home. I promised Mother Superior that I'd have the new unit in and working by midweek, and I've had to put all my men on it. Those blue nuns can be hell on wheels if you don't deliver on time."

"This isn't about that."

"Oh?"

Bromely waited for David to deposit George's order and return to the bar before continuing.

"I'm talking to you in your official role as fire marshal."

George downed the bicarbonate and belched. "Ahhh . . . that's better. Go on. I'm listening," he said, unscrewing the jar of pigs' feet.

"Before the carnival opens on Friday, it's due for an inspection, right?"

"Yeah. I'm springing a surprise inspection tomorrow morning. You've got to be on your toes with these carnival people. They're crafty, full of tricks. That's why I like arriving unannounced."

George took a slug of beer, forced a fork into the jar of pigs' feet, snagged one, and placed it on his plate. Bromley looked away as George ripped into it. He took a couple of chews, then continued. "I hope that this lot is better than the one the mayor hired last year. Remember them? I found more violations than fleas on a barn cat. Darn near didn't let them open. If it wasn't for Mrs. Holmes stepping in and hiring a licensed electrician to sort out the mess, I would have sent them packing; I don't care what the mayor said."

"I'm making an off-the-record request that you go easy with this group. Give them some wiggle room."

"Easy on them? You're kidding, right?" George exploded, grease dripping out of the corner of his mouth, a half-gnawed pig's foot dangling from his fork.

"No."

"Let me get this straight. Are you asking me to look the other way if I see any violations?"

Bromley looked him square in the eyes. "No, I'm asking that you go easy and not drive them away, is all."

Bromley could tell that George was mulling this over. The two men had known each other for years. George knew the sheriff would never try to interfere in the fire marshal's business if it wasn't important.

He looked around the empty bar, then leaned over and said softly, "What's going on?"

Fillmore had asked Bromley to keep the mission a secret, but this was Bromley's town. He knew who could be trusted. George might be an obnoxious know-it-all with the social graces of a jungle primate, but he was loyal. If the sheriff asked him to keep it quiet, he knew he would.

"I've had a call from the FBI." He shared their conversation about the drugs and the carnival's connection. "They don't want them chased out of town before they have a chance to bring them down."

"Darn drugs," George swore over his mug of beer. "My nephew got involved with them a couple years back. Nearly destroyed the kid and my brother's family." He leaned in closer. "I'm in. Tell me what you need."

Bromley hung around with George to shoot the breeze about the upcoming fair. They discussed who they thought had a better chance of winning this year's blue ribbons for prize bulls — Joe Platt or Henry Rufus. Along with their discussion, they shared a platter of buffalo wings that were hot enough to melt asphalt and a plate of cheese nachos, which would give George a case of gas that would have even Harley ducking for cover.

Around nine o'clock, Bromley left George to polish off an onion blossom and headed toward his wife's car, a silver Toyota Echo. As soon as he spied it parked beneath a streetlamp, he moaned. Inserting his six-foot-four, three-hundred-and-twenty-five-pound bulk behind the wheel was a feat better left to a contortionist.

He opened the door, leaned into the car, and swore. The interior was hot enough to scald off a pig's skin. "Sorry, buddy," he said, motioning for Harley to get in. The dog settled on the passenger seat and immediately began to pant, sending up a plume of steam that fogged the windows.

The sheriff wasn't any more comfortable. By the time he had wedged himself behind the wheel, perspiration was dripping down his neck and collecting in little pockets around his shirt collar. Finally settled, he remembered the keys were still in his pants pocket.

"Darn foreign cars," he swore, arching his back in an effort to straighten his pocket enough to slip his hand inside. The seat began to emit a strange, metallic sound. Something was giving way. Blast! The back of the seat slipped underneath him. Great, just great! Barbara would be all over him like a rash when she saw this.

Finally, he managed to start the engine, right the seat, and flick on the AC before both he and Harley succumbed to heatstroke. A blast of hot air hit him full in the face. He swore again, wondering what it was about these foreign cars that women seemed to like. Give him a good old made-in-the-US-of-A car any day.

He wished he were sitting in his Blazer right now, instead of scrunched like a roach under the heel of a boot in this thing. But since the business he needed to discuss with George was highly classified, he had thought it best not to draw any undue attention. And since everyone in town knew his car, he figured it best to take Barbara's. No one would recognize him in this. His hatred of foreign compact cars had been duly noted by the town's citizens and anyone else within earshot during debates between economy and comfort. Of course, by tomorrow, there might be a slew of rumors that his wife had taken to heavy drink.

Bromley was in no hurry to get home. He figured it would be a few hours yet before his house had been cleared of women and fabric scraps. The town was nearly deserted, except for a few cars parked outside the town hall. There was a finance committee meeting tonight. Nigel Hayes's foreign import was parked in front. Nigel was chairman of the finance committee this term. Didn't anyone buy American anymore? he wondered, slowing down to observe the make and model. The sheriff was somewhat encouraged to see that Mayor Martin still drove a Cadillac.

Fortunately, by the time he and Harley traveled to the edge of town, the AC had kicked in, cooling the interior with welcome cooled air. He let the car idle down Main Street, giving it just enough gas to crest the small bump in front of Stone's Hardware. The town crew was supposed to have fixed that months ago. It was a frost heave caused by last winter's record cold temperatures, something the sheriff hoped never to revisit.

He noticed the bulb above the entranceway to Dinova's was out. He'd give Gus a call tomorrow and let him know. Funny. It was something that Hill normally would have picked up on. Well, maybe it has just gone out recently.

Thoughts of Hill brought other concerns. It seemed that Hill was suddenly suffering from some kind of allergy, sneezing and wheezing all over the place.

Speak of the devil.

Bromley dimmed the car lights as he passed by Hill's apartment. What was that he was trotting out of his truck? Looked like a litter box. What was Hill doing with a cat? Bromley thought his landlord forbade any kind of animals. At least that was what Hill had said the time the sheriff had asked him to watch Harley overnight.

Oh, well, it was Hill's business, not his.

Bromley turned off Main Street and decided to take a ride out toward the fairgrounds. He wondered what Jed Mullen was doing tonight.

Jed never noticed the silver Toyota slowly passing the entranceway to the fairgrounds. He was too busy mulling over other things, like how he had several million dollars' worth of fine white powder hidden beneath the office trailer. He smirked. That was probably why the air-conditioning was on the blink. He had had to move some of it around to pack it all in.

He leaned back against his pickup truck and took a good drag on his cigarette, feeling rather smug. Seventy-two hours from now, he'd be out of here. No more animal dung, no more stupid old men like Sticks Hopson, and no more drain of always being on the road, setting up and taking down what felt like miles of canvas tents and stupid rides. God, how he hated this gig, but he hadn't dared back out. The money was good, and Covas's friends now trusted him. No telling where he could go once this meeting was over. He had been promised a nice chunk of change for setting this whole thing up. He could see himself now, driving a fancy sports car, living in a beach house down in the Caribbean or a penthouse in Las Vegas. Heck, he might even get himself one of those Learjets. He wondered how much those things cost, anyway. After Saturday night, it wouldn't matter. Whatever it was, he would be able to afford it. Not bad for a kid from the South Bronx.

Jed Alfred Mullen had been born to a hooker. His father had been one of her tricks. Which one had never seemed to matter.

They had lived in a small walk-up apartment with some other "working mothers." The only thing that Jed had liked about living there was the knowledge that John Gotti had been born three lots over. Jed used to see him sometimes wandering through the neighborhood, a string of local hoods trailing behind him like he was the Pied Piper. He was always dressed to the hilt — two-thousand-dollar double-breasted Brioni suits and four-hundred-dollar hand-painted silk ties. They didn't call him the "Dapper Don" for nothing.

Other than an occasional Gotti sighting, life in the South Bronx had been hell, especially for a kid like Jed with a hooker for a mother. At sixteen he had been kicked out of school for repeated absences. He liked to hang around the racetracks and watch the ponies. He hadn't been particularly bereaved at having been expelled. For the last two years he had used it mainly as a means of picking up girls.

A few months later, his mother had kicked him out of their apartment. Some john had been using her for a punching bag when he got home one afternoon. Jed had returned the favor. Given him a black eye and a couple of broken ribs. Was his mother thankful? Hell, no. She'd thrown him out of the apartment for losing her a paying customer.

He'd been happy to go.

Then had come a string of dead-end jobs — delivery boy, dishwasher, gofer for a construction company. At eighteen, he'd tried his hand at boxing. He had always been good with his fists. He'd been doing quite well until he was caught throwing a fight. The boxing commission had investigated. He'd been charged and fined and told he could never box professionally again.

He'd decided to check out Miami. He had heard there was a lot of money to be made there. Part of that was true. There was no problem finding some action. He'd connected with some guys who ran a string of "businesses." They'd set him up, and for the next couple of years he'd worked hijacking cigarette trucks, holding up convenience stores, and running money for a local loan shark. He hadn't made a killing, but he hadn't starved either.

Then he'd loaned a guy he met in a bar some money and the dope had gotten hostile when Jed upped the interest. The fight had cost him fourteen months in Gainesville for aggravated assault. There, he had met Freddie Covas. They'd become friends, and when Jed got out, Covas had helped set him up. He'd been given fifty thousand dollars in cash with the instruction to purchase a share in a carnival. Freddie had needed a new transportation system.

Jed struck a match across the heel of his boot, lit another cigarette, and inhaled deeply. The air hung heavy all around him. The rain hadn't cooled things off much at all. You had to wonder, he thought, why people traveled all the way up from Florida to spend the summers here. Hell, it was just as steamy as Miami.

The heat made him think how nice a cold beer would taste right now. Unfortunately, he had downed his last one while watching wrestling on TV. That was another thing he hated about this gig. All they ever played were hick towns, which meant they rolled up the sidewalks around seven o'clock. Heck, if he really wanted a beer, he'd have to drive clear to Hartford, or visit the local dive, Kelly's. He wasn't that thirsty.

His thoughts went back to the meeting. He mentally counted off the things still needing to be done.

First, he had to get past the fire marshal's inspection tomorrow. He'd hold his breath and hope for the best. Most of this equipment was older than Methuselah. A couple of times recently the safety bars on the Ferris wheel had swung open while the ride was still operating. The catches were worn and needed to be replaced. Suzanne had given him the money to have them repaired, but he had pocketed the cash. Why bother? The Ferris wheel needed to be junked. Instead, he'd instructed whoever ran the ride to make sure to tell the passengers not to rock the cages.

The other equipment did not fare any better. Most of it had barely passed the last two inspections in the other hick towns. At least then a fifty-dollar bill passed quietly underneath the table had greased it along. But he'd heard that this George Benson was as straight as an arrow. Any hint of a bribe and Jed would find himself behind bars. He didn't relish the thought, which was why he had set Nelson, the carnival's resident handyman, to work on the faulty wiring. Jed sure hoped he had managed to patch it up enough to pass. The success of the drop depended on the fair acting as a diversion.

He threw his cigarette down and ground it out with the heel of his boot. It was too hot to smoke. A piece of tobacco had stuck to his inner lip. He dug it out with a finger, studied it, then flicked it away.

Once the inspection was behind him, there were just a few more items that needed attention. For starters, he had to make sure Nelson was kept busy elsewhere for the three-day fair. He needed the machinery running smoothly for the inspection, but he planned on creating a nasty little diversion the last night, one that would keep every law enforcement officer in town busy while he and his friends took care of business down by the river.

Hill heard the phone ring as he climbed the stairs, his arms laden with cat paraphernalia. He had left a message on the Cats for Life message machine, asking them to return his call after nine.

He let everything slide onto the floor, frantically searching for his keys, which he discovered had slipped inside the plastic

PETCARE bag. The lock was old and worn, and he had repeatedly asked John to replace it. He finally managed to unlock the door just as the answering machine clicked on. He heard his voice.

"This is Sergeant Frank Hill of the Dorsetville Police Department. If this concerns police business, please dial 555-4433. If it's personal, just leave your name and number and I'll be happy to call you right back. Wait for the beep."

*Beeeepp . . .*

"Hello. This is Marcie Hamilton from Cats for Life. I'm sorry that I missed you, but if you call back tomorrow morning after nine, I should be home from taking my kids to school unless my husband has dry cleaning to pick up . . ."

He did a wild dance, kicking his packages inside the door while trying to keep the cat from escaping. He slammed the door shut, then dashed to the phone, snatching up the receiver just as Marcie was saying good-bye.

"Don't hang up," he said breathlessly as the cat began to wind itself around his pant leg.

"Mr. er . . . Smith? I thought I might have the wrong number. Your answering machine said a Sergeant Frank Hill lived there."

"Er . . . yes . . . I can explain . . . *kerchoo.*"

He sneezed. He grabbed for one of the boxes of tissues that were stationed throughout his apartment. "I'm sorry. Allergies."

"It is that time of year, isn't it? Hay fever?" the woman queried.

"Cats," he parried.

"Oh, dear. Let me guess. You took in a stray and didn't know you were allergic to cats?"

"Yes," he said, breathless with relief. Maybe he wouldn't have to plead with her to take the cat off his hands.

"I can't tell you how often that happens. You poor dear. Cat dander."

"Cat dander?"

"That's what causes allergies in people."

"I don't suppose there's any way to get rid of it?" he asked hopefully.

He'd taken quite a liking to the cat. Of course, he wasn't sure what to do about his lease. Maybe he could figure it out if he just wasn't in such misery. His head was in a fog. His eyes looked as though he had been on a weeklong binge, and he had begun to wheeze like an old accordion.

"No, I'm afraid not. Cats just naturally produce dander."

"Then I guess I'll have to get rid of her. It's kind of a shame. She seems like such a nice cat. Not that I'm very knowledgeable about felines. I've never had a cat before. So, when can I drop the kitten over?"

"Drop her over?" The woman laughed. "Oh, Mr. Smith, I'm drowning in cats. I woke up to a box of eight kittens sitting on my doorstep this morning. And then there're fourteen older cats that are waiting for new homes. I'm afraid that we just couldn't take in one more."

"But you don't understand. This isn't my cat."

"You're trying to get rid of someone *else's* cat?"

"No, no, no . . . I found this cat."

"Yes, you found her," the woman repeated, in a voice that said she had heard this line a hundred times before.

"No, I really *did* find her. Someone put her in a box outside a grocery store. It was raining. Hard. Lightning. I couldn't just leave her there, so I brought her home. She was very sick. I took her to the vet. It cost me two hundred dollars."

He paused. Maybe he shouldn't have said that. What if Marcie Hamilton thought he was trying to pawn off an unhealthy animal?

"She's all better now," he amended. "The vet said she must have eaten some tainted food. Probably the fish heads Gus . . . er . . . the person who owns the grocery store

209

where I found her . . . throws out."

Darn. He had to be careful. He didn't want them tracking him down. What if these Cats for Life people were to discover his identity? John would evict him for sure.

"Sounds as though you've done your best for the poor stray."

Hope was rekindled. She didn't think he was a cat abuser.

"So, will you take her in? I've called the local shelters, but they said they would keep her for only a day or two before putting her down. I couldn't do that."

"I'm sorry, Mr. Smith. Like I was saying before, we don't have any more room. I'm truly sorry. I really am."

He was momentarily overtaken by another sneezing fit.

"My, you have it bad, don't you?"

He blew his nose and tried once more to convince this woman to take the cat before his bronchial tubes completely closed. She remained unmoved.

"Is there anything you can suggest?"

"Have you tried antihistamines?"

# 7

Father James was in his study Thursday morning when Mrs. Norris came rushing in.

"Mother Superior just called. It's Father Keene."

He grabbed his black satchel and darted out the side door, shouting over his shoulder, "Call the prayer chain."

"I assume the news is not good," Marion Holmes told Doc Hammon, watching his face.

She was seated in his office, dressed as impeccably as always in a pale blue Chanel knit suit with black trim. Her posture was as regal as that of a queen, ramrod straight, not a hint of the curvature the Holmeses had always considered evidence of bad breeding.

To those observing from the outside, Marion Holmes looked the picture of good health. Other than her hair, which she refused to dye, and the age spots on her hands, little revealed her age, and few would have guessed that she had turned seventy-three last month.

Her face was flawless, her skin taut. Not one wrinkle or age spot. It was rumored among her friends that this was the result of a very expensive, esoteric procedure performed by a noted plastic surgeon in Brazil. The truth was, however, that Marion's complexion was a result of a superior gene pool.

Yet for all the outward appearances, the test results that Doc Hammon now held in his hands told a different story.

Marion's blue eyes, the color of cornflowers, bore penetratingly into his as she waited to hear the report. Doc Hammon was not immune to the power this formidable lady wielded. Last year her sizable gift to Mercy Hospital had outfitted the pediatric wing with state-of-the-art bedside monitors. It was not, however, because of her great wealth and influence that he was so desperate to soften the bad news. He feared the very thing that set her apart from the common folks in town would also insulate her from receiving the comfort so many would wish to extend once news leaked out about her condition.

He sensed her impatience and began.

"The tests show that you have a condition known as systolic failure. This means that the left ventricle of your heart has lost its ability to contract normally. When this happens, your heart can't pump with enough force to push blood through your circulatory system." He waited, allowing her to absorb this information.

"Go on," she said.

"The greatest concern with this condition is a situation called pulmonary edema."

"In layman's terms," she requested.

"That's when fluid begins to leak into the lungs. As the heart's ability to pump decreases, blood flow slows down, causing congestion in the tissues of the lungs. Fluid builds up and . . ." He let his voice fade.

Marion remained stone-faced.

He removed his reading glasses and placed them on top of the report. "I had my personal cardiologist, Dr. Leventhal, review your tests just to make sure I didn't miss anything. He's top in his profession."

"And what did your Dr. Leventhal say?"

"I'm afraid that, with the advanced deterioration of your condition, there isn't much we can do but keep you comfortable."

"I see." Marion's gaze shifted to his office

window. A gentle breeze was stirring the top leaves of the trees. "It looks like we might get rain again. We certainly can use it. My prize dahlias are withering away, and I had hoped they would be in perfect bloom for the Foxhunt tomorrow. They add such a lovely touch of color to the patio area. Guests are always commenting on them."

"If you'd like, I'll arrange for a second opinion. I can recommend several excellent physicians who specialize in cardiac conditions."

"That will not be necessary," she said, rising.

"If there's anything I can do . . ."

She looked at him steadily. "How much time do I have?"

"You might want to get your affairs in order," he said softly.

"I see. Thank you, Doctor."

Shirley Olsen, Doc's receptionist, nearly knocked her over as she came rushing into the room.

"Sorry for interrupting, Doc, but Mother Superior just called. It's Father Keene. She said you'd better get over there right away."

Marion's health had been rapidly declining. Hudson was duly concerned. She'd even lost her interest in the gardens that surrounded the estate, a hobby that had once been her passion. Down through the years, no expense had been spared, resulting in a landscape that many said rivaled Versailles.

Hudson had watched with growing concern as Marion's poor health prohibited even the daily garden tours that had always given her such great joy. She had maintained her weekly meeting with the head gardener, overseeing new plantings and the reworking of her favorite rose gardens, but refused to venture past the patio. Then, last week, she had asked Hudson to take over the task.

"I don't have the energy anymore," she had confided to Hudson.

"Has madam considered the need for vitamins or B-twelve shots? If you wish, I could make an appointment with Doctor Hammon."

She had agreed.

He watched now for the familiar shape to exit the front door of the brick building. He told himself that she would be fine. Nothing was seriously wrong. She had just let herself get a little run-down, was all. Then she appeared, and he could tell instantly that the news was not good. He rushed to her side and offered his arm to lean upon. Normally, this would have brought a sharp rebuke. This time, she grabbed hold as one would a lifeline.

"Would madam like to take a drive in the country?" he asked easily, leading her toward the car. He wanted to protect her from the grimness of whatever she had been told. There would be ample time to deal with the news later. "I heard that Harriet Bedford's nursery has just received a shipment of rare lilies. I know how much you love them. I was envisioning a lush bouquet beneath the Matisse."

"Not today, Hudson."

"As you wish, madam," he said, opening the car door.

She passed him her purse as she slipped in. She adjusted her skirt, then folded her hands primly on her lap. Hudson laid her purse by her side.

"I want you to take me to St. Cecilia's," she said.

"The church, madam?" he asked incredulously. Marion had not visited the church since William's funeral eighteen years ago.

"Yes, Hudson. The church."

Hudson was lucky to have found any parking space, especially one in front of the church. Cars were lining both sides of the road. Seconds later, Doc Hammon came barreling down the street, double-parked outside the retirement home, and dashed

expect the poor Lord is having quite a time trying to convince her otherwise. In fact, if I know my Hannah, she's up there now sewing curtains for the windows, starting in on a new quilt, and making a list of things she wants me to do when I arrive." He laughed. "Not to mention having the best time catching up with all her friends and relatives who have gone before her."

"Heaven seems so . . . real to you," Marion marveled.

"Why wouldn't it be? The Lord gave His life to break the bonds of death that separate us from our loved ones."

"I wish I could conjure up your faith," she said regretfully. If only she might ask him to stay, help her sort things out. She had so many regrets. So many unanswered questions. She also had no right to ask him to help. She had never tried to make amends or destroy the wall that her father had used to separate them. How many times had she passed David and Hannah on the street? Not once had she ever tried to strike up a conversation.

"Well, you've come to the right place," David said.

"Yes . . . I suppose I have, although it's been a long time since I've stepped through those doors."

221

"God's children are always welcomed home, no matter how long the absence."

"That's comforting to hear."

He replaced the missalette he had been using and lifted the riser, genuflected quickly, and stood up to take his leave. "I'd better be going. I promised one of my grandsons I'd take him to the park," he said, turning to go. "It was nice seeing you again, Marion. I hope that whatever has brought you back will serve to enrich your faith."

What an odd thing to say, she thought.

"Yes, nice seeing you again," she answered, then quickly added, "Perhaps you could come by someday for a cup of tea."

He lowered his head, revealing a small bald spot, and smiled. The mischievous grin that she had once found so endearing surfaced, along with a flood of fond memories. "Do I get to use the front door this time?" he asked playfully.

When they were dating, the few times that David had visited Merrybrook, he had snuck in through the servants' entrance.

Marion couldn't help laughing. "I promise to have Hudson meet you in the drive and personally escort you through the front door."

"In that case, I'd be delighted to come for

tea." He squeezed her hand. She felt herself blush.

"It was nice seeing you again." David paused slightly, his gaze settling on the crucifix. "Whatever answers you have come looking for today can be found at the foot of that cross." He leaned forward and gently kissed her on the cheek. "Godspeed, Marion. I'll keep you in my prayers."

A deep ache, a yearning, clutched her chest. Marion didn't respond. What could she have said? That she had come to confess a life filled with regrets, and that he was one of them? If only she could have found the courage to disregard her father's objections. All these years, it could have been her walking along Main Street hand in hand with David. It could have been David who would mourn her passing. Who would cry as her body was lowered into the cold grave?

She watched until his silhouette was lost among the shadows and the oak doors closed soundly behind him before she allowed the bitter tears to come. She genuflected by the tabernacle and slid into a pew, searching her purse for a handkerchief.

It was entirely her fault that she was so alone. Since William's death, she had walled herself off. The cost of caring was too much to bear. Keep everyone at a distance. Guard your heart so it might never be wrenched again. She had thought that would protect her, but instead it had caused her deeper pain. She saw that now. After being repeatedly rebuffed, friends had stopped calling. Now she doubted if many knew or cared that she was still alive. There was certainly no one left she might ask to come and stay until the end. No one to stand vigil until she took her last breath. Only Hudson. She felt a small burst of electricity charge through her tired bones. Dear, sweet Hudson. He had grown to be so much more than a servant over the years. What would have happened, she wondered, if she had pursued her heart instead of adhering to the strict social mores of her era? No . . . she mustn't let herself go there.

She cast around the sanctuary, turning away from her thoughts of Hudson. The flowers beneath the altar had begun to die. She could tell that it once had been a beautiful bouquet. She spied traces of anemones and cosmos interspersed with Queen Anne's lace and plumes of golden ferns. She wondered why no one had come to change them.

Except for a few repairs and a fresh of coat of paint, little had changed since the last time she was here. That had been the day of

William's funeral. She had sworn back then not to enter these doors again until they carried her in her own coffin. So why had she come today? Why was the church the first thought that flew into her mind after hearing Doc Hammon's prognosis?

When she had buried her son, she had buried all faith in a benevolent God. No one could console her. Not ever Father Keene, who had come to comfort her immediately after hearing the news.

"What kind of God would allow my son to die when He had the power to intervene?" she'd railed.

"His ways are often not our ways," Father Keene had said.

"Then what good is He?" she'd hissed. "What good is a God that cannot be understood?"

The priest had looked at her with tearstained eyes reflecting her own grief. But she would not be moved by his compassion or his pity. She was not one of those pathetic individuals who would run to the Church seeking comfort. Besides, what comfort could it give her? Could it bring back her child?

Outside a cloud blocked the sun, casting the sanctuary into shadows. She felt if she studied the dark corners long enough, she might glimpse the ghosts of her past.

As hurtful as it was to admit, William's death could have been avoided if she had just allowed him to marry that girl. Suzanne was her name. For the first time, Marion acknowledged her part in his passing. It was a hard realization that filled her with new grief.

She looked up at the crucifix. What had David said? "Whatever answers you have come looking for today can be found at the foot of that cross." As Christ was laid bare, so must be her sins. She must accept her part in the tragedy that had sent her son to an early grave. He would never have left if she hadn't condemned the girl he loved for lack of an appropriate pedigree. How could she have been so cruel? Hadn't she suffered the same fate at the hands of her father? Why had she felt it necessary to visit it upon her son?

If only she had known the outcome of her actions back then, she would have found a way to accept the girl. Perhaps, in time, they could have become friends. The girl was not without honor, and there was no doubting it took a true love to leave as she did, convinced that doing so was in William's best interest.

Marion glanced down at her hands. She

had made so many mistakes. Not in malice, perhaps, but in hubris. Did that make it any less a sin?

She had entered into a loveless marriage more to please her parents than herself. Her in-laws were right. If she had loved Benson, perhaps he wouldn't have died a senseless death, having to seek companionship from another woman. If only she had had the courage to follow her heart and marry David. But, unlike her son, she had been too cowed by social conventions.

She was transported back to the day William, a young man, had strode into the morning room with a sense of purpose. Funny how certain moments are forever etched in one's memory. She remembered how resplendent he looked in his Italian silk suit and gold cuff links. The way his hair, bleached by the sun, was combed back from a broad forehead, the sharp contours of his cheeks, his powerful jaw. He was her Adonis. Seeing him that morning, the years had flashed back through a kaleidoscope of scenes — William, eight years old, standing by the club's pool, his face flushed with victory at having mastered the art of a perfect jackknife; as a twelve-year-old, his widening smile at having made the soccer team; the pride she'd felt when he was chosen high school valedictorian. All those thoughts made her heart swell as he delivered a soft kiss to her cheek.

"Good morning, dear. Come sit down. I haven't seen you in days. Where have you been keeping yourself? Have you been off visiting with the Stensons' new polo pony?" she teased, going back to her morning paper. "I hear that he's just acquired a new mare from Argentina with an impressive pedigree."

William remained standing. His shadow fell across the page she was reading. She glanced up. He wore a look she could not decipher. It threw her off center. Up until this moment, she had believed there was nothing that she did not know about her son. That evidently was not true. At that moment, she sensed a chasm opening across the thick Persian carpet, one she feared she could not bridge. She felt the first stirrings of alarm.

"What is it, dear? Is something troubling you?"

"There's no easy way to break this, Mother, so I'll say it straight out. I'm engaged to be married."

"Marriage? Why, that's wonderful, dear. Who is the girl?" she asked, running down a mental list of debutantes.

"You wouldn't know her, Mother," he began. "She's not from our circle of friends."

"Someone from the South perhaps, or Europe?" she asked hopefully. William had spent last summer abroad. He had casually mentioned meeting Princess Helen of Romania. She felt a trickle of excitement. "Don't keep me in suspense, William. Tell me her name and how you met. I want to hear every last detail."

To his credit, William did not try to avoid the question or avert his glance. "Her name is Suzanne Granger, and she travels with her uncle. They own a carnival."

For a moment, she thought he was teasing. He had always been a great practical joker. Hadn't he nearly gotten kicked out of boarding school for greasing the tiles outside the dean's office with cooking oil? Then came the sharp realization that this was no joke. There was no punch line. William was serious.

"Now, darling, you can't be —" she began. The look on his face stopped her dead.

"I will not be cajoled out of this," he said firmly.

This could never work, she began. They were from two different worlds. Enjoy her company, she suggested, but realize that it could never go further than infatuation. This girl was not worth throwing his life away.

William threw down the gauntlet. He said he knew she would react like this. But he did not need her approval. He loved the girl, and they would get married, with or without her consent. A terrible row followed.

In the end, she threatened to cut him off without a penny, to which he responded that he did not need her money. He had trust funds of his own and was working toward his law degree.

Finally, he stormed out of the room. She was too blinded with rage to call after him. She waited until she heard gravel flying beneath his imported roadster as he dashed down the drive before walking to the window, her heart weighed down with grief. Why couldn't he see that this union would never work?

Hudson entered the room to remove her breakfast things.

"If you say one word about this . . . ," she warned, assuming Hudson had probably overheard.

"Have I ever disclosed anything that has transpired in the house, madam?" he asked calmly.

"No, of course not. I apologize. It's just . . . I'm so very upset by all of this. I'm not certain what I should do," she confessed, wringing the Irish linen napkin still clutched in her hand. "Why doesn't William realize that if he goes through with this, it will only end in tragedy?"

"May I make a comment?" Hudson asked quietly.

She nodded.

"Master William is a very headstrong young man. He takes after his father in that respect. He will not be constrained by social mores. He will do as he pleases, and if you refuse to accept his decision and his choice of wife, or try to interfere in any way, you may lose him."

The light from a bank of stained-glass windows patterned the backs of the pews with flecks of color as Marion surfaced from her memory. She studied the patterns, thinking what would have happened if only she had taken Hudson's advice that day. Instead, she had gone directly to Father Keene, insisting that he help dissuade William from this marriage. He had listened attentively, while their tea grew cold in their porcelain cups, then looked at her sadly and suggested that they pray and let God settle the matter. "Some things are better left to work out by themselves," he advised.

She rose from the chair like a great Titan,

filled with righteous indignation. How dare he suggest that they do nothing or that she did not know what was best for her own son? If anything, he should have proposed they pray for deliverance from this horrible state of affairs.

In the interim, she said, he should talk to the girl. Convince her to disappear. Go back to her sordid little life and leave William free to embrace his true destiny.

Father Keene refused.

She left the rectory without a further word, but when she got back to Merrybrook, she had her secretary place an emergency call to the archbishop. The previous year her contribution to the Archbishop's Annual Appeal had equipped a neonatal unit at St. Francis Hospital. He immediately took her call. She explained what she wanted done, and when he began to hedge, she hinted that her generous support would be withheld should he refuse to order Father Keene to comply with her request.

Her threat worked. Shortly afterward, Father Keene agreed to set up a meeting between Marion and the girl. William had been sent to Boston to confer with the family's attorneys about a business matter while Suzanne slipped away.

Of course, Marion denied having had any hand in the girl's sudden disappearance, but William had seen right through her lies. He went in search of Suzanne, pledging that his mother would never see him again. Marion told herself it was an idle threat, made in the heat of passion. She was certain that eventually he would realize she was right. William had died a few months later.

From the bell tower, the carillon chimed out "Amazing Grace," the notes moving through the sanctuary in a prayer of their own.

She broke down in tears. Oh, why had she come here? She had sworn never to darken this church again. Unlike David, she had no faith, no sense of the reality of God or Christ or any of the other tenets of her faith. Her soul had been hollowed years ago by grief and what she feared could never be undone. If there was a God, He certainly wasn't concerned for her. Why would He be? She had abandoned Him a long time ago, along with any hope of ever seeing her son again. What did she expect to find within these walls?

She gazed up at the crucifix, her conversation with David fresh in her mind. He had lost someone he loved, yet he was not bereft. His faith assured him that he and

Hannah would someday meet again. What made him so certain? she wondered. She sighed. Faith was not something one conjured up like a magician's trick. Oh, why had she come? Once more her eyes traveled to the cross. Was it You, Lord, who drew me here?

The question startled her. She had asked it as though she and the Lord conversed regularly, as though she had expected Him to reply. How peculiar.

She was therefore taken aback when she heard an audible voice.

*"Be not dismayed. You shall see William again, for he lives because I live."*

She swung around, certain that someone had snuck in behind her. She scanned the pews, the choir loft, the altar.

"Who's there?" she asked, her voice aquiver. The church was empty. Then where did the voice come from? Was her illness playing tricks on her mind? Then something even stranger happened. She felt a presence, a warmth, enveloping her, and she knew she was no longer alone. Her rational mind went into overdrive, trying to explain what she was encountering, yet finding no explanation forthcoming. Was it possible that she was being visited by the living God?

"Is that you, God?" she asked, not at all

expecting an answer. "If so, what are you trying to tell me?"

If she hadn't seen it with her own eyes, she would never have believed what happened next. The flowers beneath the altar, which moments before had been dying, were coming back to life. Marion watched in a mixture of fascination and unbelief as the lifeless bouquet was refashioned into the most beautiful flower arrangement she had ever seen. The flowers shone with a startling luminosity. It sent a chill up her spine.

At that moment she knew, *knew with absolute certainty,* that William lived. His body may have been buried, but his spirit lived. Death came as an inevitability of life, but through Christ, her son's spirit, his essence, had been transformed from death to life just as the lifeless flowers had been transformed.

A sob rose thick in her throat. She understood now how David could endure the death of his beloved wife yet find reason to hope and feel blessed. Anyone who accepted Jesus Christ as Savior was blessed. Blessed with eternal life.

She thought of all these years she had grieved over the finality of William's death. Her son had been taken from her, she had told herself. The child she had loved more than life no longer existed; his essence had been eradicated, blotted out, leaving her with only memories of her golden-haired son.

But that was a lie; she saw that now. A glimmer of light, like those flickering in the bank of candles beneath the Blessed Mother's feet, began to illuminate a truth she had never fully grasped before. Through the sacrifice of the crucified Christ, all who believed in Him would live. Death was not a final chapter but a transition, from mortality to immortality. William lived, and when her time on earth was through, they would be reunited.

Tears streamed down her cheeks. The fear of her own death, which she had so efficiently hidden behind a mask of stoicism, fell away. Death's cold grip, which had tunneled its way through her emotions, gave way to the warmth of a great truth. The finality of death was a lie. Christ had ransomed us from death through His sacrifice on the cross.

"Whatever answers you have come looking for today can be found at the foot of that cross," David had said. She saw that now.

A Bible verse sang out in her mind . . .

"O Death, where is your victory? O Death, where is your sting?"

She was filled with regret for all the years she had wasted harboring an anger toward God when, all the time, He had been patiently waiting for her to return to the healing power of His grace.

She knelt and prayed in the silence of her heart.

"Dear God,

"I've wasted so much of this precious gift of life. I see now that instead of rejoicing in the short time that William walked this earth, I lashed out in anger at You for having taken him away. I see now that whether a person's life is long or short has no relevance. It's what one does with that time that's important. Apparently, William had finished what he had come to do. I can accept that now."

With tears of repentance streaming down her face she asked, "Would you please forgive me?"

It was a simple prayer, yet she felt its immediate connection. It was as though God had been waiting there all those years for her to pick up the phone. With a rush of joy, she felt her spirit freed from the heavy load it had carried for so long. A new prayer of thanksgiving poured from her lips as the burdens she had carried — anger, guilt, regret, shame, unforgiveness — were lifted.

*Because He lives, so does William, and so will I.*

Suddenly, a picture of Suzanne seated in Father Keene's study came to mind. Marion's momentary joy was overshadowed with a new regret. Could God forgive her this, too?

Once more she bent her head and repented. Once more, God's infinite grace washed her soul clean.

When Marion Holmes walked through the doors of St. Cecilia's, the outer woman remained the same. She still carried herself with a regal flair befitting her station in life, but inwardly she had been refashioned, filled with such a lightness of spirit that she swore if Hudson hadn't been there to take her arm, she might have drifted up and away.

Across the road, at the Sister Regina Francis Retirement Home, everyone was laboring under a heavy weight of sorrow. Father James had arrived to administer the Last Rites to Father Keene. Doc Hammon said it wouldn't be long. The word went out, and people began to pour into the home in the hope of having one last moment with the priest they thought of as their spiritual father.

One by one, the nuns found their way to the private chapel that sat on the north side of the retirement home to pray for his safe passage into heaven's halls. The space had originally been constructed as an observatory. Its tall walls of glass and high, domed ceiling provided the perfect melding of nature with the divine. In choosing this space, Mother Superior had ignored the others' repeated objections that there was no place to hang the Pope's picture or the Stations of the Cross. She had held steadfast. She knew the power of nature to connect us with God, and apparently, so did the Master Gardener. Hadn't He begun his narrative with man in a garden?

She placed Sister Bernadette in charge of the project and wasn't disappointed. The first time the sisters walked into the chapel, they were stunned into silence. Oleander, potted palms, and tender citrus trees fanned out, giving the impression that the outside and the indoors had somehow fused. Tropical and subtropical plants covered the walls, among them the succulent climber waxflower, spectacular with its clusters of star-shaped white flowers with crimson centers. Its subtle, enticing scent mingled with those of jasmine, gardenias, and bougainvillea.

The altar was stationed toward the front of the conservatory, built from four unpolished stone pillars and a crude slab of marble that seemed to spring from a tropical oasis. Gazing upon it for the first time, Mother Superior had felt as though she had been transported back to the Old Testament, to worship among Abraham's descendants as they entered the land of Canaan.

The space quickly became Father Keene's favorite, which made it even more fitting that the nuns found their way here upon hearing Doc's announcement.

Sister Bernadette seemed the most deeply shaken. Father Keene shared her love of gardening. Before he took ill, hardly a day went by that the pair weren't knee-deep in manure or compost.

She knelt in the area that provided a wonderful view of the magnolia tree she and Father Keene had planted this past spring. As they prepared the hole, they had talked about the natural optimism of gardeners, agreeing that it could hardly be otherwise. Gardeners continued to profess great faith each time they planted a seemingly dry, lifeless seed into the ground with absolute confidence that someday it would flower into a thing of beauty.

"Oh, Father Keene, I shall miss you so," she softly cried.

Then it hit her. His soul, like the gardens he had lovingly tended, had outgrown his place on earth. It was time for him to brighten Another's garden with his gentle smile, his easy gait, his tender spirit.

Tears came freely. She let them flow. Even though she knew with certainty where he was bound, the knowledge did not lessen the empty hole that his passing would leave in the garden of her heart.

# 8

Dinova's produce section was under siege. Women swarmed around the empty fruit bins with looks of stunned disbelief. Where were the freshly picked apples — Pippin, Cortland, Rome, Gayla, McIntosh — and pints of succulent blueberries, strawberries, blackberries, raspberries, and huckleberries? Loretta Baker specifically wanted to know what had happened to the crates of peaches that Gus had said were arriving this morning.

The County Fair was only two days away, and not a piece of fruit for pie, preserves, or cobblers was to be found anywhere on Gus Dinova's produce shelves. They crawled under counters in futile search for mislaid crates. Voices buzzed in angry astonishment, humming at a fevered pitch like yellow jackets about to swarm. Finally one of them clutched her empty wicker basket to her chest and shouted for someone to get Gus out here now *or else!*

Audrey Hanson, who had worked at Dinova's since high school back in 1982, had never run so fast in her life. She found Gus writing up a milk delivery order and shouted so loudly for him to *"get up front"* that he thought the store must be on fire.

Timothy McGree had been debating whether to buy Raisin Bran or Cracklin' Oat Bran when he heard the ruckus. He tucked both boxes under his arms and hustled toward the front of the store.

Lorraine Gallagher, who had stopped in for some ice cream, was asking Arlene Campbell about her husband, Fred, when they heard the noise. She threw a container of Ben & Jerry's Chunky Monkey into her wagon and raced behind Arlene to see what the clamor was all about.

Rounding a display of coffee that was on sale, two cans for five dollars, they nearly collided with Shirley Olsen, who had just dropped in for some Maxwell House for the doctor's office.

"What's going on?" Arlene asked.

"I don't know, but I think it's coming from the produce section," Shirley said. The three women hustled on over.

As they swung around the corner, they spied Gus backed between the sweet corn and fresh cut lettuce, looking as though he were pleading for his life.

"Listen. Please, ladies. There's been a slight mix-up."

"What kind of mix-up?" Marge Peale wanted to know. Because she was Judge Peale's wife, the women felt it appropriate to defer to her as their spokesperson.

"The produce order that was supposed to be here was sent to Bradbury Market by mistake. As soon as Matthew alerted me to the problem . . ."

At the sound of Matthew's name, the women turned their gaze on him, their eyes narrowed and accusing, as though he was somehow responsible for this. Matthew stepped back, melting into the gathering crowd. There was no way he was taking the fall for this one. He was just a stock boy.

"I got on the phone to try and straighten things out," Gus explained. "You just have to be patient while I untangle this."

"Mistake?" Emma Hayes shouted, her face flushed from either anger or another hot flash. It was hard to tell with the English. "Sure it's not a conspiracy?"

"A conspiracy?" The word rippled over the sea of disconcerted, fruitless women.

"Well, wouldn't that beat all?"

"As I was saying," Mrs. Hayes continued.

"Perhaps the women in Bradbury don't think they can beat us by playing fair, so they've sunk to hijacking our delivery truck."

"No one said anything about hijacking," Gus said, trying desperately to stop a rumor before it could be launched. "Listen, all of you. There was no hijacking. It was an honest mistake, a mix-up at the trucking station, that's all."

The women weren't listening. They were now deeply committed to the hijacking theory.

Gus felt a sudden drowning sensation.

"I never did trust those women over in Bradbury," Biddie Moran added. "Not since John told me that their zoning board banned clotheslines in some of the new developments."

There was a sharp collective gasp.

"Makes you wonder what they're trying to hide, now, doesn't it?" Mrs. Hayes said.

Mrs. Norris elbowed her way closer toward Gus. "All this talk about clotheslines is interesting, ladies, but none of this helps one iota with our present problem. We have entries to get ready for the fair and no fruit to cook with. So what exactly do you plan to do about it?" she asked, glaring at the store owner.

Gus looked out at the women, feeling as though he were staring down the barrel of a loaded rifle. His mind went into overdrive. What *was* he going to do about it? He had called the trucking company, which had offered to send a truck over to Bradbury and pick up the order. There was only one catch. The first available truck couldn't get there until tomorrow morning, and by the looks of this crowd, they were not about to wait that long.

Like a man about to drown, he cast around the ocean of faces desperately searching for a life raft and spied Matthew. He smiled his most confident smile. "Matthew will take the van and bring back our order."

"But, Gus, I promised to drive Stephanie to the television station during my break. She's interviewing Mr. Pipson."

"Call and tell her that she's going to have to find another ride," Gus said out of the side of his mouth. He clapped his hands and gave the restive women his most reassuring smile. "So, that settles it, ladies. Your fruit will be here by noon."

"It had better be, Giuseppe Antonio Dinova," said Ruth Henderson, his former high school English teacher, who used to call him that whenever he was in danger of failing her class.

Hudson felt as though he had been on an emotional merry-go-round since this morning.

First his heart had plummeted right down to his toes when Marion had walked out through the doors of the medical building. He knew without asking that his worst fears had been realized. His dear Marion was gravely ill.

While he waited outside St. Cecilia's, he had stormed the heavens on her behalf. Marion might have given up on God, but he hadn't. Even though Hudson was an Episcopalian, and leaned less on the community of saints than did Catholics, he sought their intervention now, and the help of anyone else up there, on her behalf. Mostly, he prayed that Marion would find healing not only for her body but also for her troubled soul.

And miracle of miracles, a portion of his prayers had been answered. As soon as she exited the church, he could sense a change. She'd paused to study a bed of hydrangeas near the sidewalk.

He'd hurried to offer his assistance, his spirits rising like incense. "Lovely flowers," he'd commented, holding her arm steady as she bent to take in their gentle fragrance.

Marion had turned to him and smiled. It was a strange kind of smile; there was a hint of mischief in her eyes. Then, like a naughty child, she'd done something that had shocked him down to his socks. The woman who had always been so prim and proper had unlinked her arm from his, cast a quick look around to make certain no one was watching, and broken off a flower.

"Run for it!" she'd shouted, making a mad dash for the car. She'd dove into the backseat. "Well, don't just stand there, Hudson. Put the pedal to the metal!" she'd demanded.

What madness was this? he'd wondered, playfully joining in. He'd told her to "duck down out of sight," then left a trail of rubber as he sped down the hill.

"That was a hoot!" she'd cried, glancing out the back window as though expecting to be overtaken by the police at any moment.

*A hoot?* His Marion never spoke in colloquialisms. She was suddenly full of surprises. He'd glanced at the rearview mirror, making certain that this was the same woman he had seen enter the church a short while ago. He wasn't sure what had happened in there, but whatever it was, it seemed to have infused her with new life.

"I've never stolen a flower or . . . anything before," she'd said, her voice as gay as a schoolgirl's. "How energizing! Do you suppose that's what motivates thieves?"

"I wouldn't know, madam," he'd answered jokingly.

"If it is, I should have taken up thievery a long time ago."

Her gay spirits had lasted all the way back to Merrybrook. "I feel as though I could run a mile," she'd said.

"Perhaps you might start with a less ambitious exercise program, madam. Say with a gentle walk down to the stables and back."

"You're right, of course, but I feel so wonderful," she'd said, glancing into a hall mirror. She'd leaned up close and studied her hair. "I think I'll call my hairdresser and set up an appointment. I'm tired of this style. I want something . . . gayer."

"Ummm . . . Why doesn't madam take a short rest while I see about tomorrow's details? I have a short list of things that must be gone over with Mr. Dinova."

"Oh, yes, the Foxhunt. I had forgotten."

"When I return, I can accompany you on a short walkabout." The transformation was amazing. What had happened inside that church?

"Promise?" she'd asked with a slight glint in her eye.

He'd smiled at this new childlike behavior. "Promise."

Now, as he turned onto Main Street, he realized that the cause of Marion's transformation really didn't matter. What mattered was how to keep that spirit alive. There was only one way he knew, and that was to give her a new reason to live, ignite a passion. Like a pond that had been cut off from its source and left to grow stagnant, Marion had allowed her bitterness and sorrow to cut her off from life. No wonder her heart was ailing. She felt there was nothing left to live for.

He needed to find something that would change that, but what? Stealing an occasional flower wouldn't fit the bill. Perhaps he should petition the saints again for an idea, he thought, locking the car and stepping onto the sidewalk. They certainly had come through with his first request.

His mind was still filled with thoughts of Marion when he stepped through the grocer's door and was nearly plowed down by a herd of angry women.

"Madams! Please be careful!" he cried, pressing himself against the door as they charged past.

He found the grocer inside his office, giving instructions to the two teenage boys who had been to Merrybrook the day before.

Gus handed a set of keys to Matthew. "Everything has been straightened out. The manager over in Bradbury is expecting you and has set our order aside. Drive around the back, load up, and then hightail it back here before those women return with reinforcements," he said, running a hand over his bald head.

"We'll be back before you know it," Matthew said.

"And thanks, Billy, for pitching in. Between the fair, family barbecues, and Mrs. Holmes's Hunt Breakfast, Labor Day weekend is always a killer."

"Speaking of the Hunt Breakfast," Hudson chimed in.

"Oh, hi, Hudson. I didn't see you standing there. Come on in and pull up a chair. I guess you're here to go over tomorrow's details."

"If you have the time."

"I'll make the time. Boys, why are you standing there? Get going. The women will be back by noon, and they expect to find the produce section filled with fruit. Now go! And drive carefully," Gus called after them. He worried about all his employees as if they were family.

"All right, we're going. We're going," Matthew told him. "Come on, Billy."

The boys scooted past Hudson and smiled. Once again, the butler was struck by the similarities between Master William and this boy, Billy. Golden, wavy hair, long neck, sharp cheekbones, the same cornflower blue eyes. He had an odd thought. What if this *was* William's child? Could that be possible?

"Hudson? Hudson?"

"I'm sorry. What were you saying?" He pried his eyes away from the boys as they disappeared behind a swinging door.

"I was asking if Mrs. Holmes is with you. I know how she likes to personally take care of the last-minute details for the Hunt Breakfast."

"Mrs. Holmes? No, she's a little under the weather today and asked that I take care of things."

"I hope it's nothing serious. I know how much this event means to her," Gus said, searching his clipboard for the Holmes order. He found it behind the order for the Sister Regina Francis Retirement Home.

"Here it is. Now let's see. It looks as though everything is in place. Fortunately, your produce order was delivered yesterday." He sighed with relief, then mumbled under his breath, "and didn't get mixed up with today's mess."

Hudson nodded noncommittally, his mind still focused on the boy.

"Emily Curtis has been in and out of here all week charging things to your account. Let's see, what else can I tell you?" Gus scratched his head. "Five dozen fresh rolls, breads, and an assortment of muffins have been ordered from Lori's Bakery. Oh, and Harry Clifford is taking care of the coffee. I know how highly Mrs. Holmes prizes his coffee. He wasn't sure if you would have enough large urns, so he's borrowing some from St. Cecilia's kitchen."

"Yes . . . yes, all of that seems fine." Suddenly Hudson had an idea. "I'm concerned we won't have enough servers."

"Mrs. Curtis is taking care of that."

"Please advise her that I wish a couple of extra boys. Mrs. Holmes doesn't like to be caught shorthanded."

Gus rubbed his chin. "This is kind of short notice. Most of the teenage boys are busy with the fair. As you know, we have a lot of 4-Hers here in town."

"What about the two boys who just left here? I believe they're the same ones who delivered to Merrybrook yesterday. I'm familiar with the Metcalf boy, but the other one . . . ?"

"Billy. He's a new friend of Matthew's," Gus offered.

"They'd do nicely. Does Billy have a last name?"

Gus shrugged. "I never thought to ask. I'm paying him off the books."

"Tell the boys that, since it's such sort notice, Mrs. Holmes would be willing to pay them each one hundred dollars for the morning's work."

Gus whistled. "A hundred dollars each? Maybe *I* should volunteer."

By one o'clock, Matthew and Billy had made the run to Bradbury and back. Much to the townswomen's relief, the produce shelves at Dinova's were now filled to the brim.

Matthew was still determined to help Billy find the missing pig and had come up with the idea of posting his picture on the local cable network. He made a quick phone call to his grandfather, who in turn talked it over with the station manager.

"Carl says to bring a photo around and he'll air it during tonight's 'Around the Town' segment."

"I sure appreciate this," Billy said as Matthew pulled into the WKUZ parking lot, fingering a glossy eight-by-ten publicity photo of Pepper Pot that Sticks had taken in the hope of getting the Charlie Chan movie deal. "I'd like to meet Mr. Pipson and thank him personally. It's really nice of him to do this."

"He'a great guy," Matthew said. "He has to be to put up with my grandfather and Mr. McGree. They're kind of technologically challenged."

Matthew told his new friend about the two men's attempt last year at editing a program by themselves and the uproarious results. Billy was laughing so hard he could hardly breathe.

"So now I'm the official senior editor of all their programs," Matthew said. "It doesn't pay much, but I get lots of experience."

"You like editing?"

Matthew thought a moment. "Yeah, I guess I do. In fact, don't tell anyone, but I've been thinking about making my own documentary."

"Yeah, about what?"

"If I tell you, you'll think I'm a nerd."

"No I won't." Billy made an *x* over his chest. "Cross my heart."

"Father James, that's our parish priest,

he's always going on about the need for more young men to enter the priesthood. So I was thinking: Maybe I should make a documentary about what it's really like to be a priest. Not their formal roles, you know, like saying mass or presiding over funerals and weddings and stuff like that, but how they make a difference in people's lives."

Matthew paused here to remember his last encounter with Father James. Although he had not completely let go of his anger over God's refusal to find the funding for him to attend MIT, the priest's words had stayed with him. "Faith is a matter of trusting when everything else tells us to do otherwise. It's about believing in a loving Father who won't let us accept anything but the best for our lives, even when it makes us lash out at Him when our plans have been derailed."

Father's comments had forced him to reexamine his own faith, not as a kid throwing a temper tantrum because he hadn't gotten his own way but as an adult who wanted to take God at His word and trust that things would work out. Matthew wasn't certain what the outcome would be, but he was willing to give it a try and see where God might lead.

"It sounds like a great idea," Billy said. "Not that I know anything about being a priest. My mom and I don't go to church much. Too bad I'm not sticking around longer. I'd love to lend a hand. I've always been fascinated with idea of taking a concept and getting it on film."

"Wouldn't that be great? We could pair up. I'm great with the technical stuff. How are you at conceptualizing?"

"You mean taking an idea and translating it to film?" Billy thought a moment. "I think I'd be rather good at it. There weren't a lot of kids my age in the carnival to hang out with, so I practically lived in a dreamworld. I was always making up stories and acting them out. I bet you didn't know that you're seated beside the kid who saved the planet from a massive alien invasion."

They both laughed.

"We'd better get inside," Matthew said, looking at his watch. It was nearly time for their meeting.

The boys opened the car doors and were met with a blast of hot air that instantly fogged their sunglasses. Although the parking lot was only a few hundred yards from the station's front entrance, the thick wall of humid air slowed their youthful gait to a crawl. The sun beat against the concrete steps, sending waves of heat rising like steam from a kettle. By the time the two boys opened the glass doors with the station's call numbers written in bold block letters, they felt as though they had journeyed through a dense tropical forest.

"Now, who is your handsome new friend?" Gracie Abbott asked as Matthew and Billy strode in.

"This is Billy Granger," Matthew said. "He's with the carnival."

"You both look as though you're about to melt." She reached underneath her desk, where she kept a cooler of sodas, and pulled out two Cokes. "Here, this should help."

The boys gratefully accepted and chugged them down while Gracie launched into one of her monologues. "So, you're with the carnival," she mused. "How exciting. Our family can't wait for opening night. We just love all those rides. And the food! Why, we just eat ourselves sick. I do hope you have one of those funnel cake stands. My little boy loves those. Of course, my husband prefers the Philadelphia cheesesteak sandwiches. You will have those, won't you?" she asked. Not waiting for a reply, she sallied on.

"Myself? I love plain old cotton candy. There's just something about cotton candy and carnivals. They go hand and hand like . . ." She frowned, trying to think up an appropriate simile, but finding none, she shrugged. "Oh, well . . . you know what I mean."

Matthew glanced up at the wall clock. Their appointment with Mr. Pipson was for one o'clock. It was nearly one now. Before Gracie could draw another breath, he asked if the station manager was free to see them now.

"Why, I don't know. I'll have to buzz him and ask. Last time I checked, he was still talking to that girlfriend of yours."

"Stephanie? So Mr. Rosenberg was able to give her a ride over? Great." It had worried Matthew the whole way to Bradbury and back. She hadn't sounded too happy when he'd called to say he couldn't drive her as he had promised.

As Gracie buzzed Mr. Pipson's office, Stephanie rounded the corner.

"Well, hello, Matthew," she said. "I see you made it safely back from your produce run." She turned to Billy and stuck out her hand. "Hi, I'm Stephanie."

"This is Billy Granger," Matthew offered, feeling his heart skip a beat. God, she looked great in a light green summer shift that showed off her tan.

259

"Hi there," Billy said, smiling shyly.

"Stephanie is working as a summer intern at the local newspaper," Matthew explained.

"Which is why I had needed a ride here," she said, pointedly turning toward Billy. "I've just finished interviewing Mr. Pipson. It's part of a series I'm doing on local businesspeople. Now, I haven't seen you around town before. Are you new to Dorsetville?"

"I'm with the carnival."

"Really?" Matthew could tell by the look in her eyes that her reporter's mind had just kicked in.

She edged closer to Billy. "I bet our readers would be very interested in what it's like working for a carnival. Would you be willing to give me an interview?"

"I guess, although I don't know what I would say."

"Don't worry about that. I'll think up some easy questions and we'll take it from there."

"My grandfather is doing a piece on the carnival for the station," Matthew cut in. As soon as the words left his mouth, he realized how lame they sounded. It was just that he didn't want Stephanie hanging around with Billy. No sense taking any chances.

"So? That doesn't mean the paper can't run something, too."

"Matthew," Gracie called, cupping her hand over the phone receiver. "Mr. Pipson will see you now."

"Thanks, Mrs. Abbott. We have to go."

"May I call you later?" Stephanie asked Billy, looking deep into his eyes. "To . . . er . . . set up a date for the interview, of course."

"Sure. Got a pen and some paper? I'll write down my number."

Stephanie handed him her pad.

Matthew leaned over, wrenched the pad out of Billy's hand, and slammed it down on the circular reception desk. Gracie jumped like she had been shot.

"Come on," Matthew told Billy. The muscle along his lower jaw began to twitch. "We don't want to keep Mr. Pipson waiting. Stephanie will just have to connect with you later."

"Are you all right?" Billy asked Matthew as he was being dragged down the hall.

"My, my," Gracie exclaimed, watching them disappear. "What has gotten into that young man of yours?"

Stephanie was hoping that it was an attack of the green-eyed monster, which would mean maybe things would work out just as she had planned after all.

■ ■ ■ ■

"Pick up, Sheriff," Betty hollered from dispatch. "It's George."

Bromley put aside the report sent over by Agent Fillmore, got up and closed his office door, then picked up the receiver.

"Got anything?" he asked. The carnival inspection had been scheduled for this morning.

"I've got a disaster waiting to happen, that's what I've got."

George's voice roared, then suddenly faded dead away. "George? George? You still there?"

"Dropped the darn cell phone. Can't understand how people can drive and talk on these things at the same time. Wait a minute. I'm pulling over."

The sheriff drummed his nails as he waited.

"You still there?" George screamed.

"I'm not deaf."

"I'm never certain if people can hear me on these things."

"George, most people can hear you clear across town without a phone."

"Funny."

"So, what happened?"

"I did my inspection like you asked. It's just as I thought. The place is an accident waiting to happen. The wiring alone was enough to give me nightmares. And that's not to mention all the codes they're breaking by running propane stoves in tightly enclosed spaces . . ."

"Tell me you didn't refuse to let them open," Bromley said, reaching for his bottle of Tums.

"I did as you asked. I looked the other way. In fact, I had to look so far away that it gave me a crick in my neck."

"I'm appreciative of your help, George. I'm sure Agent Fillmore is, too."

"Oh, and Al . . . I overheard Jed Mullen say something to a worker about having to leave before the concert on Saturday night. Don't know if it means anything or not."

"It just might," Bromley said. "I'll pass it along."

"Oh, and Al, I went fishing the other day. You know that old logging road that runs down to the river about a half mile downstream from Barry's hotel?"

"Yeah."

"There were fresh tire tracks. No one uses that road but me and Chester Platt, and I asked him. He said he'd been too busy this summer to go fishing."

"Interesting . . ."

"Well, here's something even more interesting. Mullen's truck was parked right next to the generator trailer. He's got it outfitted with those heavy-duty tires, the ones with the four-inch ridges."

"I'm listening."

"I happened to notice that those tires were caked with the same kind of mud that runs along the edge of that old logging road."

## 9

**DORSETVILLE GAZETTE**

## COUNTY FAIR

STEPHANIE COSTELLO

DORSETVILLE. The 70th annual Labor Day County Fair is gearing up to be an exciting three days beginning with Friday morning's kickoff event, Merrybrook's Annual Labor Day Foxhunt, and ending on Sunday with the Children's Pedal Tractor Pull. Chairperson Mrs. Rochelle Phillips would like to remind all parents that children must wear helmets, and that Sheriff Bromley has promised to arrest any parent who gets out of hand. For those readers who might have forgotten, last year Fred Jackson doused one of the judges with a pail of fresh manure. Fred said his son's tractor won over Ed Farridy's son's by pulling three cement blocks a good two inches farther. The judge, however, hadn't seen it that way.

Father Dennis is looking for someone to take over his bingo duties this week in the church basement hall. He's promised to help Emily Curtis, who is catering the Hunt Breakfast, so if anyone could pinch-hit for Father Dennis, please call the rectory.

Meanwhile, Mrs. Curtis is looking for help to decide whether to serve a breakfast polenta with sausage, onions, and peppers, or a breakfast soufflé with sauteed pears. Folks are invited to stop in and sample each one, but Emily warns them to be prepared to be put to work washing pots. And even though Father Keene will not be giving the blessing this year, she still plans to serve his favorite Irish soda bread.

The Hunt Breakfast is a charity event sponsored each year by Mrs. Marion Holmes. This year's proceeds will go to support the soup kitchen run by the Daughters of Mary of the Immaculate Conception of the Blessed Virgin Mary. Mother Superior expressed her gratitude for Mrs. Holmes's generosity. "Mrs. Holmes's gift will help to provide food and medical services for our guests. This is especially needed during the hard winter months up ahead," she said.

Mother Superior added that she wished to reassure all the animal lovers who have expressed their concerns that the fox would receive a special blessing for its participation in this worthy event. Father James, who is to perform the blessing, had no comment.

Mr. Joseph Platt, whose prize bull Zorro has won the County Fair blue ribbon three years running, feels confident that he'll win again this year; but Mr. Harvey Miller, who has entered his new bull imported from Montana, says Zorro doesn't stand a chance. Sam Rosenberg told this reporter that he's seen Miller's bull and feels he might be right. He would also like to remind the folks that Kelly's is giving 10 to 1 odds in Mr. Miller's favor.

As in the past, this year's County Fair will kick off with a parade along Main Street. The mayor has suggested that those wishing to get a front-row seat arrive an hour before parade time, and as a reminder, all parking has been suspended along the parade route. Nancy Hawkins says that if folks don't mind walking up the hill, they can park in her lot at Tri Town Auto free of charge.

The parade committee has announced this year's theme, "Working for a More Beautiful Environment." The Dorsetville Scouts will lead the parade with their float. Scout Leader Harry Clifford said that it is made entirely from litter the troop found along Route 202 in Torrington.

The sheriff wants to remind all those viewing the parade to stay on the sidewalks. Last year an overzealous picture taker scared Ned Knoll's (trick) horse Silver so bad that it threw him into Esther Wiggin's lap as she rode by in the backseat of the mayor's new Cadillac convertible. Esther said her back's not been the same since.

Just a reminder that all those entering the Apple Pie Contest should have their pies delivered to the center building marked "Country Crafts" no later than 8:15 a.m. on Saturday. In the interim, Father James would appreciate it if the entrants would refrain from dropping off samples at the rectory back porch. He says it's just not Christian to try and influence a judge.

Now for those who might need a reminder of this weekend's events, here's a calendar that you can hang right on your refrigerator door.

*FRIDAY*

| | |
|---|---|
| 8:00 a.m. | Merrybrook Foxhunt. Hunt begins at precisely 8:15. Hunt Breakfast to follow. |
| 5:00 p.m. | Main Street Parade |
| 6:00 p.m. | County Fair gates open |

| | |
|---|---|
| 6:30 p.m. | Stock Tractor Pull |
| 7:00 p.m. and 9:00 p.m. | Dorsetville Firemen's Flashback to the '50s Band |
| 7:30 p.m. | Pony Draw |
| 8:00 p.m. | Teen Dance (sponsored by the Salvation Army Band) |
| 10:00 p.m. | County Fair gates close |

*SATURDAY*

| | |
|---|---|
| 8:00 a.m. | County Fair gates open. Exhibit barns open |
| 9:30 a.m. | Junior Dairy and Sheep Shearing Show |
| 10:00 a.m. | Official Blue Ribbon Ceremony |
| 11:00 a.m. | Old Tyme Fiddlers — Main Stage |
| | Oxen Show followed by Oxen Draw |
| | Antique Tractor Pull |
| 11:30 a.m. | Hollerin' Contest |

| | |
|---|---|
| 12:00 NOON | Cow Plops Throwing Contest |
| 12:30 p.m. | Pony Cart Club Display |
| 1:00 p.m. | Woodchopping and Power Saw Carving Contest |
| 2:00 p.m. and 4:00 p.m. | Fly by Night Jugglers — North Stage |
| 8:00 p.m. | Night Hawk Concert — Main Stage |
| 10:00 p.m. | Fireworks Display |
| 11:00 p.m. | County Fair gates close |

## SUNDAY

| | |
|---|---|
| 8:00 a.m. | County Fair gates open |
| 10:00 a.m. | Chicken Race |
| 11:00 a.m. | Box Lunch Auction |
| 12:00 NOON | Community Picnic |
| 1:00 p.m. | Box Car Race |
| 2:00 p.m. | Family Line Dancing |
| 3:30 p.m. | Ice Cream Social |
| 4:00 p.m. | Children's Pedal Tractor Pull |

| | |
|---|---|
| 4:30 p.m. | Closing Ceremonies |
| 5:30 p.m. | County Fair gates close |

During the night a thunderstorm had rolled in. Lightning slashed the sky, and thunder clashed so loudly that it sent the sheriff's dog sailing into his room to hide under the bed. But by Friday morning, the skies had cleared and a northern breeze had swept into the valley, bringing cool, dry air tipped with the hint of fall that the Dorsetville folks had so craved.

Just about everyone in town was up and bustling around their kitchens by the first light. Today was the opening of the County Fair. Why, it was all anyone had talked about for weeks, and now that the big day was here, there was plenty for everyone, adults and children alike, to do, and not a moment to be spared.

Livestock had to be washed and brushed to a high sheen. Bakers had to ready their entries. Quilters were still fussing over last-minute details. Barbara Bromley awoke bleary-eyed, having stayed up half the night to finish her entry, a double Irish chain with a quilted medallion center.

Lori Peterson was also up at first light.

The Lady Baltimore cake she had baked after putting Paul to bed needed to be iced. It would be her first try in the Decorated Cake division, and she was a little nervous. She had seen last year's entries and knew that the competition would be stiff. Fortunately, she had finished the needlepoint pillow that would be entered in Handcrafts. It was her own design and had come out quite lovely, if she did say so herself. She glanced at the kitchen clock. It was nearly 6:00. She felt an adrenaline rush. There was so much to be done and so little time. There was breakfast to be made, the baby bathed and dressed, and somewhere in between all that, she needed to fix her hair and put on some makeup. Suddenly she felt like a marathon runner just before a big race. Since little Paul had arrived, there never was a moment to spare.

The thought of her infant son brought a smile. He had certainly complicated their lives. It had been so long since a baby had resided in their home. Lori had forgotten how exhausting taking care of an infant could be.

In truth, she loved every moment she spent with her new son and refused even to hear about placing him in day care while she worked. Instead she brought him along each morning to the bakery, where Paul was never lacking attention. Half the time he was missing from the portable crib she kept behind the display case. Women were always scooping him up and parading him around the adjoining restaurant. Little Paul loved it, and Uncle Harry constantly thought up excuses for the baby to keep him company by the front counter. Even tough-talking Wendy seemed to turn to mush when the baby appeared. Just the other day, Lori had overheard her say that Paul was the sweetest baby she had ever seen. Lori wholeheartedly agreed. Paul seldom fussed or cried.

Lori placed the baby's bottle in a pan of hot water to warm, then went to see about her son. She walked barefoot down the hallway, feeling the polished wood, and slipped into Paul's room. He was sleeping with his legs tucked beneath his chest, his cute little bottom sticking up in the air. His tiny thumb was in his mouth, and he was making little sucking sounds.

The sight of his innocence filled her heart with the warmth of love only a mother could know. Although it was only four short months ago he had come into her life, it felt that he had always been there, tucked somewhere hidden within her soul.

She closed her eyes and paused, as she

did every morning, to thank God for sending her this precious parcel. She may not have given birth to this tiny creature, but she was as tightly bonded to him as she would have been to the child she had miscarried a year ago. The fact that Paul was a special needs child made him that much more endearing, especially since the child she had lost (a boy she had named Ephraim) had been diagnosed as severely handicapped.

When she had lost Ephraim, Lori's faith had been severely tested and she had questioned God's love. How could a loving God allow the death of this unborn child? Hadn't she come to terms with his handicap? Hadn't she wrestled with what it would be like raising a child who would never function as normal and resolved that she would love him just as much as any other child, perhaps even a little more?

She hadn't understood why she had been made to suffer back then. Her deep grief had shut out God's love, but with Paul's arrival, she felt closer to understanding. As with all suffering, it had been a prelude to a greater plan.

Ephraim was more than just her baby. He had been a special messenger sent directly from heaven's hall, bearing a unique gift.

During those few months he had been in her womb, he had opened her heart, made it ready to love all the unwanted handicapped children that would come after him. Ephraim's passing had been the catalyst to a wonderful new ministry.

Didn't Father James always say that our spiritual paths should be highways built upon service to others? She and Bob had discussed this in depth. Bob felt the same way. They were already talking about adopting another special needs child when Paul grew a little older. Bob said he would welcome as many as their hearts and their home could hold.

A soft beam of sunlight streamed through the nursery's window, laying a golden path across the floor, reflecting onto the sleeping child. Lori stepped silently into the room and gently caressed the tiny form, thoughts of cakes and blue ribbons drifting away as she stared in wonder at her sleeping child.

Father James had rushed through mass as quickly as he dared under the heated glare of St. Cecilia's regulars, who liked him to keep a certain pace. When things sped up, they tended to get confused, some standing when they should be kneeling and kneeling when they should be sitting. One time he had been in a hurry to make a meeting with the archbishop and overheard his head usher, Timothy McGree, complaining to Ben Metcalf that "I felt like I was doing some new kind of Catholic aerobics."

Under normal circumstances he happily obliged, but there was nothing normal about today. In less than an hour he was due to give the official blessing to the horses and riders for Mrs. Holmes's Foxhunt. Throughout the mass, he kept his eyes off Ethel Johnson. He didn't have to look at her to feel her steely gaze boring right through him. He strongly suspected she was behind the flood of daily e-mails denouncing the inhumane treatment of foxes during foxhunts. Yesterday he had gotten forty-two.

Honey was curled up on the pew next to her mistress. He caught the dog's eye. She turned away. Good grief! Even the dog was against him. Could things get any worse? He walked to the lectern to deliver his very brief homily, wondering how long it would take to find favor with the dog or her mistress again.

After mass, Father James didn't bother to disrobe. Instead, he hightailed it out of the church, blowing right past Timothy and jumping into his Jeep. The Holmes estate was less than five miles away. He used the travel time to pray for the safety of the fox and to bargain with God. If God would just get him out of this mess, he vowed never to let himself get into this pickle again. Mrs. Holmes would just have to import herself a priest from another parish, politics be darned.

How *had* Father Keene managed to take part in this event year after year and not incur the wrath of animal activists like Ethel? It must have been simply because he was Father Keene, and so dearly loved that even Ethel was willing to keep her angst to herself.

Thoughts of Father Keene brought a lump to his throat. Father James had spoken with Doc Hammon just before mass. It seemed his beloved friend was quickly declining. "I doubt he'll make it past the weekend," Doc had said, his eyes misting with tears. "I know it's his time, but I'm not finding any comfort in that knowledge."

How could any of them?

Father Keene had faithfully served St. Cecilia's most of his priesthood. Normally, priests remained only ten or twelve years in a parish and then were ordered to move on. But somehow, miraculously, through a succession of archbishops that came and went like the wind, Father Keene had been allowed to stay. And down through those years, there wasn't a parishioner who hadn't been directly affected by his heartfelt love for his flock, or his lilting Irish brogue as he delivered both homilies and words of comfort, shepherding God's people through the ups and downs of life's rocky paths.

Harriet Bedford often said that without him she would never have gotten through the sudden disappearance of her granddaughter Allison and her son, Peter, which had come on the coattails of losing her daughter-in-law and Allison's baby sister in a car accident. It was too much grief in too short a time for anyone to handle. Father Keene had helped her, stopping for a chat or wangling an invite for supper. And over leisurely cups of strong tea (which he always insisted upon brewing) or shared walks down the back country lanes, he had quietly listened to her pain-filled words and helped her climb up out of the valley of tears as he shared his unshakable faith in God's compassion. "For the sufferings of this present time are not worthy to be compared with the glory which shall be revealed in us," he had said, quoting Romans: 8:18.

Later, when the woolen mills closed down and the town struggled under economic hardship akin to the Great Depression, his role as shepherd had been sorely tested. It was hard to maintain your spiritual bearings when those whom God had entrusted to your care were being tossed about like flotsam through turbulent seas. He was the first one the men called when they lost their jobs or women sought with tearstained cheeks when bank officials came to foreclose on their homes.

Father James was so centered on past memories that he had nearly missed the turnoff at the junction along Route 202. He drove a few more feet, then pulled into a nearby field, overcome with an almost insurmountable swell of sorrow. He could hardly breathe.

It hit him straight on. The priest who had nurtured him, inspired him to be more than just a pastor and a sturdy foundation for God's people, a light of hope in darkness, was dying. A sob rose from the depths of his soul. It didn't matter that his faith assured him of eternal life. The sorrow did not come from doubts. It came from the knowledge that for the rest of his journey here on earth someone he deeply loved would no longer walk beside him. Father James would no longer sit beside his mentor on the altar, no longer hear his assurances that he was using God's gifts wisely or his oft repeated phrase "And this too shall pass."

The memories of Father James's early priesthood, leading up to his arrival at St. Cecilia's, rose like a gentle mist.

He had been in a terrible frame of mind. He had been assigned to another parish that was slated to be closed. It was to be his third in ten years.

His previous assignment had been at St. Bridget's, once a lively parish that had spawned an elementary school. Over the years, the city neighborhood had decayed and the more affluent parishioners had fled to the suburbs. St. Bridget's was now smack-dab in the middle of one of the state's poorest areas, a place where despair bred like lice.

If there ever was a place where a Catholic church should have fought to remain open, it was this one. It was immediately apparent to Father James that its closing would deliver a devastating blow to the already downcast people. It would also mean that the schoolchildren, who had thrived in an environment founded on the Church's principles, were about to be funneled into the public school system, where only 25 percent of students made it past eighth grade without getting either shot or pregnant.

Father James felt strongly that the Church should do everything in its power to save this parish. These people needed its guidance more than the members of hundreds of parishes sprinkled throughout the state. In fact, by removing this beacon of light in the pit of despair that they had been forced through economics to call home, the Church would effectively be plunging an entire community into total darkness.

His heart was filled with compassion for the people and anger at the surrounding Church community. Why hadn't the pastors from affluent parishes been apprised of their condition and encouraged to help? Hadn't Christ given us the directive to care for the poor? Wasn't their role as priests to inspire their congregants to higher roles of service? As St. Paul had written, "Faith without works is dead." If just one outlying church were to make a pledge, it might very well save the parish from extinction.

He voiced these issues to his superior, Monsignor Ryzak, a doughy, pockmarked man whose response had been to remove himself from all except essential duties. "It saves me from having to hear their complaints about the closing," he had told

Father James that first week.

But Father James was not about to let the church close without a fight. He rallied the parishioners to start fund-raisers. He called his seminary friends and put on a 1950s revue that sold out both nights and made a profit of over $3,400. Father James dressed like Marilyn Monroe and sang an off-key version of "Diamonds Are a Girl's Best Friend." It brought down the house.

The money raised was hardly enough to make a dent in what was needed to repair the church and school buildings, but at least it was a beginning and sent a message of hope. More important, it showed that, if the people had a leader, they would rally together and make it work.

His pastor, however, didn't want to hear any of this. In fact, the more Father James pushed, the more bellicose the monsignor became, spewing angry words at him as he drank his way into oblivion. The man had only a few years left till retirement, he said, and felt no compulsion to try to change things. Furthermore, he resented Father James for hinting that he should. "You're still young to the priesthood. Filled with unrealistic, idealistic beliefs. Dreams? Fantasies? You need to bring your head down out of the clouds," he said, making a circle above his head. "This is reality."

"At least I'm trying to help," Father James retorted hotly.

He knew he was risking being labeled a troublemaker within the archdiocese by running up against his superior. He just didn't care. Let them banish him to a parish in the backwoods of the state; anything was better than sitting idly by and seeing a needed parish go down.

"How many years has it been since your ordination? Ten? Fifteen?" the monsignor asked with hauteur in one conversation.

"Twelve. What does that have to do with anything?"

Monsignor Ryzak poured himself another large Scotch. "Come back and talk to me when you've been at this job as long as I have. We'll see then how willing you are to try and buck the system. Churches close because they don't make money. Pure and simple. No matter what you may think now, the bottom line is cold, hard cash."

The improvised parish had lingered for another four years, then closed. As much as Father James had tried not to allow his superior's attitude to rub off on him, toward the end of his assignment, he had found it difficult to maintain his faith in both the Church and a merciful God.

When the final day came, he felt only a great relief. The last few years had been like trying to roll a boulder up a steep incline. As much as he would miss the people and felt laden with guilt that he hadn't been able to save their parish, a secret part of him looked forward to starting over someplace fresh, with the hope that he might rediscover the peace of soul he had known before coming here.

Therefore, nothing could have prepared him for the discovery that he was being sent to yet another troubled church. He pleaded with his adviser to release him from the assignment, insisting that he would take a position as an errand boy, anything rather than have to face another church closing. But his pleas had landed on deaf ears, and for one sober moment, he had considered leaving the priesthood. He felt he just couldn't go on, but he did.

It was with a heavy heart that he pulled up in front of St. Cecilia's, with its chipped and frayed facade, its listing railings and peeling front doors. A section of the stone stairway had been roped off. Several portions had been torn away. The rectory alongside the church had fared no better. The front porch railing was missing several spindles, and the structure looked as though its last coat of paint had been applied at the turn of the century. Several of the upstairs windowpanes were cracked, and sills had rotted, leaving large gaps between shingles and frames.

In contrast to the decaying buildings, the lawn and gardens were well tended. It was late spring when he arrived, and a profusion of daffodils and tulips encircled the grounds. Hedges were neatly trimmed and planters filled with a colorful assortment of pansies, which lent a kind of bravado, as though hope still bloomed among the ashes. It was a cheerful thought and one that helped to motivate Father James to get out of the car, walk up the front steps, and ring the bell.

He heard a thick Irish brogue shout, "I'll be getting the door, Mrs. Norris. You mind the kettle."

The door was opened with such force that it nearly sucked him inside, and a small, gray-haired priest with a twinkle in his eye and a mischievous smile opened wide his arms and exclaimed, "Why if it isn't he himself, the new cleric come to give aid to a weary and overburdened old priest! Come in, come in! The saints be preserved. We don't want the Congregationalists down the way thinking we don't know how to properly welcome a man of the cloth. Mrs. Norris, put out another cup, we've got ourselves a new member of God's army come to aid us in the war against the devil, and none too soon.

"The bishop said Flaherty is your name, right?" he rambled on as he lead Father James toward the rear of the house. "Now that's a fine Irish name. Had a childhood friend named Peter Flaherty — any relation? He lives in County Cork now. You know, I should give him a call. He still owes me a fiver from the last Irish Derby."

Father James never did get to say much at their first meeting. Father Keene was kissed by the Blarney Stone, as the Irish say, and loved to regale listeners with stories of his boyhood back in Ireland, or the parishioners who made up the parish, or just life in general. Since Father James was a good listener, they were nicely paired.

Although the conditions of both buildings were dire, Father Keene described the spaces in warm, optimistic terms as they moved from room to room, not ignoring the desperate needs for rebuilding but couching each statement with his firm belief in God's ability and willingness to right the situation. The older priest finally summed it all up by saying, "The Good Book says that the testing of our faith is to instill trust. I'd say by the look of things here, that by the time He is finished with this test, we will have enough faith to move any future mountains that come our way."

From that moment, their relationship flourished. Father James found his faith being renewed through the mentoring of this dear, old saint. By example, Father James learned how to quietly trust in God's mercy and grace, not by looking to the outward signs for comfort but by opening his heart and soul to His leading; by waiting in confidence, not rushing ahead of God, knowing that the Father knew of his needs and that He *would* meet them in His time and in His way. Even when St. Cecilia's looked certain to close and the buildings were about to fall down around their ears, Father Keene's faith that God would work a miracle never wavered, and that faith had been justified.

The memories Father James lingered over the longest were those of summer evenings. They would be seated on the back porch. Mrs. Norris would serve them tall ice cream floats with homemade ice cream, thick and sweet with a dollop of freshly beaten cream, the glasses wet with condensation. He and Father Keene would lean back in the green wicker chairs that creaked under their weight. The town park ran behind and to the right of the rectory, its lush foliage swaying gently in the breeze. Walking trails wove through the thickets, and often the priests would hear their names being called out as folks took an evening stroll. The priests would smile and wave, often stating that they, too, should take some exercise, although neither ever made any effort to move off their porch rockers. They preferred to sit quietly, letting the day's events settle in their minds, like sediment in a pond. Some, innocuous, would sink to the bottom and not be thought of again. Other, more memorable moments would float out over the evening, sailing onto topics of conversation.

Father James would always remember these quiet moments, two priests sharing their spiritual journeys, not in lofty ecclesiastical terms but in simple parables of God's response to prayers through the everyday events of common lives. They would ponder new ways to convey God's love to those in trouble or without hope and talk about mysteries like apparitions, spontaneous healings, and visions, wondering out loud why more weren't experienced by modern man. "Jesus is the same yesterday, today, and forever," Father Keene would quote. "The same Jesus who healed the sick in

Jerusalem is available to heal today."

Then why weren't more experiencing divine healings today? The silent question hung in the air.

Hours seemed like mere minutes as night rolled its shade across the sky, obscuring the woods, the gazebo in the center of the park, and the steeple of the Congregational Church beyond, leaving just two men alone on a porch against a backdrop of soft, yellow light that filtered from a kitchen window. At some point, both would grow silent, each absorbed in his own secret thoughts until a gentle breeze would stir, like ice cubes on the bottom of a glass, cooling a layer of air that would circle their legs, forcing them back inside.

Those were the memories that Father James held close to his chest. How lonely it would be without him once Father Keene was gone, he thought, staring out into the field. A movement in the tall grass caught his attention. It must be some kind of animal, he thought, leaning over to the passenger side for a better view. He watched with fascination, trying to catch a glimpse of the creature as he traced its travels. It seemed to be heading toward the Holmes estate. He prayed it wasn't a fox.

*Fox!*

Good grief! The Foxhunt. He glanced at the dashboard clock. Gripes! He was supposed to have arrived fifteen minutes ago. He threw the Jeep into drive and hightailed it out of there, sending a pack of squirrels scurrying to get out of his way.

Matthew Metcalf, dressed in a white dress shirt, tie, black slacks, and apron, watched Stephanie Costello approach the riders with a writing tablet in her hand and an all-business look in her eyes.

"Hot water, coming through," Father Dennis called, filling the trough beneath one of the covered sterling silver serving dishes.

"You'd better move or you're going to get scalded," Wendy said.

"Sorry, Father Dennis." Matthew moved aside and went back to removing a crate full of cups and saucers while stealing furtive glances over at Stephanie.

"What's the matter with you? You haven't smiled all morning," Wendy asked, neatly setting out a row of perfectly folded napkins. "You two have a fight?"

"I don't know what we had," he said, with a sigh. "I'm just confused."

"Well, get used to it. That's what romance is all about."

"Where do you want these glasses?" Billy asked.

"Put them under the table by the glass pitchers, and make sure they're hidden behind the table skirt. Hudson the Horrible has already told me he doesn't want any *superfluous accoutrements* visible. Who talks like that, I ask you? There's something about that man I just don't like."

"Who don't you like?" Emily asked, carrying a basket of rolls.

"The butler," Wendy said.

"Hudson? Oh, he's okay. A little too prim and proper for my taste, but he seems like a nice man."

"Oh, yeah, then why is he spying on us?"

Emily looked around. "Where?"

"He's behind the rose trellis. Maybe he thinks we common folks might take off with the family silver."

Hudson had hidden himself behind the trellis to get a better view of Billy. He still couldn't get over the resemblance the boy bore to Master William. It was absolutely uncanny. It was as if they were mirror images. If his suspicions were correct, this might give Marion a reason to fight to live.

Billy had been given the task of setting out the teacups. Amazing. Even his motions reminded the butler of William. After watching him for several minutes more, Hudson was convinced. This boy *had* to be William's son. Hudson only wished that he could have come up with more information about Billy's mother. He was pretty certain that she would turn out to be the girl William had planned to marry. Hadn't her uncle owned a carnival? And the boy's name was Billy, a nickname for William. All of this just couldn't be coincidence. Still, he wished he had been able to gather proof.

"Hudson, what are you doing in there?" Marion asked. "I've been looking all over for you. The grocer has sent cream instead of half-and-half for the coffee, and Mrs. Curtis has informed me that the left jet on the stove refuses to light. And Father James still isn't here. I was quite clear that he was to give the blessing at precisely at seven forty-five. It's almost eight o'clock."

"I'll see to everything," Hudson said, stepping out from behind the trellis. "Please, don't get yourself upset. Why don't you come over here and sit down? Have a cup of tea while I sort things out."

"Yes, a cup of tea sounds lovely. I don't know what I'd do without you, Hudson," she said, looking up into his face.

He caught a hint of something unfamiliar.

There was a tenderness to that look. For just a moment, hope rushed in. Was it possible that she had feelings for him, too?

He steered her toward a seat on the patio and called to Billy. "Young man. Would you please bring Mrs. Holmes a cup of tea?"

"Sure, how do you like it? Cream? Sugar?" Billy asked.

Marion looked up at the boy and gasped. Hudson leaned down. "You see the resemblance, too, don't you?"

She looked at him with confusion. She whispered, "How could this be?"

"Ma'am? How would you like your tea?" Billy repeated.

"Oh . . . just cream would be fine," she managed to answer.

Billy carefully assembled the tea and brought it over.

"Here, ma'am," he said.

"Thank you." Marion's hands shook as she took the cup and saucer.

"Hey, Billy! Come help me with the cases of champagne," Matthew called.

"Run along, young man," Hudson told him. "Go help your friend."

Marion watched him disappear, then turned to Hudson. "It's like William has returned from the grave."

"When I first saw him, I had the same reaction. Do you suppose that William had a son?"

"A son?" She considered this. "You mean I might have a grandson? How could that be?"

"Wasn't Master William enamored of a young girl whose uncle owned a carnival?"

"Yes, but that was so long ago. I don't remember many of the details."

"Billy comes from the carnival. His mother runs it. I was just wondering whether it might be the same woman . . ." He let the thought fall or rise on its own.

"Oh, Hudson, do you think it could be possible?" Marion watched the boy as he and Matthew hurried to stack plates and cutlery. The first round of riders had arrived.

"I think it warrants investigating."

"I agree."

"We don't have much time. The fair is over Sunday evening, and they will be leaving."

"We must find out before then. You will help me, won't you, Hudson?"

"Certainly, ma'am."

"Hello, Marion. I see you've outdone yourself again this year," Henry Clarkson, president of one of New England's richest private banks, yelled from atop a chestnut quarter horse.

"How nice of you to come, Henry," she said, rising to greet her guest. She handed her teacup to Hudson and whispered, "I think I'd better exchange this for a mimosa. In fact, make it a double."

"Why I'll be darned!" Sticks shouted, throwing his arms around Pepper Pot and smothering the pig's face with wet kisses. "How did you find him?"

Billy and Matthew stood looking down at the reunion, smiles as wide as the Grand Canyon stretched across their faces.

"The riders found him," Billy told him, laughing at the memory.

"What riders?"

"At the Foxhunt. The dogs must have gotten a little confused. Instead of finding a fox, they led the hunt straight to Pepper Pot."

"The lady that ran the hunt, a Mrs. Holmes, was fit to be tied, but the priest who gave the blessing couldn't stop laughing. He told everyone that the Lord sure works in mysterious ways," Billy said, chuckling.

Sticks suddenly grew still. "Did you say Mrs. Holmes?"

"Yeah, she owns a big mansion at the end

of town," Billy said, scratching the pig beneath the chin. Pepper Pot closed his eyes and enjoyed the attention.

"Does your mom know where you were this morning?"

"She was busy with payroll, so I just took off. Why, was she looking for me?"

"No," Sticks said. The elation over having found his precious pig was draining away under a new concern. Aside from Suzanne's uncle, no one other than he knew the identity of Billy's father, or the true reason she had fought with Jed over accepting this gig.

"And guess what?" Billy continued. "Her butler paid Matthew and me a hundred dollars each just to help serve the breakfast. Can you believe it? I guess some people have more money than they know what to do with, eh, Sticks?"

"Yeah, I guess so," Sticks said, suddenly growing suspicious. No one in his right mind would pay a couple of teenage boys that kind of money to help hand out platters of sausage and eggs, unless . . .

He'd better find Suzanne, and quickly.

# 10

By 4:00 p.m., folks had started arriving to claim front-row seats along the parade route. Cars double-parked and flipped open trunks piled high with folding aluminum chairs and ice chests overflowing with crispy fried chicken, ham sandwiches, deviled eggs, potato salad, icy cold bottles of root beer, and jugs filled with iced tea. The men labored under their weight, lamenting loudly to anyone who might be passing that they couldn't understand why their wives had to pack so much food. It was just a curbside picnic, not a church banquet, for Pete's sake!

The store owners took advantage of the crowds and lined the sidewalks with goods. In front of Second Hand Rose were racks filled with summer clearance items. Women gathered around the merchandise, admiring this or that, wondering if they should take a chance on purchasing something now and whether it might still fit next summer.

Stone's Hardware had a special on lawn mowers and bamboo rakes, which Mark Stone had neatly arranged in front of the window. While men poked their way through the row of John Deeres and Toros, their eyes drifted up toward the front window, with its display of this year's newest in snowblowers. Men gathered round like eager puppies, hoping they could somehow convince their spouses to let them add one of these high-powered machines to their collections of what wives affectionately called their "yard toys."

Among the clamor and confusion, Sergeant Hill tried to maintain a semblance of order as the town's crew began to cordon off Main Street. A large dump truck drove along the curb, filled to overflowing with wooden sawhorses painted bright yellow and stacks of orange cones.

Hill admonished children to stay clear of the truck and asked adults if anyone knew who belonged to the two cars still parked in front of the Country Kettle even though every lamppost in town sported a bright orange sign stating that cars parked along the parade route after 4:00 p.m. would be towed. Well, he'd give them ten more minutes, then he was calling Nancy over at Tri

Town Auto and having them towed away. Just before making the call, he would run the license plates through DMV. Last year the Lincoln he had towed ended up belonging to a sheriff over in Manchester, one of Sheriff Bromley's poker buddies. Hill had thought his boss would have a coronary over that one.

In the distance, dozens of fire engines rumbled, their diesel engines roaring like prehistoric beasts. Dorsetville's Labor Day parade brought fire departments from all over the state. This year, Southbury was especially proud to attend. They had a new top-of-the-line tanker with a 2,000-gallons-per-minute water pump, a 1,250-gallon tank with rear dump chute and rear direct fill, and an eight-man cab. They were the envy of half the state.

While everyone was assembling, this year's parade director, Nigel Hayes, fought hard to keep order among chaos. The Scouts' float was supposed to have preceded the Shriners, but two of their cars had broken down and had to be pushed to one side for repairs. Harry Clifford was fit to be tied. It was decided that the quilters' float depicting quilts hung on a front porch would have to take their place, but their float was being pulled by a set of Joe Platt's Morgans, which hadn't yet been harnessed.

Meanwhile, folks were arriving in droves, and by 4:30 there wasn't an open space anywhere along Main Street. Lawn chairs cascaded along the sidewalks. Children tightly lined the curbs like birds along a wire fence. Every so often, one of the children would dash out into the street, trying to spy the high school marching band that always led the parade, only to be scolded by watchful parents.

As kickoff time drew closer, the air fairly crackled with excitement. At 5:00 sharp, the sirens sounded, blasting the crowds into silence. The parade had officially begun.

Everyone rose from their seats to recite the Pledge of Allegiance. Reverend Curtis from the Congregational Church offered a short prayer over the PA system, which had been set up by the reviewing stand stationed in front of town hall. He asked for good weather, hesitating only briefly over this petition to add his silent pleas, since last time he had been asked to give the official blessing, it had rained like in the days of Noah. Fair officials had later whispered among themselves that Father Keene's prayers always brought halcyon skies.

The reverend concluded with the admonition that, although folks had spent a great deal of time preparing for the various blue-ribbon events, it was a matter not of who won or lost but rather of the joy one received from taking part in a community event. Chester Platt leaned over and murmured in Doc Hammon's ear, "Obviously the good reverend doesn't have a twenty riding on Miller's bull to come in first."

Mary Williams, who reminded everyone of an ancient Nordic warrior priestess, sang "The Star-Spangled Banner" with gusto but slightly off key. The mayor offered a reminder that he was running for reelection this November but said he would keep his comments short, since folks hadn't come to hear him give speeches, they'd come to see a parade. That got rousing applause.

"Shall we begin?" he hollered into the mike.

The crowd roared their assent and waved their miniature flags.

The mayor aimed the starting pistol straight at the sky and pulled the trigger. The high school band picked up the cue, which was immediately followed by the sound of feet marching in place to the beat of snare drums. The head majorette, dressed in a uniform fringed with tassels, faced the band and raised her baton. The horn section raised their instruments to their lips in quiet readiness. With a flourish, the baton came down, and the sounds of a Sousa march filled the air as folks joined along, clapping enthusiastically to the foot-stomping beat.

The Labor Day County Fair Weekend festivities had officially begun.

The strains from the high school band wafted over the landscape, fading as they traveled up the mountainside toward Merrybrook. By the time the music reached the back terrace, where Marion was seated sipping a glass of port, only the snare drums' insistent beat could be faintly discerned.

"Short of a DNA test, how can we possibly know if the boy is truly William's son?" she asked, twisting the flawless square-cut emerald ring adorning her right hand, a throwback to the days when exquisite jewels had meant so much to her. She wasn't sure why she had put it on this evening, along with the perfectly matched double strand of pearls and the matching earrings. She hadn't opened her jewelry box for years.

Hudson, sitting near her on a wicker sofa, watched the new enthusiasm play across her face and felt his own spirits begin to rise on the wings of hope. How long had it been since Marion had been so animated?

"There must be some way of finding out," she insisted finally, leaning forward to light a candle. It had begun to grow dark. Hudson immediately apologized for being so remiss in his duties and set about lighting several others.

"Oh, for Pete's sake, Hudson, sit down. You're making me nervous. We must come up with a plan. As you said, the carnival is leaving on Sunday. That doesn't give us much time." She went back to twisting her ring.

The term *we* did not go unnoticed by the butler. Marion had never crossed the servant-mistress boundary before.

"I think we should begin with the other boy, Matthew Metcalf," he suggested. "He and Billy seem to have struck up a friendship. Perhaps he can provide a little more information."

"Excellent idea, Hudson!" she said, rising.

Hudson, who had never remained seated in the presence of any employer, quickly got to his feet.

"Sit down," she told him, pointing to the wicker sofa with a long, tapered finger. "If we're to work together on this, I can't have you continually springing up like a jack-in-the-box. You'll give me nervous prostration."

"Yes, madam," he said, sinking back onto

303

the sofa with a slight grin. He was enjoying their new camaraderie.

"Now let us both have a glass of port and let's brainstorm. We haven't a moment to waste."

"Yes, madam."

"And, Hudson?"

"Yes, madam?"

"I think, considering the circumstances, that when we are alone, you might call me Marion."

Sergeant Hill was as tired as a one-legged man in a two-legged race. It seemed as though he hadn't stopped for a second during the parade. There were people to direct, streets to be kept clear, and then the general melee that follows any town gathering, as lines of impatient motorists tried to make their way across town. It had taken all of his crowd management skills to keep things flowing, and except for the unfortunate incident of Ruth Henderson running over her sister's walker, things had gone along smoothly.

In fact, he was so tired that he decided to forgo the trip to the fairgrounds, figuring he'd see everything tomorrow. He was scheduled to work the fair from 3:00 p.m. to closing. Right now all he wanted was a shower and eight hours of uninterrupted sleep. He hadn't gotten much the night before.

For some reason, the cat had refused to settle down last night. She'd roamed the apartment from end to end, screeching at the top of her lungs to be let out. By three o'clock in the morning, he'd been almost tempted to comply, but in the end he'd decided against it. What if John Moran spied her climbing back up the fire escape?

Hill's mind was in such a fog he didn't notice that his apartment was unlocked as he let himself in or see the figure standing in his kitchen doorway until he heard a voice ask, "How long has that cat been here?"

His hand flew to his revolver until he realized the question had just been posed by his landlord. Hill felt his heart skip a beat. There was no use denying it. The cat was wrapping herself around his legs. He was busted.

John's nose began to twitch. He drew in several short breaths. He grabbed for his handkerchief as a violent sneeze erupted, sending his glasses sliding down to the tip of his nose.

He swiped his nose and glared at Hill. "I wondered why my allergies had suddenly flared up," he said, adjusting his lenses. "What part of the no-pet clause in your lease did you not understand?"

Hill tried to think of something to say in defense. "Did you know that it's pet dander that causes allergies, not cat fur?"

The cat had moved on to John and was now rubbing against his leg. He eased the cat away with the tip of his shoe.

"I'm not here to talk about my allergies. I'm here because I found this cat wandering the stairwell. Apparently, when you left this morning, the door wasn't completely closed and it got out."

Hill took offense at the term *it* but figured this was not the time to debate the matter.

"Her name is Mittens and I've tried to find her a home," he said, scooping the cat up into his arms. She began to purr, rubbing the top of her head along his chin. "But no one wants her."

"That's not my problem," John retorted. "Our agreement specifically stated that you were not to keep animals in your apartment. I'm sorry, but there are no exceptions."

Hill rubbed Mittens between the ears. She folded like putty in his hands.

"But where will I take her?"

"I suggest to the pound."

"I can't do that. They'll put her down."

"Look, I don't mean to sound hard-hearted, but a policy is a policy. Either the cat goes or you do."

Hill looked down into Mittens's trusting face. He had never had a pet before. In fact, he had always thought pet owners were kind of foolish, talking about their dogs and cats as though they were human. But something had happened since Mittens came into his life. He no longer looked at her as just a cat. When he glanced down into her eyes, he saw a soul.

"I'm sorry, John, but I just can't do that. I'll have to move out."

"I'm tired and my back hurts from lugging all this equipment around from one end of the fair to another. I don't care what kind of footage Carl wants, I'm tired and I want to go home," Timothy McGree complained, plopping down on a bale of hay outside the Mother Goose pavilion.

"Me, too," Ben Metcalf said, tucking the station's heavy camera out of the way of the crowds who jostled by. "Besides, I think we have enough. All he really needed was the shots of the Ferris wheel lit up at night for the opening segment. We got that. The rest we can come back and shoot tomorrow. Heck, the next segment of *Around the Town* doesn't air until next week. That should give Matthew plenty of time to edit it," Ben added, watching his friend kick off the battered pair of high-top sneakers.

"Geez, Timothy, put those back on before I pass out from the smell," Ben said, waving a hand across the air.

"Can't smell worse than that wagonload of manure over there."

"Want to bet?"

"All right, I'll put them back on," Timothy said, his voice laced with martyrdom.

It was dark as pitch, and the mosquitoes were out in full force. Timothy finished tying his sneakers while the pesky insects snacked hungrily on his exposed hands. He swatted the air.

"Got any more of that bug spray?" he asked Ben.

"Nah, you used it up down by the sheep corral."

"Where the devil is Sam?" Timothy asked, looking out into the crowd.

"He said he had to drive Harriet home." Although Harriet Bedford and Sam Rosenberg insisted they were just friends, everyone knew they were as close as any married couple. He drove her everywhere, and Harriet made certain to include Sam in all of her plans. Tonight it was toting a truckload of plants she had grown in the exotic nursery she had with her granddaughter, Allison. The plants were going to be a decorative backdrop for the gardening competition. Harriet had been asked to help judge.

"Yeah, but that was an hour ago. He should have been back here by now. If he doesn't hurry, I'll miss tonight's lotto drawing."

Timothy had a good feeling about tonight's game. The prize was $6.5 million. He had bet the numbers listed on a fortune cookie, the way he'd heard those eight folks in the Midwest who had won a hundred thousand dollars each had done. He had gotten the cookie from Mr. Ming, who was being featured in an upcoming special entitled "A Taste of Dorsetville." There were only two eating places in town — the Country Kettle and Ming's — so it was going to be a very short special, but what they lacked in content they made up in footage. He and Ben hadn't left a square inch of Mr. Ming's restaurant unturned.

In appreciation, Mr. Ming had given Timothy and Ben each a fortune cookie and a cup of green tea. Timothy didn't much like the tea — which was served without milk or sugar — but he tried to act as though he did. He didn't want to offend Mr. Ming. Ben drank his right down, but then Ben would eat or drink anything put in front of him without complaint. Timothy had even seen him once eat a piece of a Henderson sister's cake without checking for bugs.

Finally they spied Sam and waved him over.

"What took you so long?" Timothy asked with an edge to his voice. "How long does it take to drive someone who lives just two miles from here home?"

Sam was used to Timothy's bad moods and never took them personally. He winked at Ben and teased, "Harriet and I decided it was such a lovely night that we would go parking."

"Everything's in place for tomorrow night," Agent Fillmore told the Sheriff.

Bromley and the FBI agent were seated in Barbara's Toyota to avoid detection. Fortunately, Barbara was still at the fairgrounds and didn't know her husband had borrowed it again. She was still miffed over the broken front seat.

They were parked beneath a Route 8 underpass that sat beside an abandoned farmhouse. The steady sound of commuter traffic whizzed overhead.

"I'll have a dozen ground agents deployed in strategic locations around the spot your fire marshal says he thinks might be the drop-off point. A half a mile upstream, we'll have a boat standing ready, and I've put in a request for a helicopter in case we need to give chase."

Fillmore swatted a mosquito. "These bugs are thick as thieves this season," he said, flicking the dead bug off his forearm. "I sure hope your marshal is right about the location. If the drop is going down elsewhere, we could lose precious minutes trying to regroup and end up jeopardizing three years' worth of work."

Bromley studied the heavens. The skies hovered on the edge between dusk and nightfall. Venus flickered, playing counterpoint to the moon.

"I can't give you a guarantee, but what George said made sense. That old logging road can be accessed at the edge of the fairgrounds, which makes it easy for Mullen to disappear without being spotted. There's a deep-water dock at the end of that road. Logging company built it for freighters that used to come in and haul away the logs. The dock's not in terrific shape, but it's usable. And that area of the river is deep enough to accommodate a good-size boat.

It's also tucked away in a small cove. Unless you're looking for it, it's hard to spy from the river."

"I hope you're right," Fillmore said again, getting ready to leave. "There's nothing we would like better than taking down that group of thugs."

Sticks's animals were all properly fed, brushed, and bedded down for the night before he headed toward Suzanne's trailer. Opening night always tired him out, and tonight was no exception. He was exhausted from handing out small bags of feed, collecting the money, and making sure that no one mistreated his animals.

It was nearly midnight, and he had been on his feet for seven straight hours. His legs were ready to collapse. His joints felt as though they were on fire. What he needed was a hot shower and a couple of Advil, but that would have to wait. He had to tell Suzanne what he had discovered about Billy meeting Mrs. Holmes.

The fairgrounds were quiet. Most of the other carnies had finished refilling their stock for tomorrow and were now tucked into bed. The fair opened early Saturday, which meant it was going to be a long day. Everyone wanted to make sure they had a good night's sleep to see them through. Carnival work was often hard and grueling.

Sticks trudged along the empty aisles past the silent roulette wheel and the food concession stands. Suzanne's trailer was parked in the gulley behind the machinery. There was a small decline as he rounded a row of parked cars. He took tiny steps, always fearful of tripping and breaking a hip.

His heart sank at the sight of Suzanne's trailer. All the lights were out. Looked like she was already in bed. He paused with uncertainty. Should he wake her up? What he had to tell her was important, but what if Billy was also asleep? He couldn't chance having the boy overhear what he had come to say.

Finally, he decided it could keep until morning. He'd just have to get up a little early and make certain he caught her before things started getting crazy. The first full day of a fair, Suzanne was always running around putting out fires. He had to make sure he caught up with her before then. She needed to know that Billy had been to visit Merrybrook. Sticks had met William only a couple of times when he and Suzanne were dating, but time could not lessen the memory of his clean, aristocratic features, the ones mirrored in Billy's face. If Marion Holmes had spied Billy today, she was bound to see the striking similarity between Billy and her dead son. There was no telling what kind of trouble would come of it if she had.

Sticks was about to head back the way he'd come when he spied a small beam of light shining out from the generator trailer. Nelson must have forgotten to turn something off. It was his job to make sure all the equipment was shut down for the night. No need to wake him up just to shut off a light, Sticks thought, heading that way.

As he walked, he thought about Suzanne. She seemed so down in the mouth lately. In some ways, she was like a daughter to him, which was why he was concerned about Billy's meeting with the Holmes woman. Suzanne didn't need any more trouble. She already had enough with Jed as her partner.

Just the thought of that man set Sticks's teeth on edge. He hadn't liked him from the start and had tried to warn Suzanne. But she'd said there wasn't much she could do. They were due in Daytona for a big gig, and their main driver had just been arrested for driving while intoxicated. Jed had happened to show up. Said he'd heard about their predicament. He had a commercial driver's license and could he help out? She had hired him on the spot.

Sticks had always thought it was strange how things started to go wrong the moment Jed hired on. Machinery began breaking down; fights broke out at several of the events. One resulted in a lawsuit. Then there was that incident with a teenage girl and one of the guys Jed had recommended for a job. Towns they had played for years got wind of things and started canceling. Instead of working the big-money jobs, they were forced to take on the penny-ante stuff no one else wanted.

As he drew closer to the trailer, Sticks heard a tool drop to the floor. Someone was tampering with the equipment. That's all Suzanne needs, he thought, feeling his temperature rise. Next to the sale of food, the rides produced the most revenue, and without the generator, they were sunk.

Sticks cursed his arthritic joints. He had to get help.

He began to shuffle back the way he had come when the trailer's door burst open and Jed Mullen stepped out. The beam from the flashlight he was carrying swept across Sticks's back. The older man thought about running, but his legs refused to obey.

Jed pounced on him like a tiger, clamping

315

his fingers around the old man's throat.

"What are you doing out here? You spying on me?"

Sticks shook his head no, his eyes wide with fear.

The last thing he remembered was the sneer on Jed's face; then he lost consciousness and slid to the ground.

Just what he needed, Jed thought, Sticks slung across his back as he climbed deeper into the woods. Things had been going according to plan before the old geezer had showed up.

Jed had made certain that Nelson was well on his way to another binge. Suzanne's ace mechanic was now holed up in a motel in Brookfield and out cold. All it had taken was a couple six-packs of Bud and a quart of Jack Daniel's. That was the great thing about alcoholics. Once an addict, always an addict.

Jed's whole plan revolved around keeping the Ferris wheel off-line until late tomorrow evening. He would show up around eight. Tell Suzanne that he had found the problem and make sure the ride was running before he headed down to the river. Shortly afterward, the old part would make the generator overheat, and the Ferris wheel would come to a screeching stop, leaving dozens of folks stranded in midair.

Next, a call would go out summoning help. The local police force, composed of just one sheriff and another officer, would be summoned, leaving Jed and Covas free to go about their business down by the river.

It was an ingenious plan. Flawless, until the old man had shown up.

Sticks moaned. He was coming to. Jed swore under his breath and plunged faster and deeper into the woods. He had to get rid of him. There was no telling how long he had been outside the trailer. He could have seen Jed exchange the old, worn parts for the new ones. Jed couldn't risk him blabbering to Suzanne. He'd come too close to finally realizing his dream of wealth. The kid who had grown up poor and unwanted in the South Bronx was just about to hit it big. He wasn't about to let some arthritic old man mess things up.

The moon had slipped behind a bank of clouds, and it was getting as dark as pitch. A couple of times, Jed nearly lost his footing, but still he plowed on. He wanted Sticks's death to look like an accident. It was one thing to be wanted for dealing drugs, but it was entirely something else to be charged for murder.

Jed had decided to take Sticks deep into the woods, then dump his body off the side of the mountain. The old man wouldn't make it through a fall like that. Then, when Jed got back to the fairgrounds, he would take Pepper Pot into the woods and let him loose. That way it would look like Sticks had discovered the pig missing, gone out looking for him, and fallen down the mountain. No one would ever suspect it was murder.

But Jed needed to get up high enough to make sure Sticks didn't survive the fall. He saw a path leading to a higher summit, turned in, and snared his shirtsleeve on a pricker bush. He swore, startling a herd of deer, who took off. The sound of branches snapping beneath their feet was like gunshot in the still night air.

Bugs were swarming all around him, attracted by sweat and the carbon dioxide he exhaled. He willed himself to ignore them. All of this would be behind him in another twenty-four hours.

By this time tomorrow night, he would have ditched his truck on the side of the interstate, then hitched a ride to the nearest bus station. From there he'd take a bus into New York City, then the subway to Queens, where he'd rent a car under an assumed name (the new license and credit cards were hidden in the heel of his boot); then he was off to Las Vegas, en route to Mexico. He'd heard you could still buy some oceanfront property for a song there. Not that he would have to worry about money again after tonight. Still, he figured he'd lay low for a while. No use pushing his luck. Let Covas find another setup man. He planned to enjoy the fruits of his labor, not work until he was busted or shot.

He finally made it to the top of a ridge. He shifted the body off his shoulder and got ready to heave the old man over the side. Sticks's eyes flew open. He gave a startled gasp as Jed pitched him headfirst down the side of the mountain.

# 11

Saturday dawned bright and clear, much to Father James's chagrin. He had been hoping for a rainstorm of epic proportions. He looked outside his bathroom window, his face lathered with shaving cream. Not a cloud in the sky. He was definitely dead meat.

Today he would have to help decide which of the dozens of apple pie entries — several St. Cecilia's participants among them — had won the blue ribbon.

He went back to shaving. He probably shouldn't ask God to intervene again. He had already dodged one bullet with the Foxhunt. He smiled through a beard of shaving cream, remembering the looks on the riders' faces when they had returned to the estate with a very live and vocal potbellied pig in tow. He had never felt such a sense of relief in his life.

The news had traveled fast, as all news

did in Dorsetville. When he'd passed Ethel's car on his way to the rectory just a few hours later, she'd honked her horn and waved. Even Honey, with her head sticking out of the passenger side window, had barked a greeting. Apparently, he was back in their good graces again. At least that was something to be thankful for.

Father James rinsed his face, put the cap on the shaving cream, and tidied up the sink. Mrs. Norris complained bitterly when he left hairs. He walked into his bedroom, where his clothes were laid out on a chair. Plaid shirt, beige trousers. He was going as a civilian. No use bringing attention to the fact he was a priest. He dressed quickly, enjoying the freedom of an open-collared shirt. Those plastic tabs chafed something terrible in the heat.

Why did women have to take these things so seriously? Since his name had been announced as a judge, not a day had gone by that he hadn't found a prayer request slipped beneath the sacristy door, imploring him to pray for someone's success, along with enough apple pie samples to turn him off all pastries for life. Well, maybe not *that* long.

Then there were the not so subtle hints dropped en route out of the church.

"The Congregationalists are saying that even without the help of our saints, they're going to win this year's contest."

"Melanie Hatchet is entering her great-aunt Birdie's recipe this year. Back in the forties, it was the state's winner five years running. Don't you think she should be disqualified?"

There were still rumors flying like a migrating flock of geese that the women over in Bradbury had hijacked Dinova's produce truck in order to keep the choicest apples for themselves. Many of those women were also entered in the contest. He sure hoped a fight didn't break out between the rival groups when the winner was announced.

He stood combing his hair in front of his dresser mirror and looked himself straight in the eyes. Why couldn't women just rejoice in the fact that God had blessed them with the gift of baking and leave it at that? Instead, they had to pit one woman against the other, laud it over one another which church affiliation had won in the past, and harass a poor, beleaguered priest nearly to death with requests for prayers and blessings.

He was still concerned he might have crossed the line yesterday when one of his parishioners had asked that he extend a blessing over her ingredients. Maybe he should speak to the other judges. This might be construed as having extended unfair influence.

He slipped into a pair of loafers that no longer had any shape left to them. He had worn them since college. They were the most comfortable shoes he owned. Mrs. Norris kept trying to get him to throw them away. Twice he had had to pull them out of a Goodwill bag.

The bedside clock read 7:30. The fairgrounds opened at 8:00. The judges were to meet at 8:15.

He glanced out the bedroom window. The morning regulars were already inside the church. Father Dennis was saying mass this morning. Father James joined his prayers with theirs, asking for a double helping of patience. He'd sure need it if George Benson was on his team. "Weren't things already bad enough?" he asked the Lord. "Did you have to include him?" The Lord remained silent on the matter.

He grabbed his car keys and headed downstairs. As he suspected, the kitchen was as quiet as a graveyard. Mrs. Norris was probably on her way to the fairgrounds with her preserves. He grabbed a stale piece of white bread, slathered it with peanut butter, and went to find some jam. He was somewhat surprised to discover the pantry shelves empty of all jar fruits. What had the woman done with the dozens she'd been making these past few weeks?

The bright, sunlit morning helped bolster his sagging spirits as he walked to his car. Just think, he told himself. In a few hours, it will all be behind you. Thank God. The stress was enough to make a poor priest take to strong drink.

By seven-thirty that morning, the main route leading up to the fairgrounds was clogged with traffic. It seemed most of the county had turned out for the fair. The adjacent five-acre plot being used for parking would be filled to overflowing in no time.

Although the traffic snaked along the county road for nearly a mile, folks remained in a festive mood and patiently waited. All, that is, except George Benson, who was driving the official Fire Marshal Chevy Blazer and pumping a plume of smoke from his cigar through the open window as traffic inched along. Every few minutes, he would flash his emergency lights and sound his siren, but no one budged. Many of the cars up ahead were being driven by Dorsetville Fire Department volunteers, who knew that there was no emergency; if there had been, their beepers would have sounded. No, it was just George trying to cut ahead, afraid that the other judges of the Apple Pie Contest might start without him.

George wasn't the only one anxious about getting to the fair on time. The judge's wife, Marge Peale, who headed the town's Clothesline Quilters' group, was concerned that the traffic tie-up might hinder members from getting their quilts registered in time to be judged. She was especially anxious for Barbara Bromley, who was determined to win a ribbon, and it would be well deserved. None had worked harder this year than Barbara. But what could Marge do? At this rate, quilters stuck in traffic would miss their chance of entering. All entries had to be signed in in less than forty minutes. No doubt the entrants for other categories were just as anxious. Several cars back, she saw Lori Peterson looking very concerned.

Marge looked behind her and spied the Richters in their green Subaru Forester. Leah and Linda were hanging out the back windows, waving to all their friends. Suddenly, Marge had an idea. The shoulder alongside the road had been kept clear and was wide enough to accommodate her minivan. What if she turned her car into a shuttle? It might work. The women's husbands could take care of parking their cars. She threw her minivan in park and hopped out.

"Would you happen to have any ideas on how I might make a makeshift banner?" she asked before the Richters could say hello, then quickly told them her idea. Valerie worked as a graphic designer. Stephen was a talented portrait and landscape artist. If anyone could help, they could.

"You have anything we can write on?" Valerie asked.

Marge thought a moment. "Would some old muslin do?" There were several yards in the bottom of her quilting basket.

Stephen looked at Valerie, who nodded her assent. "Sounds like it would do just fine," he said with a grin. Like most artists, Stephen loved an artistic challenge.

He pulled over. Then the couple went into high gear as they scrounged around their car for Magic Markers and colored pens. The girls caught the sense of excitement and eagerly offered to help. Leah found an entire box of glitter pens that had slipped out of her schoolbag and beneath the back-seat.

As the traffic inched forward, Marge watched how the couple quickly fashioned a sign that read: FAIRGROUNDS ENTRIES SHUTTLE, complete with a cartoonlike bus filled with women hanging out the windows, holding pies, quilts, and jars of preserves. The design had taken under five minutes to create.

"You are amazing," she told them, shaking her head in wonder.

"You're going to need some way to attach this to your car," Stephen reminded her.

"I hadn't thought of that," Marge said, biting her lip.

Harry Clifford and his wife, Nellie, were several cars behind. Nellie taught fifth grade. Teachers usually carried a carload of supplies; maybe she would have something that could help. Marge took off on a run. Time was running out. As it worked out, Nellie hadn't a thing that would help, but Harry saved the day with a roll of duct tape he kept in the glove compartment.

Moments later, the banner had been taped along the side of Marge's minivan, and her impromptu shuttle was in business. Soon the minivan was piled with baskets of canning jars, preserves, produce, flower ar-

327

rangements, and quilts that had been carefully covered in plastic. She even picked up a man from Woodbury who had baked the most heavenly scented apple pie. If the aroma was an indication of its taste, she feared the women in Dorsetville wouldn't have a chance of winning this year's blue ribbon.

By the time Marge had deposited the last entrant at the front gate, the fairgrounds was buzzing with activity. Most families had split up to go their separate ways. Men headed toward the rear of the grounds to watch the tractor events. Women made a beeline to the metal sheds that housed the needlework and baking displays, while children old enough to fend for themselves dashed from one side of the fairgrounds to the other, determined not to miss a single event or food stand.

As they did every year, folks complained that events overlapped. This year the pony cart parade was up against the owner and dog look-alike contest. It was a quandary. Stephen Richter would have preferred to stay and sketch the beautifully painted pony carts that had begun to stir his imagination. What a wonderful subject for a painting, he thought. His daughters, however, were anxious to get on to the dog contest and kept pulling on his shirt. "Come on, Daddy," they whined. "We're missing the beginning." The girls had heard that their principal, Mr. Kemble, was entered. They were dying to see what kind of dog might resemble a man with elephant ears and a bulbous nose.

And so it went throughout the fair. So many choices. So little time.

The PA system crackled to life: "Will the contestants entered in the Apple Pie Contest please come to the judges' tent? They're about to announce the winners. And if anyone has seen George Benson, will you please tell him that Father James is looking for him? One of the entries appears to be missing."

Suzanne Granger was barely cognizant of the messages being spewed over the PA, or the woman who had stomped out of the judges' tents carrying a second-place ribbon and murmuring to a group of equally disappointed contestants that she should have known Loretta Baker's grandmother's preserves recipe would take the blue ribbon. Suzanne sidestepped the heated conversation, her thoughts returning to her concern for Sticks. Where could he have gone? It wasn't like him to just disappear.

She had been to the petting zoo. Complaints had found their way to the office trailer shortly after the fair opened. A line of parents and anxious children had formed outside the fenced-in area, but there was no one around to let them in. In all the years that Sticks had run the kiddie attraction, this had never happened before. It had her deeply worried. What worried her more was Pepper Pot's empty cage.

She looked up at the mountain range surrounding the fairgrounds. What if the pig had broken loose again and Sticks had gone out looking for him? He was nearly crippled with arthritis. If he had gone in search of the pig, he could easily have fallen and broken a bone. What if he was now lying helpless up there in the woods?

Of course, all of this was speculation. Jed's truck was also missing. Maybe he and Sticks had taken a ride. Maybe something had happened to the pig during the night and Jed had offered to give Sticks a ride to a local vet. Then she caught herself. Yeah, right. Jed? Help anyone? When it snowed at the equator.

Meanwhile, she was left with a conundrum. Sticks would have to be missing for forty-eight hours before she could report it to the police. The only ones who would go looking for him were the other carnies, which meant that she would have to close down. But she desperately needed the revenue. If they didn't take in at least four thousand dollars today, she'd be forced to close down for good, and then what would happen to the others, including Sticks? It wasn't like there were hundreds of jobs out there just waiting for them.

Crowds were pouring into the fairgrounds. It was going to be a nonstop day. Maybe, just maybe, she could pull in enough cash to keep them afloat.

Oh, Sticks, why of all days did you have to be missing today? she silently asked.

Of course, they wouldn't have been in this financial fix if Jed hadn't dipped into their cash reserves. Well, he wasn't going to be doing that anymore. She'd had a locksmith change the combination to the safe earlier this morning.

The walkie-talkie attached to her belt came to life, startling a baby in a stroller. The mother bent down to comfort the child. "It's all right, Paul. Mommy is here," Lori Peterson said, reaching in and scooping up her crying child.

"I'm sorry," Suzanne apologized, buzzing past.

"Suzanne? Are you there? We have a problem."

She recognized Organza Petri's voice. He ran the rides.

"I'm here. What's the problem?"

"The Ferris wheel isn't working, and I can't find Nelson anywhere. You'd better get over here right away."

They'd never make it without the revenue the Ferris wheel generated. She took off at a clip. Thoughts of Sticks's whereabouts had flown right out of Suzanne's head.

Hudson had been trying to chase down Matthew Metcalf all day. At first, he was told that the boy was working at Dinova's, but when he arrived he found he had just left with several delivery orders. Gus said he'd be back around two-thirty.

Two-thirty came and went, and still no Matthew. Hudson went back to Gus and this time was told that the van had broken down and had to be towed to Tri Town Auto. Hudson rushed right over, thinking this might be a blessing in disguise. He would pretend to have pulled in for gas and offer Matthew a ride.

When he arrived, however, the van was on a lift and some pretty young girl named Harvest, who he later discovered was

Nancy's newest mechanic, informed him that Sam Rosenberg had given the boy a ride.

Tracking down Sam had proven to be even more difficult because he, too, had experienced several setbacks today.

Sam delivered noontime meals for Dorsetville's Meals on Wheels program. All the homebound senior citizens within a fifteen-mile radius literally depended on Sam for their daily bread. Sam loved the job. He liked to be of service to others, which was why he never missed a day, not even in the winter, when the roads were thick with ice.

Although weather could sometimes muck up his delivery schedule, nothing proved more challenging than a three-day holiday. The kitchen was closed on holidays. Instead of delivering just one noontime meal, he must deliver three, two of which would be wrapped in heavy pieces of aluminum foil for reheating later. Problems arose since his 1972 gold Plymouth Duster could carry only a limited number of meals, forcing him to make several trips between the clients' homes and the senior center, where the food was prepared, and stretching his delivery time from two hours to sometimes five. If not executed correctly, this routine might leave some clients receiving their lunch at dinnertime. The whole thing took a great deal more planning. Sam usually enlisted Ben Metcalf and Timothy McGree to act as runners, although the term was loosely applied. But with their help, the delivery time was cut in half.

Today, though, Sam had a problem. Ben and Timothy were working the fair, interviewing all the blue-ribbon and events winners. Sam had tried to think of who else he might call but so far had come up empty-handed. Most of his social circle were either too feeble to dash about delivering meals or involved at the fairgrounds.

Sam, a man of quiet faith, finally took his problem to the Father of Abraham and humbly asked if He could send a little assistance. He wasn't at all surprised that, when he pulled into Tri Town Auto to fill up his tank with gas, he happened to meet Matthew, who offered to help.

"I can't finish my deliveries until the van's fixed. I might as well lend you a hand while I'm waiting," the teenager said.

"I accept gladly," Sam said, tightening the gas cap and wondering once again why more people didn't trust in God's care.

The two made all Sam's deliveries and were finished a little after two o'clock. When

Sam dropped Matthew off at the garage, the van was just coming off the lift.

Sam offered to help Matthew with *his* deliveries, but he declined. "It won't take me more than a half an hour or so. You go and enjoy the fair. Tell my grandfather I'll catch up with him later."

Meanwhile, Hudson continued to try to track Matthew down. He kept Marion abreast of his non-progress. She was growing fearful that they might run out of time.

"The carnival leaves tomorrow," she reminded him.

"Perhaps, madam, a more direct approach is called for," he suggested.

"You mean track down the woman?"

"I don't know what else we can do."

"You're right. Come and get me. I'll search the fairgrounds, but you continue to try to find the Metcalf boy."

Jed had made certain to stay clear of the fairgrounds until well after seven in the evening. As he suspected, Suzanne was breathing fire when she spied him pull his truck in beside the office trailer.

"Where have you been?" she raged, hooking her hand onto the driver's side door and yanking it open before he could throw the truck into park. "I've been looking all over for you."

"Since when do I have to clear my where-abouts with you before I take off?" he asked, flipping a cigarette butt over her head and jumping out.

"Why is there a padlock on the electrical trailer?"

"I put it on because some kids were messing around there yesterday. I was avoiding trouble."

"I had no way of getting in there short of breaking off the lock, which I also couldn't do" — she reached back into the bed of his truck and removed the large pair of pliers — "because you took off with all the tools."

She threw the pliers back into the truck. They landed with the sound of metal dinging against metal.

"Hey, watch it. This truck is brand new."

"I care as much about your truck as you do about the carnival. Why did you take off? You know we're shorthanded." Four people had quit over the payroll incident. "You are, after all, part owner of all of this. I'd think you'd be more concerned that things run smoothly."

He leaned against the hood of his truck and dug into his shirt pocket for his pack of Marlboros. "You're so good at taking care

336

of things that I figured you wouldn't miss me."

He bent over slightly, cupping the flame of his match, and lit a cigarette. He blew a ring of smoke, watching it drift away. He was sending a smoke signal, he mused. It said, "Jed doesn't give a good Go' damn."

"I'd love to stand here and spar with you, but I don't have the time," Suzanne said heatedly. "The Ferris wheel has been down all day. Something's wrong with the generator. You need to fix it."

"Where's Nelson?" he asked innocently.

"Your guess is as good as mine."

"I told you a month ago that you should have fired his ass."

A woman from one of the concession stands came running over. "Suzanne, we need change. We're out of ones."

"I'll take care of it." Suzanne turned back to Jed. "Well?"

"Well, what?" he asked.

"Don't just stand there. Go and see if you can get that darn thing working. We've already lost a bucket of money."

He clicked his heels and gave her a salute. "Yes, Drill Sergeant. I'll get right on it."

She gave him a look that said she was not amused.

■ ■ ■ ■

Sergeant Hill patrolled the fairgrounds. His mind felt drugged from lack of sleep. All night long he had tossed and turned. Where were he and Mittens going to live?

At the moment, the tabby was locked inside a pet carrier in the back of his pickup. He had parked it way down at the edge of the fairgrounds by the woods beneath a tree so Mittens would have lots of shade. He also figured that no one would disturb her there. He hadn't had time to search the real estate ads. They'd have to camp out until he found something. He just hoped the weather would hold.

He sighed and kept walking.

"Good evening, Sergeant," said Reverend Curtis, who was accompanied by his wife. The reverend was beaming from ear to ear. A blue ribbon was pinned to his lapel. "Isn't it a glorious night?"

"Yes, I suppose it is," Hill said, looking up into the star-studded sky. He really hadn't noticed. What was to become of him and his cat?

*His* cat? He stopped dead in his tracks.

A vision of her heart-shaped face, those sweet, soulful eyes, the way she greeted him as though he were the most important person in the world made his heartbeat quicken. Whatever the inconvenience she might pose, she was worth it because somewhere along these past few days, she had, indeed, become *his* cat.

His stomach started to growl. He had been so absorbed in his troubles he had completely forgotten to take a dinner break. He'd do one more loop around the fairgrounds, then call it quits. Maybe he'd buy a Philly cheesesteak sandwich and take it down to Mittens. He wondered if she was partial to beef.

A soft nest of branches had softened Sticks's fall. He slid onto the ground like a snake and lay there trying to figure out if anything was broken. Mostly his legs hurt. Every joint felt like it was on fire. He had tried standing once, grasping hold of a tree trunk. The pain had been so unbearable that he had collapsed in a heap.

He lay there wondering if he should try calling out for help. Would anyone even hear him? He had no idea how far the fairgrounds were. Then there was the risk that Jed might still be near enough to hear him and come back and finish the job.

Sticks decided to try standing again. This

portion of the forest was dense with trees, their branches low to the ground. Maybe he could grab hold as he made his way along. One more time, he got painfully to his feet. He waited a few minutes for the spots before his eyes to go away. His knee joints screamed out in pain as he forced himself forward.

His progress was painfully slow, but he kept at it. He figured he was about half a mile from the edge of the fairgrounds. Once he got out into the open field, he felt fairly confident that someone would spy him.

You can make it, he told himself. Just keep putting one foot in front of the other. Briars dug into his pant legs, and his hands were bleeding from the sharp, shell-hard fungus that grew on the tree branches in this part of the woods. He was making slow and steady progress until his foot sank into a groundhog's hole and he went crashing down on all fours. Pain like a two-hundred-watt jolt tore through him. He lay there panting, trying to stifle a scream.

He knew he had to get up again. He had to get moving, make it down the mountain and warn Suzanne. Jed had tampered with the generator. There was going to be an accident. Folks had to be warned.

He must have lost consciousness right

after that. When he awakened, it was mid-afternoon and something was nibbling on the nape of his shirt. He rolled onto his back, his heart racing, ready to battle. Anything could be roaming around these woods. He had heard reports of bobcats and black bears.

The sun shone directly in his eyes. All he could make out was a set of brown eyes and a pair of sharp, pointy ears. The hum of people's voices and tractor engines drifted up from below.

Pepper Pot leaned in closer and began to rub his snout along Sticks's cheek, squealing and snorting, happy to have found his best friend.

"Pepper Pot!" Sticks threw his arms around the pig's neck and hugged him nearly to death. "Well, I'll be dang."

The television studio was quiet. Except for the guy who ran the programming, everyone was at the fair.

Matthew's mind wandered like an unattended kite, freely sailing over his relationship with Stephanie as he rewound the tape. Although next week's edition of *Around the Town* didn't need to be edited until Monday, he preferred hiding out until the fair was over. Their friends were all meeting before

Night Hawk's concert. What would he tell them when he showed up alone or, worse, when they saw Stephanie with someone else? They'd know that he had been dumped. He just wished he knew why.

At times it was hard for him to believe that this once shapeless preteen with braces that he and her brother Dominic had used as a model to create a hologram of the Blessed Virgin had won his heart. Back then she had hardly warranted a second glance. Then one day she had shown up transformed into a chestnut-haired beauty. Half the guys at Dorsetville High would have given anything to date the gorgeous freshman. Now they'd have their chance, Matthew thought wryly. Good thing he didn't plan on sticking around town. He didn't think he could bear to watch Stephanie in the arms of someone else.

But if that was the way she wanted it, then it was good riddance. She had better not expect him to hang around and watch.

He had finally made a decision. MIT might not want him, but there were lots of other colleges in other towns. He'd send out his applications again, and the first acceptance that rolled in, he'd take. There was plenty of time to enroll in winter classes. He might even move out early. Get a part-time job.

A light on the editing panel flashed, which meant the last cut had been inserted. Matthew hit a few more switches, threw another tape into the console, and watched the images fast-forward across the screen. He was searching for footage of the Ferris wheel. Mr. Pipson wanted to use it as the opening shot. His granddad said it was on this tape. They had filmed it last night.

Matthew watched with growing disappointment. Glare from the lights encircling the Ferris wheel blurred several otherwise good shots. He focused all his attention on the small editing screen, hoping he might be able to salvage something.

"Oh, man . . ." A man walked in front of the camera carrying a crate of chickens. You could hear Timothy McGree swearing in the background, telling Matthew's grandfather to begin taping all over again. Seconds later there was a loud crash, followed by the sounds of frenzied voices and chickens clucking about. A few stray feathers floated across the lens.

The camera swung in that direction. The man who had been carrying the crate and another man, whose walker was now being used as a perch by two bantam roosters, were sprawled on the ground. Chickens were everywhere, dashing through the crowds of startled fairgoers.

"Come on, we'd better help out," Ben Metcalf's voice said off camera. "You help Artie with his walker, and I'll see if I can help to round up some of these chickens."

The camera must have then been placed on something high for safekeeping. It was focused on the top of the Ferris wheel. The Gallagher twins were seated inside one of the top cages.

"Matthew?"

He nearly jumped out of his seat at the sound of his name. He swung around. Hudson stood in the doorway.

"The outside door was open. Do you have a moment? I'd like to speak with you."

"Sure, come in."

"I see you're busy editing some film," Hudson said.

"Tape," Matthew corrected.

"Yes, tape," Hudson repeated. "Mind if I sit down?"

"No, here, take a seat." Matthew cleared off a chair filled with videotapes, silently wondering why Mrs. Holmes's butler wanted to speak with him.

"You're quite a multitalented young man," Hudson said, adjusting his jacket. "You work at Dinova's, go to school, and help out here."

"I like keeping busy."

"You're to be commended for your work ethic." Hudson paused briefly before zeroing in on the real reason for his visit. "Your friend Billy seems a hard worker, too."

"He's an okay guy," Matthew replied, keeping a close eye on the screen, which now showed a close-up of the Gallagher twins rocking in their chair high above the fairgrounds.

There was a slight pause before Hudson continued. "I was wondering if you knew anything about him."

"Like what?"

"Oh, let's say . . . his background?"

"No, I just met him. Excuse me a moment." Something on the tape had caught Matthew's eye.

Hudson had seen it too and asked, "Isn't that a tad bit dangerous? Those boys could have fallen out."

"Let me back it up a few frames," Matthew said. He ran the scene again, only this time at slow speed. They both edged closer to the screen.

The safety bar holding the Gallagher twins inside their chair had snapped open. The boys' faces registered instant delight. It looked as though they were having a great

345

time pretending to push each other out into space. Several times, Hudson gasped.

Then the scene began to dim. The camera battery had run low.

"Do you think they test the rides every day?" Hudson asked, greatly troubled.

"I don't know," Matthew said, pushing back his chair and grabbing for his keys. "But we'd better get over there and alert them just in case."

As he flew across the parking lot with Hudson tight on his heels, Matthew had another terrifying thought. What if Stephanie decided to take a ride?

Somewhere between handing the Ferris wheel attendant her orange ticket and sliding alongside a chestnut-haired teenage girl who later introduced herself as Stephanie, Marion realized that this was the first time she had ever ridden on a Ferris wheel. The prospect filled her with a delightful new sense of adventure.

Her intent was to ride high above the fairgrounds and see if she might spy Suzanne walking through the crowds. It was a foolish plan, she knew. Marion had met the girl only that once. She would be a middle-aged woman now, and trying to pick her out from the crowd below would be like trying to find the proverbial needle in a haystack. Still, she felt she must try. Besides, it was better than doing nothing.

The air grew chilly as they made their ascent. Marion wished she had brought along her shawl. She had left it in the limousine. Hudson had suggested she take it, and as usual, she hadn't listened. In fact, she should have listened to a lot of things he had suggested down through the years.

*Hudson* . . . Something stirred deep inside her, a yearning to be caressed, cherished. The thought made her blush. She sat up straighter in the metal seat and berated herself for such foolish imaginings. What had gotten into her lately, fantasizing about . . . of all things . . . her butler? Why, it was shameful. Yet at the same time, the feelings they evoked felt so good that she let new images range freely through her thoughts. She imagined his strong arms encircling her waist. The coarseness of his wool suit as it brushed against her cheek. The sensation of his lips seeking hers. With each image, she felt a slight thrill, like that of an adventurer exploring new and untrodden territory.

A trace of a smile played on her lips as she remembered last night's conversation. There was something so intimate about having Hudson seated so near. He was really a remarkably handsome man, with his tall, stately bearing, the shock of gray hair, and those crystal amber eyes, so penetrating yet so filled with concern for her welfare. It was a feeling that she sensed went much deeper than that of an employee for his employer.

She looked across at the girl seated alongside her, who seemed rather intent on jotting something down in a spiral notebook. She wondered what the girl might think if she could read Marion's thoughts. She supposed that, like most teenagers, this one thought romance was exclusively a product for the young.

Marion might have agreed two days ago. But then a lot of things had suddenly changed since that day in the church, although she would be hard-pressed to explain this transformation. She knew only that she had entered the sanctuary with a soul bound in sorrow and left a free spirit, no longer fettered by a life filled with regrets. That freedom had produced a joy that seemed to be bubbling over into every facet of her life. It was as if a spirit had been awakened. Suddenly, she wanted to live life to the fullest, not just observe it from the sidelines.

Was it just two days ago that she had been

resigned to her fate? Strange, a part of her had felt relief at Doc Hammon's prognosis. She was tired of living. When William had died, so had her will to live. Then two incredible events had happened in rapid-fire succession. First, through a chance encounter with David Kelly, she had been open to receive a miracle. Just the thought of those dead flowers suddenly coming back to life filled her with a new understanding of God's great love. He had sent her a powerful message about the reality of resurrection faith in His Son, Jesus Christ. With that insight had come a sense of peace that truly *surpasseth all understanding.* Suddenly, the burden of grief, anger, and unbelief that she had carried for years had lifted, replaced by the quiet assurance that since *He liveth,* so did William, and so would she when her time here on earth was through.

Then, quick on the heels of this epiphany, dear, sweet Hudson had pointed out Billy and given her another reason to hope. The resemblance between the boy and William was startling. He had to be William's son. All they needed to do was prove it. If it were true, there was much that needed to be done. Papers must be signed. New trusts created. Regardless of how she felt at the moment, Marion was a realist. Doc Hammon had been very careful to point out the seriousness of her condition. She could die at any moment. If Billy was her heir, then she must make certain he received his rightful inheritance, which was considerable. Thanks to her diligence and business savvy, the family's estate was now worth several billion dollars. Any grandson of hers would be a very wealthy man.

The Ferris wheel continued to fill, two to a seat, as they sailed higher and higher above the crowds.

I wonder how Hudson is doing? Marion thought as a slight breeze ruffled her hair. The basket gently rocked in the wind, and she leaned back to steady it. The girl beside her seemed unfazed. She was still bent over her notebook.

In the distance, the lights surrounding the huge bandstand came to life, accompanied by a deafening cheer. Seconds later, the sound of a steel guitar rang over the fairgrounds to a round of applause. The concert had begun.

# 12

It had taken Jed about ten minutes to get the Ferris wheel up and running. He figured in another twenty it would grind to a halt, stranding its riders. Too bad he couldn't stick around. He would have liked to have seen their faces.

Eventually, someone would figure out what he had done, but by then he'd be sampling margaritas down in good old Mexico. Let them try to find him. Life after tonight was going to be a wild ride. He couldn't wait to hand over his ticket and climb on.

He looked around, making sure no one was watching before he headed for the woods. He had parked his truck along the old logging road, safely out of sight. The bags of coke he had earlier removed from beneath the office trailer were stored inside. There was still plenty of time to get down to the river before Covas and the others showed up. Not that he had to hurry. After all, *he* had the goods.

Father James had been enjoying a philly cheesesteak sandwich with extra cheese, fried onions, and a side of chili fries, feeling like a man who had just been released from death row. He was finally free from foxhunts and apple pie contests and had twelve months to think up excuses to avoid having to do either ever again.

He munched happily on his sandwich, which would probably raise the roof on his cholesterol, but at this moment he didn't care. At the very least, he should be allowed to enjoy his feast, guilt free, considering that one of his cojudges, George Benson, had probably gotten them blackballed by every woman in a thirty-mile radius.

George hadn't been content to sample each entry and *quietly* list its rating on the tally sheet. Oh, no . . . not George. Nigel Hayes and Father James watched as George made a big show of running the sample around his tongue, rolling his eyes heavenward (if it gained his approval) or scowling (if he thought the entry lacked a little "something"). All of this was done under the watchful eyes of the contestants. One man in particular looked as though he wanted to hit George.

George also took it upon himself to offer suggestions. "This one could have used a little more cinnamon." Or "That pastry's so heavy it could anchor a ship." That particular comment had sent a poor woman fleeing in tears. At that point, Father James had thought about taking George aside and suggesting he tone it down a little, but as he started to rise, he looked out over the sea of women — fists clenched by their sides, their anger aimed at George like a sonar missile, and it had dawned on the priest. George's obnoxious behavior was setting him up as the perfect fall guy. No matter who was chosen this year's blue-ribbon winner, the losers would naturally place the blame squarely on George's shoulders. That meant the heat was off him! Hallelujah!

So when the winner, a man from Woodbury, was chosen, Father James felt no guilt whatsoever in hinting to the Dorsetville ladies that it had been all George's doing.

Father James was savoring the last of his sandwich and wondering if he should order an onion blossom (What the heck? He had gone this far, hadn't he?) when Ruth and June Henderson came rushing over. It was quite a sight, these octogenarian sisters pushing their walkers with the speed of a

Tasmanian devil, sending showers of dust swirling up around their feet.

"Hello, ladies. Want to join me? I'm buying," Father James said, feeling rather dapper. Amazing how wonderful it felt finally to have these last two days behind him.

"No time," Ruth said breathlessly.

It was then that it hit him. In all the years he had known the sisters, he had never seen them so overexerted. An alarm bell went off in his head.

"What's wrong?" He stood, wiping his mouth.

"It's the Ferris wheel," Ruth said, taking in a mouthful of air.

"It's stopped," June added, no less winded.

"Yes, well, it's supposed to stop to let people on and off," he explained, thinking that they simply had gotten a little confused, which happened often with the senior crowd.

Ruth gave him the look she had once reserved for the mentally challenged in her classroom and shouted, "Not that kind of stopped! It's stuck. No one can get on or off."

It took a few seconds for this information to register.

"Well, don't just stand there," Ruth said,

banging her walker against the ground, sending up another cloud of dust. "Get over there! Timothy, Ben, and Marion Holmes are up there, and you'd better do something fast before one of them has a heart attack from fright."

For the last ten hours, Pepper Pot had not left Sticks's side. It was as if the pig knew that his survival rested on his ability to keep his master moving toward the fairgrounds for help.

His owner had made most of the trek on his hands and knees, crawling like a rather large reptile. Several times he had cried out in pain, and the pig, who was using Sticks's sleeve to guide him along, would stop and deliver several wet kisses to the old man's cheeks as though to encourage him along.

As the sun went down, Sticks finally gave up. "Just let me die," he told the pig.

Pepper Pot either didn't understand or refused to accept such pessimism and continued to push and pull and prod and generally make such a persistent nuisance of himself that Sticks had no recourse but to keep on inching his way along.

By now, Sticks had lost all concept of time. He was lost in an eddy of pain. In moments of desperate despair, he would look into the soft, pink eyes of his stubby-legged pig. Who would take care of him if Sticks didn't make it? The question drove him on.

The pair finally made it to the edge of the fairgrounds. Sticks collapsed, tears running down his cheeks. He reached out and petted his pig, thinking that if he died at that moment, he'd die a happy man. No one had ever had such a loyal friend.

Then he heard a man's voice coming from behind a clump of tall grass. "See what I brought you for a snack? It's a piece of steak, your favorite."

Sticks tried to call out, but all he could manage was a whisper. He was terribly dehydrated, and his lips were as parched as the desert floor.

Normally, Pepper Pot was shy around strangers, except in the confines of the petting zoo, where treats were involved. Sticks watched amazed as the pig moved cautiously through the tall grass. He could tell by the way Pepper Pot's tail twitched that he was studying the situation.

Sticks would never know if it was the smell of that steak or his devotion that made the pig finally decide to charge through the undergrowth, squealing like his tail was on fire.

"Well, I'll be," Hill exclaimed. "What do

we have here?"

Pepper Pot squealed even louder and dashed back through the bush. He stationed himself right next to Sticks, continuing to snort at the top of his lungs.

"Where did you go?" Hill asked, twigs snapping beneath his boots as he followed Pepper Pot into the woods. "You shouldn't be out here all . . ."

A ray of moonlight stretched across the forest floor, outlining the shape of a man lying prone on the ground. His arm was draped across a potbellied pig. Hill rushed over and bent down to console him.

"It's all right, sir. You take it easy." The sergeant reached for his walkie-talkie. Seconds later, a burst of screams rose from the fairgrounds. Hill assumed it was some kids having fun on one of the rides.

"Dispatch. Over," Betty answered.

"Betty, I have a badly injured man on the edge of the woods, north of the fairgrounds. I need an ambulance. Over."

There were several bursts of static before he could decipher Betty's reply.

"I'm dispatching one your way. Boy, am I glad you called in. I couldn't raise your signal. You won't believe what's been happening. We've had a major incident at the fairgrounds. Over."

"What kind of incident? Over."

"The Ferris wheel is broken, and Timothy McGree fell out of his chair and is hanging on for dear life. I just hope the hook and ladder gets there in time. Over," she sobbed.

Hill asked Sticks, "Can you hold on here by yourself for a few more minutes?"

Sticks nodded.

"Betty, I'm on my way. Tell the ambulance crew that I'll aim my headlights on the victim. He's in bad shape, but he says he can hold on alone until they get here. Have you contacted the sheriff? Over."

"I've tried, but he's on a stakeout. He's not answering his page. Over."

"I'm headed there now. Over and out."

Hill clipped the walkie-talkie back to his belt. "They'll be here shortly. Just hold on."

Sticks motioned for him to bend closer.

Hill strained to hear.

With all the energy he had left, Sticks said in a hoarse whisper, "Jed Mullen tried to kill me."

As Timothy dangled thirty feet above the crowds, he swore that if he survived this, he would do whatever it took to end his muscle cramps once and for all, even if it meant taking up yoga and living on a steady diet of bananas. They were not his favorite fruit, but Ben insisted they were rich in potassium, the lack of which caused the cramps.

"Hold on and don't look down," Ben yelled.

"That's what I'm *trying* to do, you idiot!"

"Idiot? Who you calling an idiot? I'm not the one dangling out in space. I told you to sit down and ignore the charley horse. Now see what you've done."

Timothy hadn't meant to jump up like a jack-in-the-box, but his calf had felt as though it were clamped in a vise. He knew from experience that the only way to get the muscle to release was to stand and stretch. He had grabbed hold of the safety bar to steady his balance, and it had flown open, taking him with it.

Sirens sounded in the distance.

"Hold on, Tim. Help is on the way," Father James yelled up.

"I hope it gets here soon. I can't hold on much longer."

"What if I lean over and try to grab your hand?" Ben offered.

Timothy screamed, "Don't! You'll pitch the basket forward, and I'll go with it."

"Mr. McGree," Marion Holmes shouted. She and Stephanie were seated in the chair below. "I have an idea."

"I'm open to anything," Timothy yelled

back. The muscles along his arms felt as though they were on fire.

"I'm going to reach up and grab hold of your trouser legs; then, on the count of three, I want you to let go of the bar. Stephanie will pull us both back to safety."

An old joke flashed through his head:

Man has fallen off a cliff and catches a tree branch on the way down. He calls out to God. "God, I can sure use your help. I'm about to plunge to my death."

The heavens open, and a voice calls out, "Let go of the branch."

The man figures God mustn't have understood the gravity of his situation, so he explains. "God, I've fallen off a cliff, and I'm holding on to a mere branch. There's a hundred feet between me and the canyon floor. Please . . . send help."

"Let go of the branch," the voice repeats.

The man thinks about this for a while, then looks up to the heavens.

"Is there anyone else up there?"

Timothy looked down at the crowd gathering below.

"You got any other ideas?" he asked.

When Hudson and Matthew arrived at the fairgrounds, the crowd had fallen as silent as the grave. Everyone was holding their breath as they watched the horrible drama unfolding above them.

Next door, the merry-go-round played a merry tune as children strained to see what was going on when they circled in that direction. One parent finally had the presence of mind to suggest the children be taken elsewhere, *just in case.*

Hudson nearly fainted when he saw Marion standing up, trying to grab hold of Timothy's trouser leg. "Madam, sit down!" he yelled.

She turned slightly to see who had just given the command. Her eyes softened when she saw Hudson. "Not to worry. Stephanie and I have a plan," she shouted back. "Mr. McGree is going to let go, and we're going to catch him."

"Good God, she's lost her mind," he said.

"Stephanie . . ." Matthew felt a cold chill snake up his spine. What if the safety bar to the basket they were in gave way? He couldn't stand to watch, knowing that there was no way he could help. He needed to do something with his hands before he lost it. He spied the station's camera sitting to the side of the man who ran the rides. He grabbed it and started filming.

Hill arrived, quickly sized up the situation and shouted up to Marion. "Ma'am, I don't think that's a good idea. Why don't we wait for the hook and ladder? They'll be here any minute."

The sirens were growing louder. They couldn't be more than half a mile away.

"That's fine with me; however, I don't think Mr. McGree has many more minutes left," Marion said.

"Move out of the way," Suzanne shouted to the crowd tightly packed around the scene. She and Billy were lugging a huge piece of canvas. She had been visiting the petting zoo when she got the call that a man was dangling from the top of the Ferris wheel. It had been Billy's suggestion to fashion a safety net out of the piece of canvas used to repair the tents.

Suzanne explained to the deputy what they planned to do. "We'll need some help setting it in place."

Several strong men stepped out of the crowd and helped to carry the canvas over to the spot beneath Timothy's dangling body.

Hill went into overdrive, forcing the crowd back to make room. Folks instantly obeyed. This was not the Frank Hill they knew. This man spoke with authority. Strangely enough, no one dared question his commands.

"Father James," Hill called. "Keep the crowds back. You . . ."

Hudson looked around. The sergeant was pointing directly at him.

"Yes, you. Find some rope and cordon off the area."

"Billy, I'll help set up the canvas. You help this man find some rope," Suzanne said.

"Sure, Mom. This way, Mr. Hudson."

*Hudson?* The name brought back a rush of memories. William's butler was named Hudson. Their eyes met.

"Suzanne?" Hudson asked.

She nodded.

"Mrs. Holmes and I have been looking for you," he said.

He pointed to the Ferris wheel, where Marion was getting ready to enact her rescue plan.

Suddenly, it was as if time had stopped for Hudson and Suzanne.

"Mrs. Holmes, you're going to fall out!" Stephanie said, holding on tightly to the woman's waist. The plan had *seemed* like a good one when Mrs. Holmes had proposed it. Right now, however, she wasn't so sure.

"Just hold tight and don't let go. I've almost got him," Marion said.

Down below, the crowd was forced back

farther. The fire department had arrived. Chief Billy Halstead was calling out orders faster than a short-order cook at Coney Island on the Fourth of July, although he knew that he'd never get the hook and ladder into position in time. He hoped the makeshift safety net that had been put in place would hold if Timothy didn't make it.

"Mr. McGree, you really must trust me," Marion said, finally snagging hold of a trouser leg.

Timothy felt his hands begin to slip. It was now or never.

Father James pulled a rosary out of his pocket and began to pray. "Hail Mary, full of grace . . ."

The Catholics among the crowd picked up his refrain.

"Now on the count of three, I want you to let go. Stephanie, hold me steady, then when Mr. McGree releases his hands, pull us both in. You got it?"

"I got it," the teenager said, thinking that if this plan worked, it would sure make an awesome newspaper story.

Up above, Timothy was saying a farewell to Ben. "In case I don't make this, you've been one heck of a best friend."

"You, too, old buddy," Ben replied with a catch in his voice.

"All right, on the count of three," Marion called from below. "One . . ."

Timothy said a quick prayer and hoped that God would forgive him for occasionally cheating at cards.

"Two . . ."

He looked at the crowd below. Everyone down there was either a friend or a neighbor. He had been a lucky man to have been born and raised in Dorsetville. He cast about for Father James's face. When it came to priests, he sure was the pick of the litter; next to Father Keene, of course. The old priest was slowly slipping away, Mother Superior had told him when he called right before he and Ben left for the fair. The way things were looking, however, Timothy might be arriving in heaven slightly ahead of the old cleric.

*"Three . . ."*

Timothy closed his eyes and let go. He felt Marion's arms grasp his waist and give a firm tug. At the same time, he felt *Another* set of arms pulling him to safety.

A loud and boisterous cheer went up from the crowd below.

"I guess we don't need this any longer," Billy said, dropping the canvas. Matthew walked over and joined him. "I hope your girlfriend's all right," Billy said. "That was sure a brave thing she did."

"It sure was," Matthew said, feeling an immense relief. He had almost lost her. He knew at that moment that, no matter what it took, he planned on winning her back.

"Billy, I need to talk to you," his mother said, coming up from behind him. Hudson looked anxiously over her shoulder.

Sheriff Bromley rocketed the Chevy Blazer onto the fairgrounds, lights flashing, sirens going full blast, just as the cheer went up. He jumped out of the Blazer with Harley tight on his heels and hightailed it over to the scene as fast as his six-foot-four, three-hundred-pound frame could allow. He felt flush with relief as soon as he saw Timothy seated between Marion Holmes and Stephanie Costello, waving like a movie star.

"Hi, Al, glad you could make it," the fire chief teased. "You missed one heck of a high-flying act. Chester! Have the men secure those ropes before swinging the ladder over."

Dorsetville's fire department was getting ready to evacuate the Ferris wheel. Ben Metcalf, whose knuckles were white from hanging to the sides of the basket, would be the first to be brought down.

"So, where've you been?" the chief asked,

keeping his eyes pinned to the ladder now being moved into place.

"Stakeout," Bromley answered.

"Stakeout? I haven't heard you utter that word in a long time. I hope it paid off."

"Not as good as I had hoped," the sheriff said, watching the men tie the thirty-foot ladder in place.

The drug dealers had been rounded up, and it would be a very long time before the Covas family was back in business, but they didn't have enough on Jed Mullen to keep him behind bars for long. "He'll probably get off with a three-year sentence," Fillmore had said, watching four of New England's major drug dealers being hauled away. "At least we nabbed the big guys."

Bromley wasn't feeling quite so philosophical. He didn't want thugs like Jed Mullen coming into his town and using it as the backdrop for their drug deals. He wished there was some way of charging the guy with something more than possession.

"Hi, Sheriff," Sergeant Hill said, coming up to stand beside the two men.

For the first time, Bromley took a good look at the scene. Sections had been cordoned off with rope to keep the crowds away. A medical station had been set up to one side. Nancy Hawkins was manning it, although it seemed none of the riders needed her help.

From the laughs now issuing from the Ferris wheel, it appeared the crisis was over. Some riders even looked as though they were enjoying the drama. One thing was for sure: This was an event that would go down in the annals of Dorsetville history.

The sheriff turned to his sergeant. "You've done a first-class job here tonight."

Hill lit up like a sparkler. Bromley didn't give out compliments often.

Nancy walked over. "I thought you'd like to know that the man you found is on his way to Mercy Hospital," she told Hill. "I hear he's going to be all right."

"What man?" Bromley wanted to know.

"Some old guy who works for the carnival. I think he runs the petting zoo."

"How did he get hurt?" the sheriff asked, watching Chester Platt help Ben climb down the ladder.

"Someone threw him off a ravine."

"Why?"

"The old man saw a guy messing around with the generator." Hill turned around and looked over the scene. "I guess he's the same one who's responsible for all of this. Can't figure it, though. According to the victim, this guy's a part owner. Don't that beat all? Sabotaging your own business?"

"This guy's name wouldn't happen to be Jed Mullen, would it?"

"Yeah, how'd you know? I called dispatch and had Betty put out a bulletin for attempted murder."

"Attempted murder, hey?" Bromley said, a smile creeping across his face. "Get Betty on the horn. Tell her to cancel the all points bulletin. I just happen to know exactly where he can be found."

# 13

No one wanted to go home after the harrowing evening. Folks were too keyed up. Harry Clifford offered to open the Country Kettle and fire up the grill. So now half the citizens of Dorsetville were stuffed inside the restaurant. The place was wall-to-wall people. Some had dragged in chairs from the storage shed outside and created makeshift tables out of plywood carried in from Stone's Hardware Store. A row of such tables was now lined up in front of the bakery's display cases.

"I'd say that this definitely exceeds the legal limit of people allowed in this space," Mayor Roger Martin declared, nudging George Benson. "What are you going to do about it?"

Roger, a Congregational Church trustee, was still miffed at the fire marshal's refusal a year ago to allow his fellow parishioners to exceed the legal occupancy limit during their church's rededication.

"Nothing," George said, mopping up the cream he had just spilled with the edge of his sleeve.

"What do you mean, 'nothing'? You're the fire marshal. It's your *sworn* duty, remember?" the mayor teased.

"The fire marshal has clocked out for the night," George said, leaning back in his chair, the wood creaking like old ship timbers beneath his weight. He was seated at the round table by the front window, along with the town crew and the sheriff. The men watched the exchange with amusement.

"Right now, I'm just an ordinary citizen enjoying a cup of coffee and a burger, if it ever arrives," he said pointedly to Wendy.

"You want it faster? Then put on an apron, get behind the grill, and start flipping," she sparred.

A group of women flew through the doors, arms filled with cardboard boxes containing an assortment of apple pies. Ethel Johnson led the parade. "These are the ones that didn't make the grade," she said, referring to the Apple Pie Contest. There wasn't a woman in town who didn't have a freezer full of rejects.

Men jumped up to clear some counter

space. They didn't care a fig if the crust had flaked off the edge or the filling had run over the side.

"Tastes just as good," Nigel Hayes said, returning from the deep freeze with a five-gallon container of vanilla ice cream and several ice cream scoops.

Father James was seated with the St. Cecilia morning regulars. Both Sam Rosenberg and Harriet Bedford, who had left the fairgrounds before Timothy's flying circus act, had driven into town to join the celebration.

"Betty called Mildred Dunlop, and she called Shirley Olsen, who lives near Harriet," Sam began to explain, dropping into a chair. "Harriet called me, and I got right back in my car, and here we are. We couldn't miss out on all of this."

"Tell us everything," Harriet ordered Father James, scooting in closer. "And don't leave out any details."

As best he could, Father James related the night's events, from the stalled Ferris wheel through Timothy's aerobatics to Sticks Hopson being found by Sergeant Hill, who had gone to his truck to feed his cat, continuing on to the reunion of Marion Holmes with her grandson.

By the time he had finished relating all

that had happened, he was nearly out of breath and ready for a second helping of pie.

Harriet listened intently, occasionally throwing a furtive glance toward Hudson and Marion Holmes, seated in the booth alongside the far wall. Suzanne and Billy had left a few minutes ago to get some sleep before the fair opened again in the morning. Billy seemed overjoyed with the discovery that Marion was his grandmother and her invitation to both mother and son to consider making Merrybrook their home.

"After all, one day it will be yours," she had told the wide-eyed teenager.

"Do you see what I see?" Harriet whispered to Ethel, nodding toward Marion and Hudson. The couple were holding hands and staring into each other's eyes like starstruck lovers.

"It's about time" was all Timothy had to say on the subject, rubbing his hands with Ben-Gay. They ached something terrible from holding on to that bar for so long.

"Anyone with half a brain could have seen he was stuck on her for years," Ben said, helping himself to another scoop of ice cream. He'd worry about an attack of gout later.

"You never know about people, do you?"

Ethel mused. "Who would have guessed that Marion Holmes could fall in love with her butler?"

"Especially since she broke up her son's engagement because he was in love with a girl she thought beneath their social standing," Harriet reminded them.

"Well, not anymore," said Mrs. Norris, who had just arrived. "Scoot over, Ben. I also heard that Marion is throwing a big party at her estate in honor of her grandson. The whole town is invited."

Father James drained his mug. Amazing how his housekeeper knew these things. Oh, well, that was life in a small town for you. Gossip spread faster in Dorsetville than floodwaters, he mused. How long had it been since the incident tonight? Less than a couple of hours? Yet Mrs. Norris already knew about a proposed celebration and who was invited. He supposed if he asked, she could tell him what Marion planned to serve.

He held up his cup as Wendy passed with the Pyrex pot.

"Suzanne has done a good job in raising that boy," Ethel said. "I met him the other day at Dinova's. What a nice young man. I'm sure Marion will have to agree."

"It's not about pedigree," Sam said.

Everyone grew quiet. Sam Rosenberg seldom offered an opinion. "It's about common decency and love. Suzanne might have lived in a trailer and had to work for a living, but she is a good and decent person. Her son reflects that."

Father James concurred.

"Hi, Gramps," Matthew said, racing in with Stephanie. The two were holding hands. Stephanie was wearing his senior class ring on a chain.

"Hi, Matthew," everyone chimed.

"Here, have a seat," Sam said, pulling out a chair.

Matthew sat down, pulling Stephanie onto his lap. She giggled.

"Guess what, Gramps. Mr. Pipson was at the station when I delivered the tape. I thought they might want to use it tomorrow for the morning news. Well, he liked what I had shot so much that he offered me a full-time paying job."

"No kidding?" Ben said.

"And we work for free," Timothy lamented.

"Doing what?" Father James asked Matthew.

"Setting up some new programs. Editing."

"What about college?" his grandfather asked.

Matthew shifted Stephanie's weight to his other knee. "I discovered something tonight."

"What's that?" Father James wanted to know.

"I liked telling a story through film. I think I might want to give up my dreams of MIT and go to film school. I hear Columbia has a great film department."

Father James smiled. Columbia was his alma mater.

"Matthew is going to be a big producer, like for *60 Minutes* or something, and I'm going to work in front of the cameras, like Leslie Stahl," Stephanie piped up. "We have it all planned. We're going to make a dynamite team, don't you think?"

Everyone confirmed that, indeed, they would.

Sheriff Bromley walked outside, feeling every one of his fifty-plus years. It had been a long time since he'd raced around like a rookie, chasing after crooks. His legs felt like they were being held down with forty-pound weights, his back ached, and the muscles along his shoulder blades could use a good massage. Maybe he should have borrowed some of Timothy's Ben-Gay.

Harley raced up ahead, closely sniffing the

sidewalk. He was tracking something. Whatever it was, Bromley hoped it had nothing to do with criminals or law enforcement. He loved his job, but after tonight's events, he could use a few days of peace and quiet.

Harley sniffed around the tailgate of a parked truck. A small screened tent had been erected inside the truck's bed. The dog jumped up onto the bumper and began to whine.

"Come over here," Bromley commanded.

The dog ignored him and continued crying as though his best friend was locked inside.

"You're going to wake up the whole town with all that caterwauling." The sheriff grabbed Harley's collar and yanked him off the tailgate.

"Hi, Sheriff," Hill said, unzipping the tent's screen.

Bromley heard a soft *meow*. Harley heard it too and jumped back up to sniff inside.

"It's just Hill and his cat," the sheriff explained to the dog.

Harley and the cat sniffed noses.

"So what are you doing here? Too hot inside your apartment?" Bromley asked.

"Nah. I — that is *we* — got kicked out."

"The lease?"

"Yeah. John's allergic to cats."

"Bummer. So what are you going to do? Sleep in your truck?"

"Until I find a new place."

The sheriff looked up into a sky filled with stars. "What are you going to do if it rains?"

"I'll cross that bridge when I get to it," Hill said, rubbing Mittens behind the ears. The cat's purrs could be heard clear down the street.

Bromley thought a moment. "Why don't you come home with me? We have a spare room, and Barbara won't mind."

Fact was, Barbara wouldn't mind if he brought home Genghis Khan. She had finally won a ribbon for one of her quilts. It was only second place, but she didn't care. She said it gave her something to aim for next year.

"If you're sure it won't be an imposition."

"I wouldn't have asked if it was."

"In that case, we'd love to be your house-guests. I *can* bring Mittens, can't I?" he reiterated.

"Sure. Right, Harley? You don't mind sharing your place with a member of the feline family, now, do you?"

Harley gave three short barks in approval.

Hill carefully placed Mittens inside her carryall, and the two men headed down the hill. The sheriff's Blazer was parked by Tri

Town Auto. There hadn't been a vacant parking space in town.

"I meant it tonight when I said you did a good job out there," Bromley said, nodding in the direction of the fairgrounds.

"Why, thanks, Chief . . . I mean, Sheriff."

The two walked along in silence.

"I think it might be time to put you back on patrol."

"You mean in the cruiser?"

"No, Hill. I mean on a bicycle. Of course I mean in the cruiser. I'm warning you, though. Just one dent and you're back beating the sidewalks."

Suddenly, Hill felt as though he were made of helium. Any minute he might lift off.

It was after two in the morning before the last customer, who happened to be Father James, was told to go home.

"I'm sorry, Father, but I've got to get some shut-eye," Harry said, shooing him out the front door.

The priest hadn't intended to stay so long. It was just that he had been too wired to sleep. So much had happened in the span of a few hours that he needed someone to help him sort it all out.

He turned the corner, heading toward

home, the light of a thumbnail moon resting on his shoulder. He couldn't get the image of Marion and Hudson out of his mind. This was the first time that Marion Holmes had ever graced the inside of the Country Kettle, and he was pretty sure that, before this evening, she would have died rather than been seen linking arms with her butler.

There was something else he surmised, a sense of peace about her that he knew could come from only one Source. He was willing to bet next week's collections that sometime between their meeting at Merrybrook and tonight, Marion had turned her life over to God. He wondered what had brought that on. He'd ask his housekeeper. She knew everything.

He noticed a light was on in Reverend Curtis's study as he passed the Victorian parsonage. Emily Curtis had been one of the ones trapped on the Ferris wheel. No doubt the Curtises were having a very interesting conversation. It took only a near miss in life to make people take stock of their blessings and reaffirm what they held most dear.

Yes, indeed, it had been quite a night. Father James was reminded of something Sam Rosenberg had once said: "God created man because He likes a good story."

And what a story this was!

Billy Granger had found a grandmother. Hudson a long-delayed romance. Suzanne Granger had found a home without wheels. And Matthew Metcalf had found the career that God had apparently planned for him all along.

Father James turned onto the stone path that led to the rectory's front door. "And we know that in all things God works for the good of those who love Him, who have been called according to His purpose," he quoted, bounding up the front steps. Father Dennis had left the porch light on. A swarm of moths was flittering around the bulb.

Father James felt certain that Matthew had found his true calling. Unbeknownst to him, he had also found the money to pursue the dream.

As soon as the sun rose, Father James planned to give his best friend, Jeff Hayden, a call. Jeff's father sat on the Board of Trustees for Columbia University. Between the three of them, he felt certain that they would find the means for Matthew to attend.

Silence finally settled over Dorsetville as folks fell into their beds, exhausted from the weeks of preparation and the excitement of the County Fair.

Reverend Curtis and his wife, Emily, made a firm commitment to take that romantic weekend they had been postponing for months. "Let's go to Vermont. I could make reservations at the Equinox in Manchester," the reverend suggested, grasping her hand. How close he had come to losing her tonight. He made a solemn vow never to take their marriage for granted again.

Warm tears gathered in the corners of her eyes. They had spent their honeymoon there. "Perfect," she whispered, breaking off the last corner of her scone and passing it across the table.

Before going to bed, the reverend placed his blue ribbon in a Ziploc bag for safekeeping. He had waited for this moment for so long that, now that it was here, he could hardly contain his joy.

He removed his wristwatch and laid it beside his glasses on the nightstand, thinking he really must remember to visit Ethel tomorrow and thank her. Her hydrangeas had made all the difference. Funny, he thought, slipping between the freshly laundered sheets that smelled of lavender. The ones that grew in her garden were soft pink. The ones she had delivered were a show-stopping mint. Oh, well, he'd figure it out tomorrow. Right now he could sleep for a week.

"Emily? Are you coming to bed?" he called, ready to turn out the light.

"In a minute, dear," she said. "I just want to finish writing out this recipe."

Emily had received so many compliments on her English scones with mock Devonshire cream at this year's Hunt Breakfast that she'd decided to submit the recipe to the *Dorsetville Gazette.* Why shouldn't the rest of the town enjoy these scrumptious treats? she thought, placing the recipe alongside her husband's blue ribbon. The reverend could drop it off at the newspaper when he went to have his blue ribbon framed.

Sharing recipes seemed to be in the air tonight. As soon as Loretta Baker had gotten her husband, Donald, his cup of hot chocolate and settled in bed, she had snuck back downstairs. The women at St. Cecilia's Altar Society meeting were going to be quite surprised this week when they discovered a copy of her grandmother's blue-ribbon peach preserves recipe on each of their chairs. Like her grandmother always said, "When the Lord gives you a gift, share it."

Joseph Platt's prize bull, Zorro, had taken

the blue ribbon again, leaving many of the men in town short on cash. With the odds 10 to 1 in his opponent's favor, David Kelly had raked in a sizable amount, which Joe had decided to spend on a European vacation. His wife had been talking about it for years, and well, after seeing Timothy hanging from that Ferris wheel, Joe had decided life was too short to keep postponing the good times.

Altogether, the folks in Dorsetville would have enough to talk about till spring, which pleased them immeasurably. Winters are long and hard in New England, and nothing warms the soul more than sharing a good memory.

Perhaps that was why Father Keene had been so busy these past few days remembering. While onlookers thought he was deep in a coma, he had been gathering memories like sheaves of wheat. He planned to review them often while he waited for the others to join him in heaven's hallowed halls.

*"Thank you, Lord, for the privilege of calling Dorsetville my home,"* he prayed as the first threads of dawn wove their patterns across the sky. *"I couldn't have asked for a better place to live, or for better friends. Bless them all without limits for making this old priest's life so rich.*

*"And thank you, Lord, for helping me take care of that last piece of business. I can rest now knowing that Marion, Suzanne, and Billy are united. May the coming years of friendship erase all bitter roots of the past.*

*"Now my final prayer . . .*

*"Bless Father James. His gentle heart and kind spirit are the balm to many a weary soul. And when it is his time to cross over, may I be given the privilege of being the first to greet him at heaven's door."*

The morning light grew brighter, filling the room with its golden rays. On the nightstand stood the candle that Sister Bernadette had placed beside Father Keene's favorite picture of Our Lady of Medjugorje. A gentle breeze blew over the still form. The candle flickered several times, then blew out.

Father Keene's spirit rose along with the last whiff of smoke. Morning had come.

# RECIPES

### BLUE RIBBON APPLE PIE

Here's an apple pie recipe from Mr. John Ray Osuch, winner of the 2004 Association of Connecticut State Fairs, who was most gracious to share his winning recipe. Mr. Osuch lives in Bethlehem, Connecticut.

**Never Fail Pie Crust**

4 cups flour
2 teaspoons salt
2 cups shortening
1 egg
1 teaspoon sugar
1 teaspoon vinegar
1/2 cup cold water

Combine flour and salt; cut in shortening. Beat egg. Add sugar and vinegar to water. Add liquid mixture to flour mixture and mix well with wooden spoon.

Dough keeps in refrigerator for several

weeks if wrapped in waxed paper and foil. It may also be frozen.

Before using mixture, refrigerate for at least 1 hour. Roll out thinly.

YIELD: 3 double or 6 single pie crusts.

## Apple Filling

8 to 9 apples (a mix of Granny Smith and Empire)
1 tablespoon lemon juice
1 cup sugar
1/2 teaspoon nutmeg
1 teaspoon cinnamon
1/2 teaspoon salt
2 tablespoons flour
1 tablespoon butter

Cut and toss apples with lemon juice, then add dry ingredients. Fill bottom crust, top with butter. Add top crust, brush with beaten egg, and flute.

Bake 15 minutes at 450 degrees. Reduce to 350 degrees and bake for an additional hour.

# Loretta Baker's Grandmother's Peach Preserves

4 cups finely chopped peaches (approximately 3 pounds)
1/4 cup freshly squeezed lemon juice
7 1/2 cups sugar
1 tablespoon cinnamon
1/2 teaspoon each nutmeg and ground cloves
1 bottle fruit pectin

Remove skin from peaches by submerging peaches in boiling water for 30 seconds or until skin begins to separate from fruit. Immediately place peaches in bowl of ice water. Skins will slip off quite easily.

Peel and pit peaches. Chop very fine or grind. Measure 4 cups into large saucepan. Add lemon juice, sugar, and spices.

Place over high heat. Bring to rolling boil and boil hard for 1 minute, stirring constantly. Remove from heat and at once stir in fruit pectin.

Stir and skim for 5 minutes. Ladle quickly into sterilized jars (Loretta uses the dishwasher). Paraffin at once, or keep refrigerated.

YIELD: eleven 6-ounce jars.

# Emily Curtis's English Scones with Mock Devonshire Cream

## Scones

4 cups all-purpose flour
1/2 cup sugar
4 teaspoons baking powder
3/4 teaspoon salt
12 tablespoons (1 1/2 sticks) chilled unsalted butter, diced
1 cup whipping cream
3 large eggs
1 tablespoon vanilla extract
1 tablespoon lemon peel
2 teaspoons water

Preheat oven to 400 degrees. Line 2 baking sheets with foil.

Sift dry ingredients into large bowl. Add butter. Use your fingers to rub butter into flour mixture until it resembles coarse meal.

Take another bowl and whisk together cream, 2 eggs, vanilla, and lemon peel. Add to flour mixture. Stir until just blended. Do not overblend.

Gather dough into large ball and knead lightly on a well-floured surface, incorporating surface flour just until dough is no longer sticky. (Don't spend a lot of time on this. The more you work it, the tougher the scones.)

Roll out dough on floured surface to 3/4-inch thickness. Use 2-inch round cookie cutter to cut out scones. (You can continue to regather leftover dough, roll it again, and cut out more scones.) Place scones on foil-lined baking sheets about 2 inches apart.

Whisk remaining egg and 2 teaspoons water in small bowl. Use pastry brush to lightly brush over tops of scones.

Bake until golden brown, about 20 minutes. Transfer to cooling rack. (Can be made 8 hours ahead.) Cool completely before storing. Serve at room temperature.

## Mock Devonshire Cream
3 ounces cream cheese (room temperature)
1 tablespoon sugar
1/8 teaspoon salt
1 cup whipping cream

Blend cream cheese, sugar, and salt. Stir in whipping cream and beat until stiff peaks form. Refrigerate until ready to serve.

## FATHER KEENE'S FAVORITE
## IRISH SODA BREAD

3 cups sifted flour
3 tablespoons sugar
3 teaspoons baking powder
1/2 teaspoon baking soda
1/2 teaspoon salt
1 cup raisins
1 1/3 cups buttermilk

Preheat oven to 375 degrees.

Sift dry ingredients and toss in raisins (this keeps them from sinking to bottom of batter). Add buttermilk until blended. (Dough will be sticky.)

On floured board, knead just enough to be able to handle dough without it being sticky (about 10 times). Shape into 8-inch round loaf. Place on cookie sheet. Cut cross in top of dough with sharp knife.

Bake 45 minutes. Remove from oven and cool.

**Lemon Glaze (optional)**
Mix 1 1/2 cups confectioners' sugar with 2 teaspoons lemon juice (or just enough to make a glaze). Spread over cooled bread and let set.

# ABOUT THE AUTHOR

**Katherine Valentine** is the author of the Dorsetville series, which reflects the beautiful New England landscape and its people, whom she dearly loves.

The employees of Thorndike Press hope you have enjoyed this Large Print book. All our Thorndike and Wheeler Large Print titles are designed for easy reading, and all our books are made to last. Other Thorndike Press Large Print books are available at your library, through selected bookstores, or directly from us.

For information about titles, please call:
(800) 223-1244

or visit our Web site at:
http://gale.cengage.com/thorndike

To share your comments, please write:
Publisher
Thorndike Press
295 Kennedy Memorial Drive
Waterville, ME 04901